A
**BUTCH
BLISS**
NOVEL

Also by Harry Bryant

In & Out
Hidden Palms
Snake Road

THE RIGHT KIND OF SINNER

HARRY BRYANT

51325 Books

This book is published by **51325 Books**, a division of Firebird Creative (Clackamas, OR).

Flow like water across stones . . .

Book Design by Firebird Creative.

First **51325 Books** edition: February 2021.

THE RIGHT KIND OF SINNER

CHAPTER 1

"Hey, you know what I'm gonna do this weekend?"

I had been surveying the selection of beer in the EZ Quickie Mart's cooler, and Gavin's question interrupted my train of thought. I had narrowed my choices down to three . . .

Gavin stood near the end of the front counter, rocking back and forth on his heels. He was barely able to contain his excitement. If I didn't play along, he might explode.

"No, Gavin," I said. "I don't know what you're going to do this weekend."

"I'm going to ask Katie to marry me."

"Well, that's exciting," I said.

He kept nodding like he was a tea kettle about to explode. The only reason his head didn't come off was because all that *Wheeee!* was venting out his ears. Gavin worked the swing shift at the EZ Quickie during the week. It was his second job—he also did dishes on the weekends at Three Hares. During the day, he was studying film at UCLA. Somehow he found the time (and energy) to date, and apparently, it had been going well between the two of them.

I had met her a couple of times at the store. She was a willowy girl with big eyes and an innocent earnestness. She didn't talk much—not to me, at least—but the way she watched me, it was like being stared at by a baby panda.

I grabbed a six pack of the IPA that had become my default and brought it over to the counter.

Gavin was still venting out his ears. "You always stand there like you're going to pick something new, and then you don't."

"It's not the choice that matters," I said. "It is the illusion of choice."

"Uh-huh, whatever, Zen Master. From over here, it looks like you have a problem with commitment."

"Well, one of us should," I countered.

He giggled, a toothsome grin stretching his face. Gavin was perpetually sleep-deprived, which made him look like a dozing sheep dog. The glee lighting up his face was a nice change. "I got a ring," he said. "Do you want to see it?"

"Of course," I said, supressing a bit of panic about what was expected of me. What did guys say to one another in situations like this? I didn't have the right experience to be a good wingman. One didn't do big romantic gestures in prison, and prior to my decade with the California Department of Corrections and Rehabilitation . . . strictly speaking, it wasn't a romantic sort of business.

Gavin dug a black box out of his back pocket. I took it and opened it carefully. Inside, there was a simple silver loop jammed between black velvet stays. The ring was topped with an unpretentious setting that held a single diamond solitaire.

"What is that? Half carat?"

"No, man. Full."

I put the box down on top of my six-pack. "That's a lot of late nights, ringing up beer and snacks," I said.

"I'm not going to be doing this forever," he said. "I only have a year left. And then—"

The motion detector at the front door buzzed as two guys came into the tiny store. They caught my attention because they were wearing ski masks and carrying guns.

"Nobody do nothing stupid," the taller of the two said. He waved his gun at us. It was short and ugly, with a long magazine hanging off the front. Some kind of cheap semi-automatic. A spray and pray sort of gun.

Sensibly, Gavin and I put up our hands.

The second gunman, a short guy who moved in quick bursts—like a weasel hyped up on sugar—darted over to the counter. "Anyone else here?" he demanded. His hair was long enough that tufts of it stuck out from under the back of his mask.

Gavin shook his head.

Weasel looked at me. His eyes, framed by the black ski mask, were tiny and brown. Just like a weasel. His gun was a snub-nosed revolver, the sort of weapon that was only accurate at close range. Like the distance between us now. "Asshole," he snarled. "I should—"

"Check the back," his companion snapped.

Weasel grumbled about being ordered around, but he did as he was told. Spray and Pray covered us while Weasel went to the back of the store. I watched him check the coolers. There was something familiar about him, but I couldn't put my finger on it. I hadn't seen his face, but that's not the only way you know someone. You can recognize a person from the way they walk, or the manner in which they speak.

"Open the cash drawer," Spray and Pray ordered. He had come closer to the counter. The barrel of his gun drifted toward me. "You got any money?"

"Some," I said. "It's in my front pocket."

"Get it out," Spray and Pray said. "Slowly," he added as I dropped my hand toward my pocket.

Gavin hit the *No Sale* button on the cash register, and the gunman's eyes flickered toward the sound. They flicked back just as quickly, but there was anger in them now.

My fingers were poised at the top of my pocket. I hadn't moved. I didn't need to make him any more nervous. He was looking for an excuse.

"Put the money in a bag," he snarled at Gavin.

"No one," Weasel said as he returned. "Just these two assholes." He was breathing fast, and he extended his arm as he came, making sure I knew he had a weapon.

Gavin pulled bills from the register and shoved them into a paper bag. There wasn't much there; Gavin knew the rules. Anything larger than a ten dollar bill got dropped into the safe bolted to the floor behind the counter. This wasn't a secret. It was written on the sign mounted on the wall behind him.

If you're thinking about robbing this store, there are three things you should know: 1) your actions are being recorded on video tape; 2) there's not more than $100 in the cash drawer; and 3) this establishment is owned by Chow Enterprises. Don't be stupid.

The family—or more accurately, Chow Enterprises Inc.— owned eight stores in total. Three along Pico, two in West Los Angeles, and the rest made a lazy arc from Santa Monica to Venice and then over to Inglewood. If you were to chart them on a map of the western portion of the Los Angeles metro-politan area, they would make the lower half of a circle. Not coincidentally, the nail salons run by Mrs. Chow inscribed the upper half of the circle.

The exhortation to not be stupid was in reference to the third item on the list. Not that these two yahoos seemed terribly adept at reading posted notices.

"Aw, shit. That's all?" Weasel had been watching Gavin stuff the bag. "Man, there's barely any there," he whined.

"This guy has some," Spray and Pray said. Weasel darted closer, shoving his gun in my face.

"It's in my pocket," I said calmly. Weasel's eyes were ping-ponging back and forth. "Can I get it out?"

Weasel nodded, the motion making his gun shake. He circled to my right, which put him between me and Spray and Pray

These two haven't done this a lot, I thought as I slid my fingers into my pocket. I pulled out my money clip and held it up so everyone could see what it was. "Okay?" I said.

Weasel reached for the clip, but I held it out of reach. "I'll give you the money," I said.

He grimaced and looked like he was about to do something he'd regret later, but Spray and Pray snapped at him to cool it. Weasel listened, but his eyes were still rattling back and forth.

I pulled the bills out of my clip and peeled off a twenty before I held out the rest. Weasel grabbed it as soon as it came into range, and it was only after he had taken the cash that he realized I had kept a bill.

"All of it," he snarled.

"I need to pay for this beer," I said, nodding toward the six-pack on the counter. "You can have the rest, but I'm going home with some beer, and I'm not stealing it."

"What the fu—" Weasel drew out the syllable.

"I'm not a punk thief," I said.

"Who are you calling—"

"Rabbit." Spray and Pray interrupted the smaller man's question. "Get the cash already."

Rabbit, I thought. *Not a weasel.* I had been wrong about the sort of annoying critter he was.

"I sh-sh-shoulda shanked—" Rabbit groused as he reached for the paper bag of cash on the counter.

And that was when I recognized him. "Ralph?"

For a moment, it was as if a pause button had been hit. We were all caught in that moment, our brain trying to process what had happened. Or what was about to happen.

Gavin, with his hands in the air, had a look of utter panic on his face. Ralph—oh, I knew the little shit now—was bent toward the counter, one hand reaching for the bag of cash. His gun was pointing over my left shoulder. Spray and Pray was a couple paces closer to the door, his mouth hanging open.

Gavin, smarter by a dozen IQ points than anyone else in the room, snapped out of the freeze-frame snapshot first. He dropped to the floor, not wanting to be in anyone's line of fire.

Ralph was still thinking about the money when I grabbed him. He yip-yipped like a coyote as I spun him around. I wanted his gun pointing the other way in case Spray and Pray went wild with his gun. Ralph started to struggle, but it didn't matter. I was behind him, and I had a forearm around his neck.

We had wrestled like this once before, when we had been cellmates at the California Department of Corrections and Rehabilitation's facility in Tehachapi. Ralph had been in and out of juvie for most of his life, but this was his first time in the big league. He wanted to be a part of one of the gangs at Tehachapi, but potential recruits needed to prove themselves. Show they were capable of doing the ilicit work that might be asked of them.

Ralph had made a shiv out of a straightened bedspring and a couple of popsicle sticks. He thought he would surprise me, but I wasn't the sort who was easily surprised, especially when this dumbass had tried to smother me with my pillow two nights earlier.

Anyway, we wrestled. Somewhere during the scuffle, he managed to stab me twice with the shiv. I broke his arm when I took it away from him, and then, because I was bleeding and pissed off about the whole thing, I banged his head off the cell door a few times.

I spent a couple of weeks in the prison infirmary. Ralph, in addition to the busted arm and a concussion from all the head banging, picked up a stutter. The kind folks in CDCR transferred him down to Lancaster after that, where the day-to-day environment was less chaotic and violent.

In the convenience store, fondly recalling our last encounter, I pulled his arm back. He remembered what happened in our cell, and he started to squeal and thrash in my grip. I tried to hold him steady, but he slipped free and jammed his elbow into my chest. For a second, I couldn't breathe.

Someone shouted, and then a hard and metallic object struck me in the face. I wobbled, losing track of Ralph altogether, and then a blow to the back of the head drove me to my knees. I blinked heavily, trying to get my pupils to work. The light was all wrong.

Spray and Pray's gun went off—a chuffing chatter like a hundred locomotives all arriving at the station at the same time. There was more shouting, though it sounded like it was coming from far away, and then I heard one more gunshot.

There was blood on the floor, and for a second, I thought I had been shot, but I realized it was only a few drops. I touched my nose, which was a bad idea because the lights went all wrong again. There was blood on my fingers when I focused on them.

Using the counter for support, I hauled myself upright. There was no sign of either gunman. The six-pack of beer was still on the counter. The paper bag with the cash was gone. I glanced around, and spotted my twenty on the floor.

I didn't see Gavin.

Gradually, I realized I wasn't the one making the wheezing noise. I tried to find the source of it, and that was how I found Gavin, sitting on the floor at the end of the counter. His mouth was open, and he was trying to tell me something.

There was a hole in him, and it was leaking.

CHAPTER 2

I WAS LEANING AGAINST THE NEWSPAPER RACK OUTSIDE THE EZ Quickie Mart when Angel showed up.

More cop cars than could fit in the tiny parking lot made things exciting for awhile. The ambulance driver parked the rig on the street, and the techs hustled the stretcher across the lot. They stabilized Gavin, loaded him up, and the ambulance left. No one bothered to ask about my nose. The cops got busy securing the scene. Lots of yellow tape. Guys in blue, walking back and forth on this side of the tape, telling rubber-neckers there was nothing to see. Guys in suits, crawling around the store like they were checking all the sell-by dates.

Angel ducked under the yellow tape like a pro. When a uniform intercepted her, she flashed a business card and pointed at me. The uniform didn't care what her card read. She gave him a pitying smile and kept on walking. He went to grab her arm, but she was too quick for him. She got halfway across the parking lot before one of the suits caught sight of the cop hustling after her. He wasn't pleased.

"Hey," I shouted. "That's my lawyer."

The two men stopped. Angel kept moving. She gave the suit a smile that didn't go all the way to her eyes.

Angel wore a fleece jacket over a dark blue t-shirt and jeans that hugged her leggy frame. I was happy to see her, and not just because she looked good in jeans. She was long-boned and sleek, like her mother, but taller. She had her mother's eyes too, though hers hadn't been frosted by decades of cynicism. Her hands were more like her father's—long fingers, big knuckles.

The sort of fist that left a mark when it hit you.

Not that she had ever hit me. Her father, on the other hand . . . It was how he made sure I was paying attention.

"You okay?" Angel asked when she reached the curb.

"I'm okay."

She examined my face in the harsh light from the store, which was lit up like a studio was doing a film shoot inside. "Did they . . . ?"

"No one died." I lifted my chin toward the street. "Gavin took a round. He got a free ride to the hospital."

"He going to be all right?"

"I hope so."

"Tony called me. He said there had been a shooting."

Tony Chow was one of Angel's brothers. He wasn't the one who was running the stores, though. That was Jackie. Jackie had a couple of custom auto shops, but when his father went to prison, he had stepped in and picked up the family business. Occasionally, he would come by the house and see his mother. It took me a while to figure out why she always had some ridiculous errand for me on Sunday. That was the day Jackie came to visit. I didn't fuss about it. Jackie and I weren't all that tight. I was the guy who had spent more time with Dad during Dad's final years, and it was a bit of a sticking point. There were unresolved issues between father and son, and my presence in the Chow family orbit hadn't helped.

"Well, it's nice that someone cared," I said.

"It's the family business, Butch."

I wrinkled my nose. "So you're not here as my lawyer?"

She patted me on the shoulder. "One thing at a time."

The suit decided that was the excuse he needed to interrupt. "Ma'am, if you're not—"

She stopped him with a flip of her hand. "My name is Angel Chow. My brother owns this store." She gave him her professional lawyer look. "What is your name?"

"Detective Lorenzo. Robbery-Homicide." He was doughy in the middle and flat across the face. His eyes were quick, though, and there were laugh lines creased into his face that the job hadn't managed to erase. The detective shield clipped to the breast pocket of his well-tailored suit jacket was gold, and his tie was blue and red. "Where is your brother?"

"He's busy," Angel snapped.

"Sign in there says there are video tapes. We'll need to see them."

"Of course. But you'll have to talk to my brother's lawyers."

"I'm talking to you."

"I am here as counsel to Mr. Bliss, who I am in the process of having a conversation with."

"Fine," he said. He didn't move.

"A private conversation," she said.

He glanced at me and shrugged. Why would I need to talk to a lawyer if I was just an innocent bystander?

I gave him one of the stares I had learned in prison. Not the *fuck you, piggy pig* one. That would have been rude. I kept it civil and gave him the *Sure, you could take the last bagel, but then I'd have to have someone stab you in the shower* look. It was one of Mr. Chow's favorites.

He gave me a *I'll be seeing you again, punk* look, which was so rookie I almost rolled my eyes.

"Jesus," Angel sighed as the detective wandered off. "You men are always measuring your dicks."

"It's not the length that is important, its—"

"Okay, okay." She held up her hands. "I'm sorry I said anything."

I smiled at her. "I'm glad to see you," I said.

Some of the tension in her shoulders vanished. The ghost of a smile crept across her face. "It's been awhile, hasn't it?"

My relationship with the Chow family was complicated, but only in that *Pull up a chair and sit for an hour or two while I tell you a story* sort of way. Mr. Chow and I knew each other in prison; when I got out, he found me and offered me a job wiping his ass and making grocery runs for his wife. After he died, I was off ass-wiping duty, but Mrs. Chow promoted me to part-time chauffeur. Sometimes we visited the nail salons that were her portion of the Chow family empire. Occasionally, we took her yappy dog to get a haircut.

Angel—the baby of the family—had recently graduated from UCLA's School of Law. Instead of joining a big firm, she had opened up a small office in Ocean Park. It was a long rectangular space on the second floor of an unremarkable office building. Mrs. Chow, when she allowed herself to talk about her daughter in my presence, said Angel was doing a lot of work with young kids and families who were trying to raise themselves out of the gang culture still rampant in the surrounding area. Rising property values and gentrification had pushed some of the nightly violence south, but the change hadn't elevated the life burdens of those who were still in the area. She was busy, and I hadn't seen much of her in the last few months. I hadn't taken it personally, except for, well, the parts where it could be argued I was partially responsible for the break-up of her last relationship. But whatever, you know? Nathan hadn't been right for her.

She was chewing on the inside of her lip like she was starting to think about why we hadn't seen much of each other, and I leapt to distract her from that line of thinking.

"I stopped by to get some beer," I said. "It's on the way home from the gym. And while I was contemplating the cooler, two guys in ski masks came in, waving guns. The wanted the money out of the till. Took my cash too."

"That's it?"

"That's it."

"So why all the shooting?"

"There was shooting?"

She flicked the shoulder of my jacket. I looked where she had touched me and noticed a ragged tear in the material. "How did that get there?" I wondered.

She nodded toward the storefront. "Probably the same way that glass picked up a few bullet holes," she said.

"Well, they did get a little nervous near the end," I admitted.

"About what?"

"There wasn't much money," I said. "You know how Jackie is. All those rules. And his people follow them."

"Not everyone can be a wild stallion like you, Butch," Angel said.

"Yeah, well, these two were disappointed by what they found."

"And you didn't say anything?"

I gave her a hurt look. "Why would I say anything?"

"I'm just asking," she said. "I'm going to get a look at the tape, you know. Am I going to see something I don't want to see?"

"Oh, well, yeah. Okay. I didn't say anything . . . "

She shook her head. "I hear a 'but' coming."

"One of them was going to shoot me."

"Ah," Angel said, throwing up her hands. "Of course."

"It's not like you think," I said.

"No? What is it then?"

"You know, from your tone, I'm starting to think you're not in my corner, counselor."

"You're the one who has backed yourself into one."

"Only because I'm feeling like this is an interrogation."

"Really? So far I've asked one question, and you're having trouble answering it."

"I'm trying to, but you keep rolling your eyes."

"I'm not rolling my eyes," she said.

"Not on the outside," I said. "But on the inside . . ." I made a circling motion with my hand. "It kinda feels like you've already made a decision about this."

"I—I haven't . . ." She sighed loudly and put her hands over her face. I took the opportunity to notice how she was standing:

one leg, turned out; her hip, cocked to the side. She was doing a little posturing. Had we not put all of the awkwardness of the last few months behind us?

She dropped her hands. "Butch, what happened?" she asked.

I kept it simple. "Two guys came in and robbed the place. Things got out of hand. They shot up the store. Gavin took one the chest. I guess I had a near-miss. That's it."

"Did you have a gun?"

"Of course not."

"Gavin?"

I gave her a look, and she withdrew the question.

"What were you doing here?" she asked.

"Like I said: getting beer. It's on the way home from the gym. I've been getting beer here for several months."

"Okay," she said. "So, if necessary, we can establish a pattern of behavior for you."

My tongue got stuck on the edge of my teeth. "Yeah, we could," I said when I got it unstuck. *When you start doing the same thing the same way every day, that's when they own you,* Mr. Chow used to say.

"Gavin and I chat," I said, pushing the thought aside. "He likes to go on and on about some film he just saw."

She hid a smirk. Angel knew of my attitude toward Hollywood.

"This time, though, he was talking about his girlfriend."

"His girlfriend?"

"Are you surprised he has one, or that he would be talking to me about her?"

"Neither. Both. Maybe some other reason entirely," Angel said. "It's just the lawyer in me."

"He was going to propose to her," I said.

"Wow. Really?"

"Yeah. And now . . ."

Angel looked off into the distance. "Where'd they take him?"

"Santa Monica," I said. "Maybe UCLA. They didn't tell me."

"All right," she said. "I'll find out."

She pulled a black notebook out of her jacket pocket, and I made room for her on the edge of the newspaper rack while she made some notes. Our hips touched, and I tried not to think about that contact as she wrote.

The crowd had dwindled, and those who remained were either tourists or crime scene junkies; everyone else had graduated to that "two is more than one, and one is all I ever needed, thank you very much" stage of living in LA. There were two vans with TV call-signs on their sides. If there was a story to report, it would probably make the late news. I nudged Angel with my shoulder. "I'd like to be gone before they start looking for someone to interview," I said, nodding toward the vans.

She looked up from her notes. "Someone should talk to Detective Lorenzo about that," she said.

"Someone should."

She closed her notebook, but she didn't move off the newspaper rack.

"It kinda feels like something my lawyer should do," I said.

A tiny smile tugged at the corner of her mouth. "I guess I did put myself in that position, didn't I?"

"Got a little eager, did you?"

"Maybe."

"There's a vote of confidence."

"They're not charging you with anything right now, so you could walk away. But that might look bad."

"Especially if I abandoned you to talk to the TV folks."

"That would be real bad."

I put on a wounded expression. "I thought you were supposed to say nice things about me," I said.

"I'm supposed to be outraged when other people don't say nice things," she said. "I'm not obligated to say anything."

"Geez, can I have my retainer back?"

She smiled. "I think you're my charity case this year."

"Lucky me."

Her hand closed to a fist and she bounced it on my leg a few times. "You're not telling me everything," she said.

"Nope," I said.

She sighed.

I had no problem lying to her mother, and her mother, more often than not, knew when I was lying. For the most part, she didn't call me on it and I didn't feel bad about doing it; such was the nature of our relationship, I guess. Lying to Angel was a different matter, but I wasn't going to tell her about Ralph.

Detective Lorenzo came out of the store a few minutes later. He wandered over and stood in front of us, hands in his pockets. "I've looked at the tapes," he said.

Angel frowned. "Did my brother say you could?"

"A man's been shot," Lorenzo said. "There are bullet holes all over the place. Crime scene techs are already tagging and bagging. You want to get in my face about looking at some video tapes. I thought you weren't representing the family."

Angel shut her mouth, though she wasn't happy about it.

"Anyway, I saw the tapes," Lorenzo said. "You want to add any commentary to what I saw."

"I'm not sure what you saw, Detective," I said.

Angel put her hand on my knee. "Is my client under arrest?" she asked.

Lorenzo made a noise in his throat as he gave her a sidelong glare. "No," he said.

"Is he a person of interest in this investigation?"

"That remains to be determined."

"Really? Would his record with the State of California have any influence on your conclusion jumping here?

Lorenzo's face darkened. "I don't care for the tone of that question, Ms. Chow."

"I don't care for your tone either, Detective, so I guess that puts us on an even footing. Are we going to do a dance here?"

"I was just asking," Lorenzo said. He took his hands out of his pockets and spread them innocently. "All nice and polite like."

"Well, since you're not arresting him—which is very nice and polite, thank you—we'd like to go home." She paused a beat before playing nice in return. "Please."

"I was just buying beer," I said, trying to be helpful.

"He was just buying beer," Angel echoed.

"Fine." Lorenzo held up his hands. "You're free to go, Mr. Bliss. It's likely we'll want to talk to you again, so don't leave town . . ." He made a circular motion with his hand. "You know this routine, right?"

"I'm familiar with it."

He offered a business card. When I didn't take it, he gave it to Angel. "We'll be in touch," he said. "If he wanders off, it's on you."

"He won't wander off." Angel tucked the business card into her notebook.

Lorenzo gave her a look like he wasn't sure he believed her, and then he went back into the store.

Angel toyed with the elastic band around her notebook. "What happened in there?"

"They wanted my money," I said.

"And you gave it to them, right?"

"Well . . ."

"Butch."

"I was going to give it to them, but I needed to keep a twenty. To pay for the beer."

"Wait. This guy had a gun in your face and you said, 'Take my money, but not all of it because I have principles?'"

"What? I'm not a thief."

"Oh, Butch." Angel shook her head.

"I'm not a thief," I repeated. "Not like Ralph."

"Who?"

"Ralph . . . I don't remember his last name. He and I were roommates briefly, once upon a time."

"Roommates?"

"Upstate," I said. She knew about my stay at Tehachapi. That was where I had met her father, and he had taken me under his wing.

"And why are you thinking about Ralph what's-his-name now?"

"Because he was the one who wanted my money."

"Wait. You knew one of the thieves?" Her eyes widened. "What did you say to him?"

I gave her a hurt look. "Why do you always think it was something I said?"

"Well, it usually is."

"He recognized me," I said. "It was when he said he should have shanked me that I recognized him."

"Shanked you," Angel echoed. "So he had a knife?"

"No, back in prison. That's when he tried to stab me."

"So he didn't stab—shank—whichever."

"'Shank' usually implies success in the action, or, at the very least, an eagerness for a successful outcome in that regard," I explained. "'Stabbing' is, well, you know, *stabbing*."

"Which was it?"

"Definitely a stabbing."

"But not a 'shanking.'"

I shook my head.

"And you just let him?"

"Well, it wasn't like I was expecting it. After the first couple of thrusts, I took the knife away from him."

She shook her head at my casualness about it all. "You haven't seen this guy in what? Five years? Seven years?"

"More like eight," I said.

"Whatever. *A while.* All of a sudden, you run into him as he's robbing a convenience store in Los Angeles."

She didn't phrase it as a question, but there was definitely a question there.

"It happens," I said.

"No, it doesn't."

"It's just a coincidence."

"Sure it is." If Angel had been wearing stern lady eyewear, she would have dipped the frames and scorched my hair off with a look.

I couldn't blame her. I didn't believe the bullshit I was laying out either.

Mr. Chow's voice echoed in my head. *Doing the same thing, the same way: that's when they get you . . .*

CHAPTER 3

Mrs. Chow wandered into my bungalow while I was on hold with the hospital in Santa Monica. She left the door open and ignored my hand gestures to close it behind her. That little bark monster of hers was going to wander in.

Mrs. Chow was elegant like a swan and she wrapped herself in designer clothes and tastefully restrained jewelry. Her hair and nails were professionally done, of course, and she carried herself as if her hands were delicate china, which, once upon a time, they were. She had done modeling work for Cartier and Tiffany's—watches, rings, and bracelets, mostly.

She got a beer out of the refrigerator, which she also left open, and offered me the bottle. As I had one of my own on the counter, I knew she wasn't being polite and demure. She wanted me to open it for her.

Hand models. Can't do a damn thing that might leave a mark on the money makers.

Naturally, since I had the rugged physique of a working man, I did the hard work and twisted the cap off.

Technically, my hands were more famous than hers, screen time counting more than glossy print exposure. But the perks of my job hadn't been fancy watches and diamond bracelets.

She took a delicate sip from the beer, and it was like watching a flamingo try to drink from a bird fountain. "Why do you drink this?" she complained.

"I buy that brand because you don't like it," I said.

"You are a terrible host," she said, putting the bottle down on the counter.

I glanced over at the open door. "And you are a terrible guest."

She waved a finely manicured hand at the phone stuck to my ear. "You were on the phone. I saved you the trouble of coming to the door."

"But you couldn't tell I was on the phone from the other side of the door."

"But you are, so . . ."

"That's not how that works," I pointed out.

"How what works?"

The hold music disappeared in my ear, and a voice told me I was talking to someone at the third floor nurse's station. "Yes, hello," I said. "I'm calling about Gavin . . . Gavin . . . Uh—" I put my hand over the phone's mouthpiece. "What is Gavin's last name?" I asked Mrs. Chow.

She raised an eyebrow. "Who is this Gavin?"

"Gavin works for—never mind." I returned my attention to the woman on the phone. "Gavin, uh, I don't know his last name. He came in earlier tonight with a gunshot wound. In the chest."

"He may have," the woman said. "Who is asking?"

"I'm the guy who was standing next to him when he got shot."

"Were you? Were you admitted together?"

"No, no. I didn't go to the hospital. I wasn't—Is he there?"

"You are a lucky man," the woman said.

"Well, thank you. I was hoping Gavin had the same sort of luck."

The woman was silent for a moment. "He does," she said. "If we are, in fact, talking about the same young man . . ."

"Do you have a Gavin staying on the floor tonight?"

"I'm not at liberty to divulge that information."

"Do you have more than one Gavin?" I tried.

"Would they have gunshot wounds too?"

"That would be highly unlikely."

"It would," she said. She was silent again.

"So, is he okay?"

She answered my question with another. "Are you immediate family, or just the guy who standing next to him earlier this evening."

"Just that guy," I said.

"Well, for you, visiting hours are from ten to six tomorrow."

I thanked the nurse for her information and hung up the phone. "I think Gavin's going to be okay," I said.

Mrs. Chow made a noise that may have meant anything—it was what passed as polite-making commentary appropriate to the differences in our stations in life. Her gaze roamed around my spartan living room. "You need a girlfriend," she said. "Someone who can decorate."

"It's more than I had in prison," I said.

She shook her head. "That is the sort of nonsense my husband—may he suckle at the breast of my better self—would say."

"He said a lot of things."

A small brown shape trotted into the bungalow. It was a Pekinese who was as over-groomed as he was obnoxiously mannered. When people speak of pets being reflections of their owners, they are thinking of Mrs. Chow and Baby Baby.

"Oh no," I said. "He's not allowed in here."

"What? Baby Baby is a good dog." Mrs. Chow crouched and held out her arms for the little bastard. He jumped into her embrace and made himself comfortable. His eyes were all moist and *look how cute and innocent I am*, while his underbite locked his mouth into the sort of sneer you saw on has-been character actors who are confronted by a new kid working the valet desk at Spago's—the new one in Beverly Hills, not the old one on Sunset.

Anyway, the dog was a pain in the ass and—

"He has bladder control issues," I said.

"He does not," Mrs. Chow said. "He got a gold star from Doctor Mike just last month. He's in better shape than you, Butchy Boy."

Mrs. Chow's term of endearment was too close to the furry fucker's name for my liking, which is why she used it as often as possible, of course.

"Doctor Mike is a veterinarian," I said, trying to keep my voice calm. "I'm not sure he's qualified to speak about the state of my health."

Baby Baby let out a sharp yap. Mrs. Chow rubbed her fingers in the fur on his neck. "I know," she cooed to the dog. "He is such an unfriendly person. Always saying such mean things about you."

My beer bottle was empty. I didn't have any memory of draining it, but I could certainly imagine doing so. I reached for the one Mrs. Chow had abandoned. "I'm going to drink this," I said. "Then I'm going to find its friends in the refrigerator. You can stay and watch, if you like, but—" I chugged half of the beer and then belched loudly.

"So ungrateful," she said, still talking to the dog as if I wasn't there. "We give him a nice home. We treat him with respect. Yes, we do, don't we? We don't bark at him—"

"He does bark," I interjected. "In the mornings. When I'm trying to sleep."

"We don't remind him of the life debt," she continued, as if I hadn't spoken. "We invite him over for lunch. Don't we, my sweet boy? Yes, we do."

"Wait. What?"

She held the dog out to me. His nose quivered, and he paddled the air with his paws. "Lunch," she said. "We will all go out together."

"No, before that. What life debt?"

"My husband—may he grow so fat and complacent that fifteen eunuchs will be needed to lift him from his bed—saved your life."

"That's not what—"

"In prison. Where you were going to be what—what is that they call it?—gang raped, by a group of very angry white men."

She scratched Baby Baby behind the ears. "I do not understand why men violate other men when they are angry. How does that make them less angry?"

"That's not what happened. I wasn't in any danger of being raped."

"You were going to join them? And rape other men?"

"No, I wasn't—" I rested the beer bottle against my forehead. Cooling my brain. Collecting my thoughts. "What time?" I asked, recalling the other thing she had said, which was probably why she'd come prancing into the bungalow in the first place.

"Eleven-thirty," she said.

"Him too?" I nodded at the dog.

"Of course."

"Not in my car."

She gave me a patronizing pat on the cheek. "Who pays for the lease on that vehicle?" she asked.

"The same person who will be paying the cleaning bill if he pees on the seats," I pointed out.

"You think too much about pee, Butchy Boy," Mrs. Chow said as she swept past me with Baby Baby in her arms. "That is another reason you need a nice lady friend. She will give you something else to think about."

I had enough to think about already, and it took several of the beers to shut off all those thoughts. Eventually, it was quiet enough in my head that I got up, peed, and went to bed.

Such is the life of the unemployed ex-con.

I had been in the hospital myself for a GSW—gun shot wound, as the shorthand goes. A Mexican fellow had taken a dislike to me, and we had progressed beyond the exchanging of lewd insults. That's when I had learned that hospitals have to inform the police when someone comes in with a GSW. Though, in some parts of the greater metropolitan Los Angeles area, coming in with something *other* than a GSW caused confusion when the staff was filling out paperwork.

Gavin was in a room with two beds, but he was the only patient. A slender woman with brown hair was curled up on the other bed. Her eyes were closed. Gavin was stretched out flat on the other bed, surrounded by pillows. A thin blanket was carelessly pulled halfway up his naked chest. It didn't cover the heavy dressing.

I tried to be quiet when I came into the room, but Gavin stirred and slowly opened his eyes. "Hey," I said quietly. He stared at me like he wasn't sure I was real, blinked a few times, and then slowly nodded.

He was hooked up to an IV that was dripping a solution into his arm from a plastic bag. Leads attached to his fingers and a cuff around his wrist connected him to a panel of machines that showed a bunch of important medical information. "You going to live?" I whispered, jerking a thumb at the mechanical watchdog.

He nodded again.

He was pale and his skin was waxy and slick. The shadows under his eyes said he hadn't been sleeping very well.

"Living is good," I said. I stood near the foot of the bed and tried to figure out what to do with my hands. "Lots to look forward to, right? Graduating. Starting that film career. Getting married." I looked over at the sleeping girl. "That her?"

I asked, even though I knew it was. I was trying to engage him. Get him thinking and talking about happier stuff.

My question brought some animation to his features, but then something like grief crawled across his face. "Yeah," he croaked. "That's her. That's Katie."

"She's pretty," I said. "She stay here all night?"

He nodded.

I recalled what the nurse had told me last night about immediate family, and I liked that the staff had glossed on a definition for the kid. "Well, I was in the neighborhood," I said. "Thought I should bring you flowers or something."

This time, it was almost a smile that ghosted across his lips. "You're such a liar," he whispered.

I pretended to be hurt.

"Flowers, huh?"

I looked at my empty hands. "One of the staff is putting them in water for me," I said. "I forgot to get a vase."

"Sure you did."

I thought about patting him on the leg or something, but settled for tapping my knuckles against the mattress near his foot. "You need anything?" I asked.

He nodded.

"Yeah?" I figured he was going to ask me to smuggle him in a hot dog or something. Hospital food being what it was, and all.

He turned his head and stared at his girlfriend. "The ring," he whispered.

"Yeah? What about it?"

"He took it."

"Who took it?"

"Rabbit." The monitor next to his bed was showing jagged peaks in his heart rate. He turned his head back toward me, and his forehead was shiny with sweat.

I watched him for a moment, and he stared back at me.

"Rabbit," I said.

He nodded.

"Are you sure?"

He nodded again. "After . . . after he knocked you down." He paused, catching his breath. "He grabbed the cash, and then . . . I tried . . . I tried to stop him. That's when . . ." His eyes flickered down to the bandages on his chest.

"Ah, shit, Gavin."

"Yeah." He offered me a weak smile. "It was a whole carat, Butch. It wasn't cheap."

I looked at Katie. Her hair framed her face, and her eyebrows tweaked together slightly as if some part of her realized we were talking about her, but she was too deep in a dream to find her way back. "Well, if you're sure she's the one . . ."

"She is," he sighed.

I exhaled slowly and returned my gaze to Gavin's sweaty face.

"You recognized him," he said. "The guy at the counter. The one named Rabbit. You know who he is."

"Yeah," I said. "I know who he is."

"Get it back for me."

"Gavin—" I started.

His legs thrashed under the blanket. More lines spiked on the monitor. "I've heard people talk about you," he said. "They say you—"

I stopped him before he said something that was hyperbolic hero bullshit. "People like to talk," I said. "They like drama. They like outrageous stories. Most of what people talk about is nonsense."

"Some of it is true," he argued. "I know it is is. I know what you do. You find things. You help people out. You're a good guy."

I made a face when he said that. "Look, Gavin—"

Katie made a noise, and her hand tightened into a small fist. Gavin turned his head, and the tension in his face slipped away. His pain vanished when he looked at her. You could see it in the lines on the monitor. Everything was returning to normal.

My chest tightened as I thought about what he felt for her, about what she meant to him. To have that connection with someone was . . .

I cleared my throat. "Okay," I said. "I'll see what I can do. I'll ask around."

"Promise?" The word slipped out of his mouth like it was the last gasp of air from a deflating balloon.

I lowered my hand, and this time I let it rest on his leg. "Yeah, I promise," I said.

He let out a long breath and his eyes fluttered shut. The monitor kept charting his lines, and I stayed until all the signals were nice and calm.

Katie didn't move again, and when I left they both looked like they were having the same dream. Peaceful and serene. Like Gavin knew everything would turn out okay for them.

Bullshit hero stories. They always get you in trouble.

CHAPTER 4

Did you tell the therapist about your mother? Mr. Chow had once asked after my monthly visit with the shrink at Tehachapi. There were rules mandating regular visits with the in-house psychologist, not because the shrinks thought we needed it, and certainly not because we thought it helped. State rules. Reminders we weren't our own people.

What about my mother?

Does she know what you did?

Yeah, she does. It was in the papers. Some jackass interviewed her for the Denver Post.

And how did she feel about her baby boy being a criminal?

We were in the yard at Tehachapi, watching Dickie Boy and Tattoo Bob lift weights. Dickie Boy was doing close to three hundred on the bench.

Well, she's disappointed, I had said.

And how does that make you feel?

Look, I already had this talk with the doctor lady. Why the fuck am I telling you?

Mr. Chow shrugged. *I thought you might want to talk about it.*

I just did.

No, you didn't. You didn't tell her anything. That would have been weak.

And telling you isn't?

He tapped me on the chest with one finger. *I can feel it inside you. Locked in there. You're carrying that around like it is precious. It isn't. You should let it go.*

I'm not carrying anything.

He kept tapping me, his finger growing more and more insistent. I finally grabbed it. *Knock it off, old man*, I growled.

His head barely came up to the middle of my chest. Dickie Boy could have bench pressed him all day. He pushed against my hand until my arm was bent against my chest. *Are you going to break my finger?* he asked.

I don't want to break your finger.

He kept pushing, and I had to shift my feet to stop him from shoving me back. *What are you hiding in there?* he asked.

Nothing. I bent his finger.

He looked at me without pain or fear. There was nothing but a deep understanding swirling in his eyes. When I bent his finger a little more, a melancholic smile creased his lips. He wasn't going to stop me.

I let go, and refused to talk to him for the rest of the day.

The following month, I told the shrink about the dissolution of my parent's marriage. My father's drinking problem. The night he missed the driveway and put the car through the picture window in the living room. Mom, Cathy—my sister—and I had been watching TV, and I had been making popcorn in the kitchen when the car crashed into the house. Cathy died. Mom had her hip busted, and Dad—protected in that liquid haze that made alcoholics rubbery—came out of the car with nothing more than a gashed lip.

Two weeks after we buried Cathy, Mom kicked Dad out of the house and filed for a divorce. It got ugly, and Mom spent the rest of the year crying and popping pain pills.

Promise me, she had begged me one night when she had been mostly lucid, *promise me that you won't waste your life like your father.*

How does your son's incarceration make you feel? The reporter had asked my mother.

I'm disappointed, was all she said.

Have you spoken with your mother? the prison shrink asked.

29

Why would I? I replied.

What was I going to say to her?

I hadn't talked to my dad since he moved out. I wasn't even sure if he was still alive.

I wasn't even sure why I had suddenly thought of all of that, either.

Two guys in suits were waiting for the elevator in the lobby of the hospital. The one on the left smiled when he saw me. I recognized him as he walked on, blocking my exit, and his buddy followed closely behind him. "Good morning, Mr. Bliss," he said. "Going up?"

"Actually, Detective, I was—" I watched the other man push the button for the third floor, where I had just been. "I guess I'm going to three," I said.

"I guess you are," said Detective Lorenzo. He smiled like we were old pals and *wasn't this the most delightful of coincidences?* I didn't share his enthusiasm.

His partner had one of those faces that mothers continue to love even as the rest of the world found excuses to leave the room. His hair was short and uneven. He squinted like he was trying to burn a hole in things with the power of his eyeballs. This focus meant he was prone to missing other details, like the patch of stubble on his check that had escaped his morning shave or how the ill-fitting line of his jacket made it clear to everyone with a criminal itch that he was carrying something big and heavy in a shoulder holster. "Breaking in a new guy, I see," I said.

'Detective Nelson and I have been working together for three years," Lorenzo said.

"How time flies."

"Were you visiting someone?" Lorenzo asked.

"Sure," I said, deciding not to bother with being coy.

"Gavin Harrison?"

"You're good at this detecting thing."

He spread his hands. "Fifteen years on the force. You learn a thing or two in that time. Like how to use the Internet. You know about the Internet, Mr. Bliss?"

"I've heard of it."

"You can learn a lot of fascinating things on the Internet." He glanced at his partner. "It's all free. Just hanging out in . . . the ether or the data pipes or whatever it's called. Just hanging out."

Nelson pinched his eyebrows together, letting me know that he, too, was up on the "Internet."

"You two are still working on this routine, aren't you?" I asked. "Which of you is supposed to be the straight man? Because all I'm getting is 'Hardass Harry' from both of you."

"I'm good at paperwork," Nelson said.

"He's good at paperwork," Lorenzo echoed.

I nodded. "See? Now that's some patter. Nice back and forth."

"I also know how to use search engines," Nelson said.

"He does." Lorenzo nodded sagely. "Old guy like me? I can barely figure out how to check my email. But Nelson? Nelson knows how to find the free stuff . . ."

"The stuff that is just hanging around out there," I said, demonstrating that I was keeping up with the geniuses trapped in the elevator with me.

"On the Internet." Nelson bit off the end of the word.

The elevator interrupted our banter with an enthusiastic *ding!* The doors slid open, and there we were, back on the third floor. No one was waiting for the elevator, and neither of the detectives were inclined to step out of my way, and so we stood there. Waiting for someone to make a move. The elevator, unimpressed with our lack of initiative, started to close its doors, and Lorenzo put out his hand to stop them. He nodded brusquely at Nelson, who gave me a final squinty glance before wandering off toward the nurses' station.

"Do you want to know what he found on the Internet?" Lorenzo asked.

"Not really," I said.

"I think I'm going to tell you anyway."

I sighed and brushed past the detective. He followed me out of the elevator, which was relieved to be unencumbered by our indecision. I gave it a forlorn look as it closed its doors and went on its merry way.

Lorenzo proceeded to tell me what he learned—sorry, what Nelson had learned.

"You did some time," Lorenzo said. "Possession. Distribution. Involuntary Manslaughter."

I nodded. "Yeah, I do remember hearing those words being bandied about."

Lorenzo cocked his head. "You disagree?"

I gave him the sort of smile you gave the guy behind you in the prison cafeteria line when he got jumpy about how long you were taking with the mashed potatoes. "The City of Los Angeles and the State of California made it pretty clear my opinion was not required in this matter."

"Where'd you spend your time?"

"Tehachapi," I said. He knew where I had been incarcerated. He was being polite. Giving me opportunities to engage in the conversation. And that's how he was going to characterize it in his report, of course. A "conversation." Not an interrogation.

"Nice place?" he asked.

"Oh, yeah. Sure. Real nice. The weekly pedicures and massages were especially lovely."

He favored me with a quick grin, letting me know that he appreciated a healthy level of sarcasm. I saw some of the charm he could turn on for a jury. "I don't mind a good massage myself," he said.

"I'm sure the Internet could recommend a place or two."

"They do massages at those nail salons the Chows own?"

I did a slow four count in my head. Letting that charm slide off of me. "Lotus," I said. "The one over in Chinatown."

"They do all sorts of services there, don't they?"

"I don't know the full list off the top of my head, but yes, I suspect they do."

"You ever gotten a massage there?" He was smiling again. Letting me know he was in on whatever secret we were sharing.

I shook my head. "I'm inclined to say 'go fuck yourself, Detective Lorenzo,' but respectfully, of course."

"Fair enough, Mr. Bliss. Fair enough." He tongued his lower lip and glanced over toward the nurses' station. "How about your porn career. You want to talk about that instead?"

"Go fuck yourself, Detective Lorenzo." I didn't use my respectful voice.

His grin stuck to his lips. "I like your story, Mr. Bliss. It was some really entertaining reading."

"Yeah, well, I'm sure the right producer and the right studio could turn it into an award-winning drama," I said.

"No doubt," he said. "No doubt. Who should play you? You got any preferences?"

I walked off, leaving him there. I could have waited for the elevator to come back, but he was going to keep talking and I was done listening. I could take the stairs. I didn't mind. Walking away was a choice free men had, and it was always delightful to exercise that choice.

Lorenzo had delivered his message. *I've got my eye on you, punk.* I didn't need to stick around and play more eyeball hockey with him.

I drove by the EZ Quickie Mart. The police tape was gone, and there was plywood in the door frame. The neon signs were dark, and there wasn't anyone inside. In a couple more days, taggers would start marking the plywood.

No one cared. The shootout was yesterday's news, and in LA, that was all it took. The city had a very short attention span; usually, the cops did too.

I should let it go. *There's nothing here,* I thought. Nothing to do with me or anything.

Yeah? So who was the guy with Ralph? Mr. Chow asked.

I don't know, I thought.

Maybe you should find out, he replied. *Besides, the kid asked you to find his ring.*

"Yeah," I said quietly. "He did."

That shut Chow up, and I started up my car and left the lot.

Willie's gym had started out as the bottom two floors of an industrial office building. He hollowed out the place and turned it into the sort of gym he had grown up with in New York. A place where no one bothered to paint the walls because they were too busy working iron. A place which stank of sweat and hard work. Willie didn't give a shit about who you were in this town. If you cared about your status, Willie nosed it out fairly quickly and tossed you out. You showed up; you did the hard work. That's all that mattered. That attitude was supposed to keep the pretty preeners and mirror junkies at bay, but the gym had opened as a renaissance in self-reliance had been sweeping Hollywood. Willie found himself with more members than he had space for, and instead of franchising—which a number of people begged him too—he bought the entire building.

If they want it badly enough, they'll come here, he said. *That'll be the new membership requirement.*

Willie was a stubborn contrarian, but he wasn't stupid.

Stevie—Willie's hulking nephew—was hanging out at the registration desk when I walked in, talking with Lorraine. Stevie was a couple inches taller than me and at least a hundred pounds heavier, all of it muscle. The only part of Stevie that wasn't shaved was his eyebrows and the eighth-inch stubble on his cheeks that looked like a geometry experiment gone awry.

He had blue eyes like a newborn baby and a smile that was equally as disarming. A lot of the world was too complicated for Stevie, but he didn't notice.

The big man held out a massive fist for a tap. "Get some last night?" he asked with a smirk.

"Why? Is there some on my face?" I asked.

"No, man. I mean . . ." It wasn't nice of me to confuse him, but his default routine was a bit thick-headed, even for him. "You're usually here, you know, before the rush," he said. He shrugged, and it was like watching a mountain range struggle through a seismic shift. "I figured, you know . . ."

I glanced at Lorraine. She was a slender brunette who liked her hair up and out of the way. It plumed out of a tight band at the back of her well-shaped skull. She didn't fuss with make-up, and she looked comfortable in one of the gym-branded t-shirts and yoga pants. She was in charge of the day-to-day management of the gym, and she radiated an active vitality that inspired regular visits from a lot of members.

She was, via some byzantine tangle of familial ties, related to Willie, which made her off-limits, though that was mostly an excuse to get men to move along when they lingered at the registration desk. She and I had had drinks at the Irish pub across the street a few times, and one night, we made out in my car for awhile after I had driven her home. She had a strict rule about dating unemployed men, however, and since I wasn't in any rush to punch a clock somewhere, tangling tongues across the gear shift was as far as we'd got.

It was our little secret.

Lorraine caught me looking at her, and her impish smile deepened. I felt like smiling back at her, but I kept my cool.

"I'm thinking about repainting my bathroom," I said to Stevie. "Had to get some color swatches."

"Cool, cool," Stevie said. He smiled and nodded, signaling that everything was, once again, right in the world.

Lorraine's look said *You are not painting your bathroom.*

I offered her a *Maybe if I had some help . . . ?* look. She didn't fall for it.

Having done the meet and greet routines with the staff, I went downstairs and changed. I didn't care about the stationary bikes, the treadmills, or the weight machines upstairs. I stayed downstairs with the boxing ring and the free weights. The regulars and I nodded at each other as I wandered past the ring. There were a pair of speed bags in the back, along with a couple of large mats for activities that didn't require gloves and cups and mouth guards. There was a guy who used to come in on the weekends and practice foot juggling. Occasionally, he'd bring an assistant who he'd bounce around as she turned herself into a pretzel. After a few months, they vanished, and I figured whatever company they had been touring with had moved on.

A woman with curly red hair pulled back into a wavy ponytail was working one of the bags. She was taking it slow, learning the rhythm, and I did my best to stay out of her line of sight as I loosened up with some tai chi.

We had done it every day in the yard. Once Mr. Chow was satisfied we had learned the basic forms, we took turns leading our little cohort. We were all equals when it came to body movement and spiritual enlightenment. It was one of the little ways he kept us tight—our own little incarceration family.

Once my muscles were loose and I had let go of the noise I had brought with me, I picked up a rope and lost myself in the cyclical motion. I didn't have a watch, and I didn't watch the clock. It was how we worked out in the yard: there was no clock; you had nowhere to go; you did the work until you were done. Your body would let you know.

The redhead finished up her time with the bag. She tugged off her gloves and gathered up her gear. She made eye contact when she walked past and I nodded a simple hello. She seemed familiar—I had seen her here before, but I didn't recall seeing her downstairs. She was broad for her height, and some might have found her upper arms and back too muscular, but there was nothing amiss with the way her hips moved. When she reached the stairs that led up to the main floor, she stopped and looked back at me.

I missed the next turn of the rope, and it tangled around my leg.

After a long shower, I circled the mezzanine and knocked on the open door of Willie's office. He was sitting behind his desk, peering at his computer screen. Willie was a second generation Navy man, though, unlike his father, he had enlisted, preferring to stay below decks instead of above. He had been at sea during the Gulf of Tonkin incident—the event which had led to US troops getting sent to Vietnam. Willie finished his tour after the war was over, and he spent another decade working Merchant Marines ships before finally quitting the boats altogether.

He had boxed during school, but there hadn't been much opportunity for that during his time in the Navy. Well, not officially. Young men always find excuses to use their fists.

Willie looked at me over the top of his reading glasses. "Did you do your time?" he asked.

Willie was vehemently against the idea of building a brand for the gym. He didn't advertise in any of the papers; he didn't do flyers; and whenever Lorraine or anyone else tried to get him to put up a billboard or some equally narcissistic display, Willie would respond that they could hang his corpse from the overpass when he was gone. However, he did have a catch-phrase. He didn't say "hello" or "good morning" or "Here to work out?" He said: *Did you do your time?* The first few times I heard him say it, I had flipped him off. The question had a different connotation for me, and back then, I was still a little pissed about being reminded. Willie hadn't cared. He was like

Mr. Chow in that way. Time was time. You either used it well or you didn't. In his gym, that meant doing a good workout.

"I did my time," I said as I dropped into the leather chair opposite his desk.

"You hear about that thing at the EZ Quickie?" he asked. He nodded at the copy of the *LA Times* on his desk.

"I might have heard about that," I said.

"Yeah?" He was still watching me over the rim of his glasses.

"Yeah."

"Paper says it was gang-related."

"Do they?" I wrinkled my nose, fighting the urge to grab the paper and see what it said.

"Yeah, a couple of street soldiers interrupted a meeting. Tried to take out a lieutenant or something. It's a bit vague after that."

"Street soldiers?" Were we talking about the same EZ Quickie Mart I had been in last night? "How do they figure that?"

Willie shrugged. "Fancy pants reporting, I guess."

I reached for the paper. "Well, that's what they pay those guys for, isn't it?" The story was on the second page of the Metro section. Two paragraphs of basic facts, followed by a paragraph quoting an unnamed source with the LA Police Department— probably Lorenzo, trying to keep a handle on the story. The rest of the article veered into the weeds where it talked about long-standing issues with gang violence. It was a regular topic in the paper these days, and most of it was, unfortunately, on the verge of becoming boilerplate that everyone glossed over.

However, there was one line that brought me up short. "A hierarchy? In the Chow organization?" I couldn't believe the editor let that get printed. I checked the byline. Peter Bayance. I didn't know the name.

"What's that?" Willie asked.

"The fancy pants part you were talking about," I said. Bayance had dropped the idea that the shootout at the EZ Quickie Mart had to do with tensions between local criminal gangs and something more organized. Like internationally organized. I wondered if Mrs. Chow had seen the article. She wouldn't be too pleased about it. Back in the day, the Feds had tried to link Mr. Chow and his businesses to various international interests—Hong Kong triads, the Medellin cartels, gun-running from Africa—but, as far as I knew, they hadn't be able to build a case. All they had managed to do was dig into the financial records of Chow Enterprises. All they found were some accounting practices that were dodgy enough to convince a judge in their pocket. I never completely understood why Mr. Chow hadn't fought the case harder, but, well, none of us ever understood Mr. Chow's true motivations for what he did.

As I was thinking about triads and gang shootings and secrets men took to the grave, Lorraine came into the office with a handful of paperwork. "Oh, hey, Butch," she said.

"Hey, Lore," I replied.

She put the paperwork in front of Willie and rocked on her heels as she looked across the table at me. "So what color are you going to paint your bathroom?" she asked.

Willie asked a lot of questions with one raised eyebrow.

"I told Stevie I was shopping for paint samples," I said.

"Because you're painting your bathroom?"

"No," I said. "I'm not."

Lorraine's impish grin returned.

"What?" I asked.

She shrugged. "Maybe you should," she said. Willie saw the gleam of amusement in her eye, and when he looked at me his expression said: *Tell me my niece doesn't know what your bathroom looks like.*

I raised my shoulders in that *Maybe she broke in once to steal some toilet paper* sort of way.

Lorraine tapped the stack of paperwork she had brought in, breaking up the eyeball lock between Willie and me. "The numbers look good," she said.

Willie reached for the top sheet of the stack. "We'll recoup the initial investment in six to eight months?"

"Maybe as early as four," she said. "But six is good."

"Six is good," Willie said. "How do you feel about coffee?" he asked me.

"I like coffee," I replied.

"How about smoothies?"

"I don't mind smoothies either."

Willie nodded as if those answers were the ones he had wanted to hear. He peered at his computer monitor and clicked his mouse a few times before leaning back in his chair. He pushed his glasses up to the top of his head. "Okay, I think that's what we need to know. I'll make my decision in the morning."

"Sounds good, Boss." Lorraine paused as she passed me. Her tight-fitting yoga pants had no pockets, and so the business card she pulled from her waistband was suggestively curved by the the arc of her hip. "For the coffee *lover*," she said, putting a little unnecessary emphasis on the last word. She dropped the card on Willie's desk, within my reach. It didn't lay flat.

"What's that?" Willie asked as Lorraine left his office.

"A business card," I said. I picked it up before he could get any nosier. The card was for an espresso stand, one of those little shacks that had been popping up in the corners of parking lots. Like a spread of tiny mushrooms in a concrete forest. The card listed the owner's name—*Greta Lundgren*—and someone, possibly Greta herself, had written "the first one is on me" in a tidy script across the back.

"You know, I really do like coffee," I said.

CHAPTER 5

CURIOSITY PROMPTED ME TO DRIVE BY THE ADDRESS ON THE card. It was a miniature craftsman style house nestled in the corner of a parking lot attached to a large sporting goods store and an even larger hardware store. The shack was painted cheery colors and it had extraneous dormers that were lined with twinkling lights. There was a drive-thru lane on either side. A large sign mounted on top of the house pronounced the shack's name—Perks A Lot—and a cartoonish figure of a large-breasted woman holding a steaming cup of coffee was painted behind the letters. The wink she was giving the world was a very knowing one.

I half-expected the baristas to be wearing next to nothing, but the cheerful young woman who greeted me when I drove up was fully-clothed. "What can I get for you?" she asked.

"Uh, some sort of coffee, I guess." The menu board had three rows of options.

"Drip? Latte? Mocha?" The young woman, sensing my confusion, leaned forward and pointed at the bottom of the menu. "There's also the daily special." A slate board attached to the menu showed a fancifully decorated cup of coffee, along with a name that sounded more like an ice cream sundae than a beverage.

The handwriting on the slate was, I noticed, very similar to the handwriting on the back of the business card.

The young woman noticed the card in my hand. "You here to see the boss?" she asked.

"Yeah," I said. "I guess I am."

The young woman leaned back. "Hey, Greta," she called. "There's some guy here to see you." She smiled at me as a car pulled up on the other side of the stand. "Let me know if you make up your mind, okay?"

"Okay," I said.

As she crossed to the other side, a woman came out of the back. I recognized her, but not because we had actually met. It was the redhead from Willie's. She smiled when she saw me.

I held up the card she had given Lorraine. "I hear the coffee's pretty good here," I said.

"It is," she said. She was wearing jeans that hugged her hips nicely, and her dark green t-shirt didn't quite come all the way down to her waist. Her eyes were a lighter green than her shirt, and I focused on them instead of the tiny band of tanned skin showing at her waist. "Know what you want?" she asked.

"No one ever misunderstands that question, do they?"

"No, they never do," she said, a merry light in her eyes.

"Honestly, I'm not up on the whole artisanal coffee thing," I admitted.

"Tell people you're a purist. It's better that way."

"I'm not much of a purist, either."

"Why don't I just make you something."

"That sounds great," I said.

She grabbed a white cup and wrote a complicated notation on the side with a black marker. She put the cup on top of the espresso machine, and then, responding to an unspoken flow between herself and the other woman in the shack, she crossed to the other side and finished the transaction happening there. The young woman who had first helped me was busy with the wands and dials on the espresso machine. The two women moved effortlessly around each other, well-practiced in dealing with the tiny space inside the shack.

It was easy to watch their backsides while they worked, and I resisted the temptation and looked around the parking lot instead. The hardware store was having an outdoor sale on potted plants and tiny trees. Judging by the number of cars in the lot, business on plants and trees was brisk. Two cars parked near the edge of the lot drew my attention. A quartet of young men lounged around the cars. One of the vehicles—a custom blue Camaro—had its doors open. The cars were far enough away that the music pumping out of the heavy speakers was a distant *whub-whub-whub* of a sinuous bass line.

They didn't look like the early spring gardening types.

I saw dudes like this all the time in prison. Young guys, full of testosterone and a need to prove themselves. Most of them wound up as cheap entertainment for the lifers. Some got smart and found a way to avoid the gladiatorial circus. There were outliers, of course, men who threw themselves—body and soul—into that life until it ate them up. When they got out, they found the outside world didn't know what to do with them, and invariably, they drifted into something that approximated what they had inside.

I was thinking about what Bayance had written in the paper when Greta appeared in the window. "Here you go," she said, holding out a white cup. The notation she had written was cryptic, but my name was written in her now-familiar handwriting.

"You spelled my name right," I said.

"I figured there wasn't a silent Q or something."

"No, just like it sounds."

She put a hand on her hip, her fingers right at the top of her jeans. "I figured you were like that," she said.

"How so?"

She nodded at the cup in my hand. "You going to try that or hold it all day?"

I took a tiny sip through the slit in the plastic lid. The beverage was hot, and I didn't taste anything but foam and fire for a moment, but then a vanilla aftertaste melted on my tongue. There was another flavor too, but it vanished before I could place it. "That's good," I said.

"Of course it is." She smiled. "That's your signature drink now. Anna will remember it the next time you come by."

"The next time?"

She smiled, and I liked how the sentiment echoed in her eyes. "I'm Greta, by the way," she said.

"I figured that out," I said. "I'm Butch."

"I know."

Right. She had written my name on the cup.

We stared at each other for a minute, and then she tilted her head to the side. "There's a line behind you."

I glanced at my rearview mirror. "Oh, yeah. There is."

She bent forward and rested her forearms on the narrow ledge of the shack's window. It put her face at the same level as mine. "You're holding up the line," she said, her eyes focusing on my mouth.

I stared at her mouth too. "Yeah, so?"

"It's hard to take their money when you've got your foot on the brake, Butch."

"Should I rev my engine and pop my clutch?"

She gave me a generous grin that sent sparks shooting down my spine. "Try not to spill all over yourself when you do," she said.

"Since when do you do drink coffee?" Angel asked when I wandered into her office.

"People grow and change all the time," I said. "That's what makes them interesting."

"Uh huh." She eyed the cup in my hand. "Perks A Lot?"

"I understand the coffee stand business is crowded and competitive. Everyone is going to be drinking coffee, Angel."

"Everyone already does."

"Yes, but now it is a burgeoning craft industry."

"Whatever." Her attention drifted back to the document she had been working on. There were several file folders on her desk, along with a spread of official-looking court documents. She was wearing a gold blouse with navy slacks, and there was a matching jacket laid on the sideboard next to her briefcase.

"Did you have court today?" I asked as I went over to the brown couch by the window and sat down.

"This morning."

"Did you win?"

She gave me the sort of look one gives a small child who keeps asking for ice cream. I sipped from my now-lukewarm coffee. Cinnamon! That's what the other flavor was. *Like her hair,* I thought.

Angel ignored me, and I let my gaze wander around the long rectangular space. It made for a nice open floor plan, but it was terrible for private conversations. Right now, Angel's schedule probably wasn't so full that clients overlapped each other, but I imagined that wouldn't last.

I thought about the law office where she had done her internship. It took up an entire floor of a posh Century City address, and it was a maze of offices and conference rooms, intended to keep every encounter with every client as private and confidential as possible. I wondered if any of the lawyers who were working there had ever worked in a one-room office like this, or if they had skated into the polished wood and chrome finishes with the bored nonchalance of the entitled.

Angel's office was on the second floor of a red brick building that looked out over a major intersection in the section of Santa Monica that used to be a separate community called Ocean Park. On her side of the street, the buildings dated from the late '70s when concrete was still every architect's darling and contractors weren't paid enough to think in complex shapes. Across the street, the '80s were in proud peacock display. The buildings had scallops and swoops and fancy ironwork. They still looked like prisons to me, but then I had a jaundiced view of bars on windows, no matter how ostentatiously they were arranged.

There was no elevator in Angel's building, and access to her office and the three others on this floor was a wide staircase from the sidewalk. Downstairs was a taco shop, and the building was old enough that the smells from the kitchen crawled up through the cracks and vents. I imagined everyone on the second floor was already known by name at the restaurant.

Angel saved the document she was working on and sent it to the printer in the corner of the room. The machine hummed and spat out a handful of pages, which Angel gathered, stapled, and put on top of the stack on her desk. The stack went into the top file folder, and the whole lot went into the upper drawer of the long file cabinet next to the printer.

"What are you doing here?' Angel asked me when she was done putting her work away.

"I wanted to see the place," I said.

Angel looked around. "Well, here it is," she said.

Other than the clock, she had one picture on the wall. It was a photograph of a beach. I wondered if it was a picture she had taken or if the picture had come with the frame.

"It's nice," I said.

"It's cheap," she replied. "And functional."

"Don't let your mother hear you say that."

Angel crossed her arms and gave me a *I don't really have time to watch you drink coffee* look.

"Are we still pretending that you're my lawyer?"

She gave me a *Get on with it, already* shrug.

"There was an article in today's *Times* about the shooting," I said. "It mentioned that there's been a string of robberies at the family stores in the last month. Is that why Tony called you?"

An annoyed expression flickered across her face. "He's been a bit of a pain in the ass since the robberies started."

"And Jackie? What does he think about all this?"

"Jackie . . ." She shook her head. "Jackie's been . . . "

"You two talk that much?"

"He never liked Nathan—"

"None of us liked Nathan," I pointed out.

"Jackie and I haven't talked much since Dad died," she said. "And there's been even more distance since . . . you know . . ."

I did know. I had gotten involved in one of Nathan's side projects not too long ago. It hadn't turned out the way Nathan had hoped, and the law firm he had been working at had dropped him like an ugly lizard. I had heard that his father had left the firm too, though I hadn't heard whether he'd been fired or had left out of familial solidarity. I felt a little bad for him. Nathan had dug his hole all on his own. It was too bad his old man had felt the need to jump in with him.

"How many robberies?" I asked, getting back to the story in the paper.

"Three?"

"Counting last night?"

"I think so."

"The guy who wrote the article in the paper has quite an imagination," I said. "He thinks that a long-standing Southern California crime family is under assault, and that last night's robbery was, in fact, an attempt against the organization's hierarchy—"

"Wait. What? A hierarchy?"

"See? And here I thought you'd take issue with 'long-standing So Cal crime family' part of that sentence," I said.

She frowned, worked the expression up to an outright fume, and then went over to her desk and picked up the phone. She dialed a number from memory and when someone answered, she started talking. "Mom, it's me. No, I—Mom. Mom. There was an article in the paper today. Did you see it? No . . . Butch. Butch said—no, Mom—Yes, he's right here." She looked at me and rolled her eyes. "Yes, Mom, he knows he's not where he's supposed to be right now. Yes, I know. He's—"

She fiddled with a pen while she listened to her mother. I knew the feeling. I put my feet up on the coffee table and focused on the cup in my hand.

"Mom . . . Mom . . . Mom!" Having finally gotten her mother's attention, Angel took a deep breath and ran a hand through her hair before continuing. "Why is someone writing about us being a crime family?" she asked.

Without being too obvious, I watched her face as she listened to her mother's long-winded and evasive response. She made noises now and again—not enough to interrupt and not quite fully formed words. "Okay," she said finally, and there was a cold finality in her tone. "Okay," she said a second time as she looked over at me. "Okay. I'll tell him. Uh huh. Yes, Mom. Yes—I—No. Mother. No, I will not. Mother—" She hung up the phone with a tiny growl of frustration.

"That woman . . ." she started.

I kept my opinion to myself.

"Do you know where you were supposed to be a half hour ago?" she asked.

I glanced over at the unadorned clock mounted on the wall. Like everything else in the office, it was functional but not remarkable. I tried to recall if Mrs. Chow had made arrangements for me to drive her around today, and I eventually recalled the conversation last night. "Oh . . . " I said lamely. "We were supposed to have lunch."

"You really need to get a cell phone," Angel said.

"Why? So your mother can find me?" I shook my head.

"Yeah, well, I'm not your answering service."

"You called her," I said. "And you admitted I was here. That was all your fault."

"Fine." She crossed her arms. She was angry, but not at me.

"What is it?" I asked.

"She wanted to know why you were here, and frankly, it's none of her business."

"Well, apparently I—"

"She meddles," Angel said, interrupting me. "I'm a grown adult. Who I see, who I talk to—I can hang out with whomever I want. Whenever I want."

I nodded in agreement. "It's what grown adults do," I said.

"Right," she said.

"Right," I echoed.

Neither of us said anything for a minute, and I finally broke the silence. "Are we still talking about her being angry at me?"

"What?" Angel came out of whatever thoughts she was having. "You? No. I—I called her . . ."

"You were asking about the article in the paper," I prompted.

"Yeah," Angel said. "I was."

"What did she say?"

Angel shrugged. "She didn't say anything about it."

"Nothing at all?"

"Well, she said that was all lawyer talk and she couldn't be bothered with keeping track of lawyer talk."

"Really? And here you are, a lawyer and all."

"Yeah, look at me." She made a little gesture with her hands. "Woo."

"You need some practice with that cheerleading bit," I said.

She sat down and her shoulders slumped. "I know," she said. "Butch, I—"

"What?"

"It's—nothing."

"I think it is definitely something," I said.

She let out a long breath of air. "It's—you know how my mother gets."

"I do."

She focused on a spot on the wall, and her face went through a series of expressions. "Have you heard from the police?"

I thought about my run-in with Detectives Lorenzo and Nelson. "Nope," I said.

"Do you need me to do anything?" she asked. "As your lawyer?"

"No," I said. "I think we're all good."

"Okay. I'm—I'm going to get back to this file I was working on, okay?"

I got up from the couch. "Yeah, okay."

"You'll let me know if you need anything."

"Sure," I said.

It wasn't the most awkward exit I've ever made, but it was up there. I knew it wasn't me. Something was bothering Angel, and between her and Tony being all over the robbery last night, I was starting to wonder what was going on with the family.

I had read a book or two about statistics during my stint in Tehachapi. While I hadn't understood most of the finer details, I did follow the part which said that odds get long real quick. That made me a lottery winner. The one-time-in-a-million guy who happened to be in the wrong place at exactly the wrong time. I was a random dude buying beer at a random store, and my magic number came up. The odds were long, but it happened, you know? You get enough convenience stores and enough robbers, eventually, you'll get a robbery with bystanders in the store. It wasn't impossible.

But, in this instance, it was a Chow Enterprises store, and I was a guy who had a pre-existing relationship with Mr. Chow. The *But I was just buying beer* argument was tougher to swallow. If you were keen on connecting disparate dots and seeing bigger pictures, it was harder to see my presense at the robbery as merely a statistically unlikely event.

My relationship with the Chow family wasn't a secret; I was the closest thing Mr. Chow had had to a confidante during his stint in the California penal system. Follow the thread: Chow grooms me behind bars; I do my time and get out; Chow develops cancer and CDCR cuts him loose so he can die at home; I move into the bungalow on the property where his wife lives, and the best job description anyone could write about me is "Errand Boy for Mrs. Chow."

I could see how Bayance squinted and changed "Errand Boy" to "Bagman" in his head. That turned a boring recap of all those expert studies that say how dangerous it is to live in LA into a buzzworthy tale of warring crime families. *Hello!* Look at those copies, flying out of the newspaper racks.

Add in the fact that one of the robbers was my old roommate at Tehachapi, and the piece gets really juicy, doesn't it?

When I had met Ralph at Tehachapi, he was a squirrelly kid with light fingers who was in and out of juvie so often they didn't bother assigning his room to someone else when he scooted out the front door. Ralph celebrated his eighteenth birthday by swiping a high-end roadster. When the cops caught up with him three days later, he learned the state didn't care when he *stole* the car, they cared when he was *caught*. Legally an adult for forty-eight hours, he wasn't going back to juvie. It was the big time at Tehachapi for the belated birthday boy.

He tried to make friends, but he lacked both the sheet and the social standing that would have made him an asset. The only group who didn't threaten to eat him when he tried to make friends were the Double Zs—a tight-knuckled group of lightning bolt lovin' skinheads. The Double Zs didn't want him, but Ralph was insistent and desperate, and they finally gave him a task to shut him up. Or get him killed, it didn't matter to them, really. *Show us your balls*, they told him, and so he tried. Twice, in fact.

The first time he tried to smother me with a pillow, and that didn't work out too well for him. The second time, he used a shiv he had made himself (nice initiative, Ralphie!), and he did a little better. I still broke his arm and banged his head a few more times than necessary against the cell bars.

In my defense, he had stabbed me twice, and there was a lot of blood, and I was pissed.

Anyway, Ralph got a transfer to Lancaster, where everyone was much friendlier and gang initiations were frowned upon. He had done his time apparently. Still had that stutter I had banged into his brain, though. I couldn't blame him for holding a grudge. I had given him reason.

Who was he running with? He was a street rat; he wasn't the sort who had ideas on his own. If there was a concentrated effort to bust up the Chow family organization—not that such an organization existed—Ralph wan't going to be running things. He was the sort who followed orders, and against my better judgment, I was starting to wonder what Ralph had been up to since his release from prison.

CHAPTER 6

AFTER I PASSED THE THIRD PAWN SHOP, I FIGURED I SHOULD do something about the promise I had made to Gavin. I had been thinking too hard about Ralph's new friends. A more practical thought was: *what would a guy like Ralph do with a full carat diamond ring?* The answer was that he'd dump it.

Pawn shops are such a part of the modern urban landscape that you stop seeing them. In some neighborhoods, they have sexier names, like "resale boutiques" and "antique malls." But Ralph wasn't the kind of guy who'd boutique his way through an antique mall. He'd want someplace that wouldn't ask too many questions and wouldn't rip him off.

I stopped at a place with hand-painted signs that said they bought gold and platinum—*Best Prices in LA!* Behind the bar-covered windows, there was an array of guitars, lawn equipment, and skiing gear. Inside, the detritus of lives interrupted, unfulfilled, and frustrated were haphazardly organized: more guitars and amps, as well as drum kits and keyboards; racks of fancy dresses worn once, hastily removed, and never dry-cleaned; tuxedos in pastel colors and leisure suits that had failed to help their wearers score. At the back, there were glass-fronted counters filled with watches, costume jewelry, and engagement rings for unions never consummated. A sign on the wall repeated what the signs outside said. *Best Prices in LA!*

A guy in an old t-shirt with lank hair and a sleepy expression ambled over as I peered at the contents of one of the cases. He made noises with his mouth, and when I looked up, he gave me a sloppy grin that had missed a few dental appointments.

He grunted when I told him I was just looking. He hooked his fingers in the corners of the pockets of his worn jeans and didn't wander far. I paid attention to the rings. I wondered if Gavin had bought his ring at a place like this or if he had gone to an actual jewelry store. Jewelry was cheaper here, but the selection wasn't very good. Nothing looked like it came close to a carat.

"You ever get anything bigger?" I asked.

He snorted. "Gotta cross Pico if you want bigger," he slurred. "Yeah?"

"That kind of bling attracts the wrong sort, you know?"

I nodded. "I suppose it does." I pointed at the largest diamond. "What do you pay for something like that?" I asked, nodding toward the sign on the wall.

He shrugged, not willing to divulge trade secrets.

"Quarter?" I asked. "Third?"

He kept shrugging.

"You don't pay half," I said.

He wrinkled his nose and shook his head.

That was enough of a hint. Ralph wouldn't have gotten much for the ring if he sold it to a place like this, but it would have been more than he and his pal had gotten out of the register.

A pair of fancy earrings caught my eye. They were like a cascade of frozen water droplets—emeralds, water of pearl, and some other light green stone. I flashed on seeing them hanging against Angel's neck, and I pointed at them. "I'll take those," I said.

The guy grunted and approached the counter. I used the time while he fussed with the shelves and jewelry to look over the security of the place. There were cameras conspicuously mounted on the ceiling: two covering the door, one covering the register. The windows had bars over them, and there was a security gate that could be dropped over the glass doors at night. The door at the back of the room was solid and had two locks in it. I figured there was a bat or a gun under the front counter.

It didn't look like a lot of security, and if someone wanted to smash and grab, they'd probably be able to outrun the mouth-breather working behind the counter. Not that he'd be running after any thief. He wasn't paid enough for that sort of exercise. It was the same sort of security theater that Jackie had at the EZ Quickie Mart. Just enough to keep idiots from getting ideas. If they did, they wouldn't get much, and their audition tapes for America's Dumbest Criminals would haunt them forever.

The pawn shop guy finished fumbling with the shelves and wandered toward the cash register. He punched keys on the register and a total blinked up on the screen. I peeled some bills off my clip and passed them over. I got a paper bag in return. I grabbed one of the store's business cards on my way out.

In the car, I shook the earrings out of the bag. I had probably overpaid, but the stones sparkled nicely and the mother-of-pearl were a nice contrast. I peeled off the price tag, put them back in the bag, and slipped the bag into the center console of the car.

I wasn't sure why I had bought them. Maybe as a belated apology for messing up her relationship with whatshisname— the lawyer she had been dating a while back. Maybe as a thank you for standing up for me last night. Whatever. I didn't feel like overthinking it.

A painting of a giant red bird over a white diamond dominated the wall of a building across the street. The wall had been painted black, which made the bird and the diamond jump when you drove by. The rest of the building was utter nondescript. If you were coming from the west, you'd drive right past it and not even wonder what it was. The windows were blacked out, and the door was a heavy slab of oak that looked like it had been rescued from a old sailing ship or something.

The eagle nagged at me, and after thinking about it for a minute or so, I realized why. Tribes have their secrets codes, ways of identifying themselves to others in a crowd. It was going on all over LA—red and blue bandanas. And sometimes it wasn't as nefarious as that. Simple iconographical communication. The Dodgers cap. The Lakers shirt. The football jersey with a players' name on the back. You didn't have to know anything about the individual sport to know you were looking at a fan who wore their devotion on their sleeve.

I didn't know the team or the brand that had a red eagle for its logo, but damn, it felt like an esoteric symbol of some kind. Like the square and the compass for the Masons. Something like that.

Then it came to me: the black eagle of the German Empire. The Double-Zs liked to mix the black eagle with their lightning bolts. The bird on the building wasn't the same—this one was flying, the German bird was posed—but it looked like it might have been designed as a homage.

Which might be enough if you were looking for like-minded folks to hang out with.

I locked up my car and went across the street to see how many angry white dudes I could find.

Dive bars used to be places only the locals knew about, but which were always in danger of being discovered by tourists. *Get your authentic LA flavor here!* And then, all too quickly, what made the place attractive would vanish beneath a constant stampede of badly tanned, wide-eyed out-of-towners who would edge out the regulars.

Just look at the Viper Room in West Hollywood. Back when it was the Central, it was a perfectly nondescript watering hole where locals could get sauced without having to worry about being seen by anyone they knew. Now, you couldn't go in or out without wondering if someone was taking your picture and selling it to the tabloids.

There was no one at the door of the Red Eagle. I went in, and the smell hit me first: spilled beer soaked into shitty carpet, a lingering tang of human sweat that put me right back in the yard, and the grungy after-taste that came from licking ashtrays. My eyes adjusted to the decor and the lack of sexy lighting, and I spotted an aged bar on my left. There were a half dozen pool tables on the right, and they took up most of the open floor. Places to sit or park your beer were relegated to the spots along the wall. In the back, there was an aisle for darts. On the inside wall, the white diamond and red eagle were painted on the ugly and uneven bricks.

There were two guys at the bar and a third was poking at a cue ball like he was waiting for a signal from deep space. The waitress was a tattooed and leathered blonde who looked like she chewed diamonds to relax. I wandered up to the bar and made the universal sign for 'beer.' Eventually, she ambled over.

"You have more than one choice on tap?" I asked.

She gave me the middle finger as she walked away, but she came back with a pint glass that was mostly foam. I put a ten on the bar, and tried the local swill. It was as pale as her hair and as watery as the eyes on the dude sitting three stools over. But I was thirsty, and I plowed through the foam and drank about an inch of the cold beer.

"We know each other?" I asked the dude with the quavering gaze. He hadn't shaved in a week or six, and hadn't combed his hair in twice as long. Some of it stuck up like all the glue he'd been sniffing had made its way into his brain and out through his skull.

He was good at staring.

Back in the warm and encouraging embrace of the CDCR, there were informal seminars on the proper ways to use your eyeballs. You didn't make eye contact. You didn't stare. And if you were caught staring, you looked down as quick as you could, especially if the guy you were gawking at could shove both your arms most of the way up your rectum. That was the responsible way to deal with accidental eye contact.

There was another school of thought which argued that you should double down. You didn't look away. You met that interloper's gaze and you gave them the fucks you'd been storing up all winter. Of course, that led to arm flexing and chest thumping, as well as all kinds of shit talk, but hey, that's what afternoon free time was all about anyway, wasn't it?

Or, as Mr. Chow taught his little concrete coterie, you could stand your ground without making trouble. You didn't have to threaten. You didn't have to submit. You could be nice. *Strike up a conversation,* he said. *Ask him if he's read any good books lately.*

Tattoo Bob had a question: *Won't that—you know—escalate the situation?*

Mr. Chow looked at me. *You hear that?*

Bob's been paying attention at school, I said. Mr. Chow waved a hand, like he wanted to me to explain it to the class. *No, Bob, you're changing the situation,* I said. *Look, the guy wants to pound you. He's looking for an excuse. It won't matter what you do. Or he doesn't want to dance, and you've given him an out. Either way, the situation is on your terms now. If he was thinking about throwing down—*Mr. Chow rolled his eyes at my vernacular, but whatever, Bob knew what I was talking about—*if he was thinking that, you've confused him now. Is he supposed to answer your question? Is he supposed to call you a pussy for reading? What's he supposed to do?*

Bob scratched his head. *Is this going to be a test?* he asked.

I poked Bob in the chest. *See?* I said. You didn't know what was going on, even though you asked the question.

I waved at the bartender, and when she came over, I nodded at the guy. "He a regular?"

"More regular than you," she said.

"You dialed the charm all the way up for me, didn't you?"

She dropped her middle finger and rotated her hand until the digit was pointing straight up, showing me how far her dial went.

"Can I buy him a beer?"

"Sure, you can," she said. "But it won't make any difference."

"I'm not trying to save him. I just want to make sure he stays hydrated." I gestured at his face. "A man's eyes can get awfully dry with all that staring."

A tiny crack appeared in her facade as she wandered off. When she came back, she had two beers, both poured high and tight. She put one in front of the old dude and put the other one in front of me. She picked up the terrible pour she had brought to me, a tight motion struggling to make itself seen on her lips.

Friendliness had its limits at the Eagle.

I picked up the beer and raised it to the dude sitting nearby. He had already gulped down half of his pint glass, and he exhaled loudly when he lowered his glass.

She was right. It didn't make any difference. As soon as he finished the beer—which wasn't long—he went back to staring at me.

I finished mine a little more leisurely, paid my tab, and got up from the bar. Other than buying the weird dude a beer, I had made no lasting impact on the place. As soon as I walked out the door, it was going to revert right back to the way it was before I walked in. Just a bunch of dudes waiting for something to happen somewhere, along with their waitress who had given up a long time ago. The rest of her life was going to be spent being angry about some decision she had made two or three decades back.

The guy playing pool had finished his game, and he was standing there, the rack in his hands. He had looked past me when I had stepped away from the bar, but there had been no sign on his face that he was thinking about anything other than breaking the next rack.

Yep. It seemed like exactly the sort of place that would attract a careerist like Ralph.

☆

It was late enough that traffic was going to be bad for a few hours, and so I went to the Pico branch of the Santa Monica Public Library and checked out a few weeks worth of *The LA Times*. Bayance's name showed up regularly in the Metro section. He was the guy who the editors went to when they needed some institutional knowledge to put pieces together.

While reading the *Times*, I learned the LAPD were looking at a group called "Vista 13" for the first robbery. Bayance's background on Vista 13 said they were a splinter branch of the group that had come out Mar Vista Gardens—a sprawling project built in the 1970s when the city of Los Angeles and the federal government attempted to pave over the race issues by building tract housing in terrible areas. Naturally, these projects weren't well maintained, and things got feral and feudal.

Occasionally, Bayance would reference the *Venice Voice*, and when I asked at the reference desk, I was told it was a weekly magazine based in—guess where?—Venice, California. I checked out a stack of the *Voice* and went through them too. It was filled with the sort of fluff you'd expect from a weekly servicing a tourist destination, but one writer caught my attention. She wrote lean prose, with a fiery edge that would have pushed her content to the op-ed page at a larger paper. She was writing a series of articles about the changes the neighborhoods were suffering through, focusing on the families who had been living in the area for generations.

When I was done, I didn't have any better idea of the angle Bayance was pushing. If it was in the paper, then it went farther back than what the local library had. I could go ask Mrs. Chow—that'd be nice and direct—but she would pretend to not understand English. I wasn't fooled, but when the woman wanted to stone-wall you, there was no way of getting her to talk.

I couldn't see myself calling Jackie either. *Oh, hey, Butch. Thanks for calling. Yeah, can you believe it? I'm a criminal mastermind. I never thought anyone would figure it out.*

Which left the *Times* writer.

I found a pay phone in the lobby of the library and dialed the main number of the paper. When the receptionist answered, I asked to speak to Peter Bayance. The woman asked me to hold as she transferred my call.

It rang twice and then someone picked it up. "Hello?"

"Ah, hello? Yeah, uh, hi. I'm trying to reach Peter Bayance," I said.

There was silence on the line. "Why?" the voice asked.

"I wanted to talk to him about a story he wrote the other day," I said. "I might have some insight."

"Yeah? He know you?"

"No," I said. "We've never met. Is he there?"

"Nah. Stepped out for a minute," the voice said. "I can take a message for him."

"Yeah, okay," I said. "Tell him that Bliss called."

"Bliss?"

"Yeah, Bliss."

"Okay, Bliss. You called. You want to say anything else?"

"Tell him I'm calling about the shooting at the EZ Quickie Mart the other night."

"The EZ Quickie . . . ? Oh, yeah. I remember reading about that."

"Really?" I said. I had a suspicion I was talking to Peter. "When did you read it? Was it when you were waiting to get your colostomy bag emptied?"

The line was quiet again. "Something like that," the guy said.

"Right. Well, tell Bayance that the guy who was in the market when those dumbass started shooting wants to talk to him."

"Wait, wait. Hang on. He just walked into the newsroom. Hold on."

The line went dead. I told myself I'd give him ten seconds. He came in eight. A little breathless, like he had just run to the phone. I wasn't fooled. I could tell it was the same guy. "This is Bunko," he said. "Who's this?"

"The same guy you were talking to less than ten seconds ago," I said.

I listened to him breathe for a few seconds, and then he let out a dry laugh. "No one calls me 'Peter' except for my sister in Florida and my editor. And I don't like either of them."

I can't imagine why," I said dryly.

"So, you were there, were you?" he said. "At the EZ Q?"

"I was."

"And?"

"And what?"

"Well, you tell me," he said. "It's your quarter."

And I was starting to think I had spent the money foolishly. "Look," I said. "Whatever theory you've got is wrong. There's no criminal enterprise operating out of that store."

"Yeah? You want to say that on the record?"

"I'd rather not."

"So, you're wasting my time then?"

"No, I—"

"Look. I get a lot of calls from people who want to tell me how I got things wrong. If I talked to all of you idiots, I'd never get any work done. You're going to have to do a little better."

"You made it sound like the local Sureños chapter is taking a run at the Chow family."

"Did I?"

"Yeah, you did. But that's not what happened."

"No?"

"The guys with guns. They weren't Mexicans."

He laughed. "Of course they were. It's their territory."

"It wasn't. It was two white dudes. I was there. And I knew one of them."

That shut him up for a second. I heard paper rustling and the sound of the phone receiver being juggled. "Okay, what did you say your name was?"

"Bliss," I said. "Butch Bliss."

I did a three-count in my head and interrupted him when he started to challenge me. "Yeah," I said. "That's my name. I did a dime in CDCR. Shared a cell with a guy named Ralph something or other. He was the twitchier of the shooters."

"Okay, okay." He talked under his breath as he wrote. *Bliss. 10 years. Cali penal. Ralph.* "Where?" he asked.

"Tehachapi," I said. "Ralph went to Lancaster."

"Tehachapi. Lancaster. Got it." Paper rustled again. "Okay, look. I need some time to check this out. Can I call you back in an half hour?"

I glanced at the clock. The library was closing in twenty minutes. "I won't be at this number in an half hour," I said.

"Okay, okay. How about . . . How about . . . there's a Thai place on Pico. North side. Between 32nd and 33rd. Can you meet me there in, say, about an hour?"

"Yeah, sure," I said. "I can do that."

"Okay. I'll see you then."

He started to hang up. "Hey, Pe—Bunko—how will I know you?" I asked.

He laughed. "I'll know you. Your mug shot will be in the system if you're telling me the truth, won't it?"

I nodded, though he couldn't see me. "I'm much handsomer now," I said.

"Aren't we all?"

CHAPTER 7

THE THAI RESTAURANT WAS ABOUT TEN BLOCKS AWAY, AND since I was going to be extraordinarily early if I drove, I decided to walk. We did a lot of walking in prison, though we never went very far and we never went very fast. Walking down a long boulevard, like Pico, was still a novelty for me, even though I had been out for several years. It was that sense of freedom, that I could—if I wanted to—keep walking forever.

But I didn't walk forever. I only went up to 32nd, spotted the Thai restaurant, went past it a few blocks, and then came back again. This chewed up forty-five minutes or so. I stood on the corner of Pico and 33rd for a few minutes, watching traffic roll by. I wasn't paying attention to specific cars; I was looking at the flow. What was moving. What wasn't. Were cars parked illegally? Were peopel hanging out in their vehicles?

I had no reason to think I was being followed, but there was something nagging at me. Maybe it was a feeling brought on by reading Bayance's articles and thinking about the conspiracy he was attempting to uncover. Maybe it was something that had been planted years ago and was only now scratching its way out of a neglected field. Some seeds didn't need much care. They just needed to be ignored long enough to germinate.

Eventually, I crossed the street and went into the restaurant. It wasn't fancy, but it smelled good and about half of the tables were full. A young man with a spot of beard at the point of his chin seated me in a booth near the front, and I took the side that let me look out the windows. He brought a pot of hot tea and nodded amiably when I said I was waiting for someone.

I drank two cups of the tea before Bayance showed up.

He came in a tan sedan that had never been a sexy set of wheels. It hung low to the ground, more of an issue with the shocks than the design itself, and he half-crawled / half-spilled out of it. His short hair wisped about his head like it was mist collecting on a pale fungus, and he had a lumpy face and a perma frown that said he thought way too often about way too much. He wore a pale blue shirt under a grey windbreaker and his pants were pleated in the front. Urban tourist camouflage. Cheap sunglasses covered his eyes, and he took them off when he entered the dim restaurant.

He looked around the room. I didn't try to hide, but it still took him a few passes before he finally matched my handsome face with a mug shot from back in the day. Bayance came over to my booth and slid into the other side. "You Bliss?" he asked.

"I am," I said.

He nodded. "I did some research on you."

I spread my hands like this wasn't a surprise.

"Interesting reading."

"Less interesting to live."

"I bet. And that bit with the snake guy?"

"Overly dramatized." I smiled. "It had been a slow news week."

"There's no such thing in LA," Bayance said. "There's only a pause between acts."

"How very Shakespearean of you."

He cocked his head. "Richard II or King Lear?"

"I was thinking more *Two Goons in Denmark*."

"I don't know that one."

"Pity," I said. "That was their complaint too."

Bayance smiled, letting me know he got the joke.

The young kid wandered by, and without looking at the menu, Bayance ordered one of the combos, asking for several substitutions, thereby the whole concept of pre-packaging food items on a combination menu. When the young man looked at me, I ordered some pot stickers.

"That's it?"

"I'm pacing myself," I said.

"Like you are with Mrs. Chow?"

I toyed with my tea cup. "How about we not do it that way?" I asked.

"Which way is that?" he asked, trying to look innocent.

"The way where you keep asking me 'are you still masturbating in public restrooms?' sort of questions."

"Jesus. If you are, I really don't want to know about that."

"Sure you do, *Pete*." I put a bit of spin on his name, just to see if it would wind him up, and I was mildly surprised to see a flush creep up his neck.

Be nice. I heard myself talking to Tattoo Bob. *Change the situation. Take charge of how the dance is going to go.*

"Why 'Bunko'?" I asked.

He poured himself a cup of tea and slurped it down. "I used to surf. Big waves out in Hawaii. The name showed up one afternoon—I don't remember why—but it stuck. You know how those things go."

I thought of a conversation with a producer a long time ago. *We got one Bobby. We don't need two. Come up with something different and maybe it'll make a difference.* "Yeah, I know how those things go," I said.

He drew his finger through the moisture left by his cup. "You said something about the shooters at the market."

"Yeah, they were white."

He frowned like he didn't like that answer.

"Why'd you write that bit about me being part of the Chow organization," I said. "You didn't even know I was there."

"You were there," he said. "You live with Mrs. Chow, for Christ's sake."

"I live on the same property," I said.

He gave me a *We're playing for the cheap seats here, pal, and they aren't big on nuance* look.

"I've been working the local desk longer than there's been a desk there," Bayance said. "I was the one who kept digging on those assholes who thought they could get away with beating Rodney King. I was there when the verdict came down. I was there the following day when they started looting—stayed on the street for a week to make sure it got reported right. I've been threatened, shot at, had my cat run over—you name it."

"I'd rather not."

"I know who's who in Oakwood better than the gangbangers squatting there know. I interviewed kids in Mar Vista when no one else did. No one knows what's going on in this city better than I do. I don't give a rat's ass about petty crime. It's not worth my . . . "

"Pedigree?" I offered.

"Whatever. The stories I do are important. There are people who get nervous when they see my by-line. Folks downtown sh—"

He broke off as the young kid came by with two bowls of soup. When the young man was gone, he reached for the hot sauce and shot a healthy squirt into his soup. "It's weak," he said. "They're trying too hard to broaden their audience. Your regulars keep you in business. Not the tourists."

"Is that what your editor tells you?" I asked.

"People don't keep up their subscriptions because they think it's a civic duty," he said.

I watched him slurp his soup.

"What's the play here?" I asked. "I called you. Either I'm here for the *They really don't understand me* exclusive or I think you've got it wrong."

"Or you're one of those guys who likes the game."

"What game?"

Behind him, a dark compact rolled by. A flag went up in my head. It was moving like it was looking for a parking spot, but the lot wasn't that full. I noticed the back window was down, while the front wasn't. Why was the back window—

"Move," I snarled at Bayance. He looked at me, a puzzled look on his face. His spoon was halfway to his mouth.

The window behind him shattered, and the restaurant was filled with the stuttering noise of an automatic weapon. I dropped to the floor, covering my head as glass rained down. People started screaming. Outside the restaurant, the wheels of the small car squealed as it left a smear of rubber in the parking lot.

Bayance was still sitting in the booth. His face was down on the table. There was blood on his pants. His hand lay limply beside him. It wasn't moving.

"Did you do something you shouldn't have?" Lorraine asked as she wandered into the lounge on the second floor at Willie's. She had several bottles of water and some healthy snacks from the vending machine downstairs. The lounge was at the back of the building, and its windows looked out over the parking lot and the building across the alley. There were a couple of old couches and a ping-pong table shoved in the corner. Willie hadn't decided what to do with the lounge yet. It was the only private space at the gym.

"I don't know what you are talking about," I said distantly.

I was thinking about the back of Bunko's head. I was thinking about the glass shards I had picked out of my palms while I had walked away from the restaurant. I was thinking about guns.

I couldn't own a gun myself—thanks to the State of California's rules about what ex-cons can and can't do—but that didn't mean I was unfamiliar with them. Mrs Chow owned a Glock 26, a subcompact version of the Glock 17, and she dutifully did her time at the range every other month or so. She wouldn't hear of me sitting out in the car while she ran through a box of ammo, and since the guy who owned the range knew the Chow family, I got to practice on a variety of guns.

Mrs. Chow made a point of talking to the staff about the firmness of my stance and how well I gripped the guns while I shot. The owner made himself scarce during these conversations. The gals who worked the range usually hung around and humored the clan matriarch. Or maybe they were agreeing with her. I couldn't tell. I was busy thinking about what I was doing.

Actually, to be honest, I was trying not to think about what *she* was doing.

Maybe Bunko was right. I could argue all day that I was just a bum, soaking off an old man's nostalgia and last wishes, but it was an argument that was getting harder to say with a straight face. I mean, the only reason "bagman" wasn't accurate was because I didn't carry a bag. But that would only work for the truly pedantic in the audience. Everyone else—like Bunko had said—was buying copy because it made for good reading. Shakespeare wrote *Hamlet* for the cheap seats, because they wanted sex and death and family drama. The bits with Rosencrantz and Guilderstern were there because Shakespeare couldn't help himself. Maybe that was my excuse. I needed the illusion of my independence because the other option was to acknowledge that I owed the old man everything.

"Anyway, this was all I could find in the machine." Lorraine laid out the snacks on the ping-pong table. "It'll have to do, unless you want me to go across the street and get you a real meal."

"No, this is great, Lore," I said.

"Are you hiding out or something?"

"No, I'm dodging my fans."

She wasn't sure if I was kidding. "It's just . . . you didn't say much when you came in, and then you went and worked out on the machines—which isn't like you—and now you're . . . " She gestured around the lounge. "It's kind of a hideout."

"I needed someplace to think," I said.

Her teeth toyed with her bottom lip. "I can order you a burger or something," she said.

"This'll be fine. Really."

"We're going to have a better selection soon, you know."

"Yeah?"

"Yeah. Willie's going to do it. He's going to put in a full-service coffee bar and smoothie shop."

I nodded, happy to be talking about something that had nothing to do with a drive-by shooting at a thai restaurant on Pico Boulevard. "Perks A Lot," I said.

"Yeah, Perks A Lot is going to run it." She gave me a knowing grin. "Did you get your free coffee?"

"I did."

"How was it?"

"Hot," I said.

She raised an eyebrow.

"And delicious," I added. I levered a finger at her. "You are a troublemaker, you know."

She shot me a finger in return. "Always," she said. She gestured toward the door behind her. "You want me to remind you when it's closing time?"

"Sure," I said. "And Lorraine?"

She paused at the door.

"Thanks for bringing me some food."

She made a face. "I like you, Butch," she said. "Don't make a thing about it."

"I'm not. And don't make a thing about checking up on me."

"I wasn't," she insisted. The savage flick of her pony tail as she left gave her away, though.

I ate the snacks. I drank the water. I stared out the window. I waited for something to happen. Nothing did, and I had no great revelation about the day's events. Eventually, it was time to go somewhere else.

On the way home, I caught the local news break on the radio. They had a segment on the drive-by shooting on Pico, mostly to mention that celebrated local journalist—Peter 'Bunko' Bayance—had been the victim of the incident. Police were looking for individuals who have information about the terrible incident. No one mentioned his recent article in the paper, and no one drew any connections to the shooting the other night at the convenience store.

The only people making those connections were me and, possibly, the LAPD. And whoever had done the shooting.

Too many people thinking the same thoughts.

CHAPTER 8

In the morning, I took a long shower to loosen my lower back and thighs, which were annoyed by the workout I had done yesterday. My head was a bit fuzzy still, but cleared up when I hit the line at Perks a Lot.

"Want your usual?" Greta asked, leaning her hip against the edge of the counter. She was wearing a yellow top with a scoop neck, which revealed a lovely swath of quintessentially SoCal sun-burnished skin.

"I've only had it once, so I don't know that I'd call it the 'usual,'" I pointed out.

A car drove up on the other side of the shack. She held eye contact for a second, and then pushed off from the counter with a supple grace. "Missed your chance," she called over her shoulder.

I smiled. I wasn't in a rush.

I noticed the blue Camaro was parked in the same spot as the other day. When Greta came back to the window, I nodded at the sports car. "They there every day?" I asked.

She leaned forward. Her eyes took on a troubled shadow. "They're part of the scenery," she said. "You know how it is."

I nodded. "How about something simpler today," I said. "Not too much milk."

"One or two shots?" she asked.

I watched a guy get out of the Camearo and hitch up his pants. He was talking on a cell phone, and his free hand was making big gestures. "One," I said, opting to not wind myself tighter than I already was.

Greta made the machine do things with steam and coffee beans. I watched the easy movements of her hands and hips as she worked. She put a spoon across the container of foamed milk and made a swirling motion with the cup as she poured. She covered up her handiwork with a lid and brought the cup over to the window.

"Five bucks," she said as she handed the cup over.

"You're kidding."

"We've learned it's easier to overcharge than to convince people to leave a decent tip." She had a hand on her hip, and her tongue teased the corner of her mouth. "I rounded it up, saving you the embarrassment of doing the math."

"Rounded it up from what?"

"Does it matter?" she asked.

I dawdled, letting my engine race. She watched me, a curl still developing on her lips, and then someone impatient for their morning fix interrupted us and she was gone, like the sun fleeing behind storm clouds.

I eased around the shack and let my car roll through the parking lot. I was interested in the Camaro and its occupants. Their colors said they thought they belonged, which was the key thing to remember about gang posers. They look like they belong, but their presense is as much an illusion as is the notion perpetually floated by the men in the steel towers downtown that they really want to clean up the streets. Everyone knows the lie when they see it; the polite act is pretending otherwise.

Had these guys taken the run at Bunko last night?

He knew the place, Mr. Chow pointed out. *He didn't need the menu to order. Same place. Same routine. That's how it happens.*

I could see the how, but the why eluded me. Was it payback for what he had written? But I couldn't think of anything he had written about the Vista 13 gang in the last few weeks.

Was I asking the wrong question? What if it hadn't been the Mexicans. What if it had been someone else?

When I asked that question, suddenly the focus shifted back onto me, and I didn't like being in the spotlight like that.

I had skipped breakfast, and the coffee woke my stomach up. As I was walking past the taco shop below Angel's office, my stomach made even more noise than it had in the car. I ducked into the restaurant, figuring an early lunch would shut it up.

Angel wasn't alone, and the guy with her was well-dressed and paying a lot more attention to her than you normally see between lawyers and their clients. Except on TV, of course.

"Hey, kids," I said as I closed the door loudly. "Anyone hungry?"

Angel took several steps away from the guy, turning away as she did. The guilty turn. A director I knew used to shout this at his actors. *Make the guilty turn! Don't let us see your face. Make us feel like we should look away too.*

The guy, on the other hand, was either cool enough to pretend nothing was going on or he wasn't good at reading cues from his partner. Either way, I wasn't one to make a big deal about canoodling in the office—especially when it wasn't my office.

Angel regained her composure and offered me a polite smile. "Butch. What are you doing here?"

"I brought lunch," I said. I put the bag down on her desk.

"Butch, I—" Angel took a step toward the guy. He was wearing an off-the-rack suit, but it fit him well across the shoulders. It was dark blue, pinstriped with red, and his shirt was a lighter blue. He wasn't wearing a tie, and his shoes were a warm brown leather. Decent hair cut. Nice cheekbones. Had a bit of a dimple when he smiled. He looked like the kind of guy who drove a Range Rover. "This—this is Darnell. Darnell, this is Butch."

Darnell offered a hand. I noticed his watch. His grip was warm and not overly aggressive. "It's nice to meet you, Butch," he said. "Angel says you are a huge supporter of her efforts here."

"Well, she's easy to support."

Darnell let go of my hand and indicated the bag on Angel's desk. "I appreciate your offer, but we've—I've—already eaten."

"I know," I said. I pulled up the client chair and dug into the bag. "I was being polite."

Darnell frowned, and he looked over at Angel for assistance. She figured it out as I stacked foil-wrapped fish tacos on her desk. "Miguel," she said.

I nodded. "You know? Miguel is very polite. Really nice too. Knows everyone's name. Solid customer service. But he's not very good at knowing whether he's supposed to know something. For instance, when I tried to order lunch for you"—I pointed at Angel—"he got all flustered. I asked him if I was ordering the wrong thing, and he said, 'No, no, she likes that.'" I leaned over and glanced in the waste basket next to the desk. There was a brown bag identical to the one I brought.

"Butch—" Angel started. When I looked up, she waved a hand at the food on her desk. "Can you . . . ?"

"What?"

"Can you get a plate?"

I glanced around the office. "I wasn't aware that you had plates."

A measured smile dropped into place on Darnell's face. "I'll get one," he said.

"No, wait—" Angel sighed. She shook her head.

"How about that. The man knows his way around the office," I said. "Is he as familiar with your cupboards at home?"

"Butch. Is this—" She broke off as Darnell returned with a plate. It was green and heavy—exactly like the sort of dishware you'd expect to find in a high-end bistro like, say, Three Hares.

"Thanks, Darnell," I said, transferring my tacos to the plate. I mopped up the smear of water on the desk with a paper napkin.

Darnell looked at me. He looked at Angel. She shook her head like this was something she suffered all too frequently.

I peeled open a fish taco. "Angel and I have some family talk to do," I said. "I'll leave it up to her if she wants you to hear it." I shoved half the fish taco in my mouth and made crunching noises.

"Butch . . ." She gave Darnell a look that said she didn't know what I was talking about.

He took it in stride. "I need to get back to the office," he said, making it easy for everyone. He walked over to Angel and kissed her lightly on the cheek. "I'll call you later." He stopped beside me and put his hand on my shoulder. There was more pressure in this contact than there had been in his handshake. "She'll tell me if it is anything I need to know. Otherwise, it's not my business."

I swallowed the food in my mouth. "Good for her," I said. "And I appreciate your understanding."

Angel watched me finish the first taco as Darnell left the office. I balled up the wrapper and tossed it in the trash as the door clicked shut.

"You're angry," Angel said.

"Well, right now, I'm hungry," I said. "After that, I might get angry." I started on the next taco. "Did you happen to read the paper this morning?"

She shook her head.

"Lucky for you, I got one," I said. I pulled a copy of the *LA Times* out of the bag. It was a little stained with grease, but that was okay. The article I wanted her to read wasn't on the front page. I pulled out the Metro section and passed it over. I finished the rest of my tacos while she read.

Bayance's death made the front page of the Metro section. Most of the article was devoted to a glowing summary of Bunko's career in journalism. Details about the shooting at the Thai restaurant were three sentences in the last paragraph.

Angel put the paper down on her desk. She was pale. "Is this—is this the guy who wrote the article the other day?"

"It is," I said.

"My God," she breathed. "Why—why would someone do this?"

"That's a very good question," I said.

She looked at me, and comprehension dawned in her eyes. "You were there . . ."

I put a finger to my lips.

"Butch! How—how did—"

I wadded up the last of the foil wrappers and put all my trash into the paper bag and put the bag in the trash. "I don't know, Angel," I said. "I spent yesterday looking for Gavin's ring—got nowhere on that, by the way. Since I couldn't figure out why this guy had written that nonsense in his article, I figured I should find out if he regularly jumped to conclusions like that."

"And?"

"He's been writing for the *Times* for forever, it seems. Told me all about his bona fides—"

"So you were there."

"And—" I paused. "Yeah, okay. Look, I called him and asked to talk. He said he'd meet me. We did, and we didn't even get past the soup when a car goes by. Someone in the back seat drops the window and hoses down the front of the restaurant. Who knows who they were shooting at."

"Wait. They were shooting at you?"

"The gun was one of those cheap automatic pistols. It blows through a whole magazine in three seconds. It's got no barrel to speak of and—"

"Butch." Angel shushed me with her hands. "I don't need to know . . ."

"Yeah, right. Sorry."

She toyed with the edge of the newspaper. "What did you talk about?"

"Not much," I admitted. "He tried pushing my buttons about Mrs. Chow."

A tiny smile tugged at Angel's mouth.

"I shouldn't have been surprised, I guess. It's not like it's a state secret or anything, but come on, I'm not famous or anything."

"Except for that thing . . ."

"Which thing?"

"The thing with whatsername."

"Whatsername?"

"You know."

"I do, and I know you know too, so . . ." I gestured at the door where the handsome Chinese-American man had left. "How long have you and *whatsisname* been seeing each other?"

"Darnell," she said automatically.

I gave her a *Is it going to be like that?* look.

"Fine," she sighed. "That thing with Penelope."

"It wasn't a thing," I said.

"The papers said otherwise."

"The papers also say that the Chow family is a criminal organization You shouldn't believe everything you read in the papers."

"Yeah," she said, dragging the word out.

"What?"

"Look, I don't know anything about criminal activity that my brother might be involved in," she said.

"Gosh, counselor, are you volunteering a denial before I've even asked a question?"

She colored slightly. "I'm not unaware of who my father was, or how he made his money."

"He wasn't an upstart bootstrapping entrepreneur?"

It was her turn to give me the *Really, is it going to be like that?* look.

"Tony's—look, he surprised all of us when he came back. And he surprised us again when he said he was going to stay. I didn't understand why. He ran away so fast. Why would he come back?"

"Family," I said. "They get their hooks into you."

"Yeah, maybe." She shoved her hands under her legs and leaned forward. "He's worried about something."

"Tony?"

"Yeah, Tony."

"Okay, what?"

She didn't know. I didn't either.

And that's where we left it: questions and a vague knot tightening in my stomach.

The tacos helped a little, but not enough.

CHAPTER 9

STEVIE WAS AT THE FRONT DESK WHEN I WALKED INTO THE gym. "Yo, Butch," he called. He held out a business card. For a moment, I thought it was going to be another card from Perks A Lot, but the severe logo of the Las Angeles Police Department dashed that hope. "Some suit was looking for you."

I read Detective Lorenzo's name on the card. "Yeah?"

"Said he had some questions for you."

"I bet he does."

Stevie peered at me, his face puckering up as he tried to read my expression. "Didja boost a car or something?"

"No, nothing like that," I said.

"That's good," Stevie said. "I thought maybe you'd gone all arrivederci on us."

"What?"

He made a vague stabbing motion with his meaty hands. "You know, that thing where you . . . you know."

"No, I don't know."

He glanced at a pair of attractive young women as they strolled into the gym. He flashed them a big grin and said hello. They waved and smiled back. He beamed at their backsides as they headed upstairs to one of the workout studios.

I snapped my fingers, drawing his attention away from the pert pair rocking their hips. "What are you talking about, Stevie?" I asked.

"When?"

The big man's attention span was worse than mine. "Just now. That word you used. *Arrivederci*. What are you talking about?"

"Isn't that something you say when you're kissing your neighbor's daughter in Italy?"

"No, Stevie. It's not what you say when you're kissing your neighbor's daughter."

His eyebrows went up. "What do you say when you're—"

"Hey, Butch." Lorraine saved me from committing bodily harm to the muscle-bound doorman. She popped around the counter and gave me a broad smile. "What are you two talking about?"

"Butch is talking about frenching some farmer's daughter," Stevie said.

"I was saying no such thing."

"Wow," Lorraine said. "And so early in the afternoon too. Have you been drinking?"

"Not noticeably," I said.

She gave me a *You're not as sly as you think you are* look. "Oh, yeah, there was some guy from LAPD here looking for you."

I tapped Lorenzo's card on the counter. "Yeah, Stevie got that much right."

"You do something you shouldn't have done?"

"No more so than usual," I replied.

"Recidivist," Lorraine whispered, a wicked gleam in her eye.

"That's it," Stevie said. "Redivicist."

I left the two of them to work on Stevie's grasp of the language. I thought it was a pointless exercise, but Lorraine always enjoyed impossible projects. She might be able to get him to pronounce the word correctly by the end of the week, and I felt a flare of jealousy for Stevie's education. Lore knew how to make a man want to live up to the words she called him.

"You do your time?" Willie asked when I dropped into the chair in his office.

"It depends on who you ask, apparently," I said, which made him look up from his work. He was looking at the financial section of the paper, and a legal pad nearby had a bunch of scribbled notes.

"Recidivist," I said.

He leaned forward and turned around the daily calendar on his desk. "Good guess," he said. It was one of those Word-a-Day calendars, and underneath the word I had just used was a neat definition. *One who relapses.*

"Your staff is eagerly trying it out on paying customers," I said.

"You don't pay," he pointed out.

"I guess that means my complaint with management is going to fall on uncaring ears."

"It'll be filed in the appropriate drawer," he replied. He took off his reading glasses and examined my face. "You look like your dog died or something."

I let out a bark of laughter. "I'd be throwing a party if that mutt passed."

"Which mutt?"

"The barking pisser that wakes me up every morning."

"The what?"

"Baby Baby," I said. "He's a furry rat who makes a lot of noise and—" I made a waving motion with my hand.

Willie repeated the motion. "All over?" he asked.

"Well, not all over. Just once."

"And you're still angry about it?"

"It was a couple grand in cash, Willie."

"So, wait. This dog—which isn't yours—pissed all over a bunch of money you had lying around."

"It wasn't *lying* around."

"Was it yours?"

"The money? Yeah."

"This is why they make banks, son."

"To keep dogs from whizzing on your green?"

"And other reasons, yeah."

"I should look into that," I said, giving him a *Thanks for the hot tip, wise old feller* look.

He shook his head. "You gotta invest that stuff, Butch. It doesn't do you any good in a duffel bag under your bed."

"It's still a novelty."

He laughed at that.

We sat in silence for a few minutes. Willie toyed with his glasses. I looked at the old movie posters on the walls. "Whadya need, Butch?" Willie asked finally.

"Nothing," I said. "Why do you think I need something?"

"You've got that look."

"What look?"

"Well, apparently it's not the *My dog died* look, so it's got to be something else."

"I might need some help finding a guy."

"A guy?"

"Yeah, a guy."

"He's not in the phone book?"

"Nah, I don't think he's in the book."

"Have you looked?"

I admitted I hadn't.

"You should do that first," Willie said.

"Can we pretend I already did?"

Willie put his glasses on his desk. "What kind of help?"

"A couple of phone calls."

"And you can't make these calls yourself because . . . ?"

I smiled at him. He shook his head. "You're a really terrible detective," he said.

"I'm not a detective," I replied. "I'm an ex-con."

"Aren't you types supposed to have a network?"

I leaned forward and tapped the edge of the desk calendar. "That's the sort of things these people have."

"And you're not recidivising?"

"I don't think that's a word," I said.

"Awfully literate of you."

"Nothing but the best education the California penal system could provide."

He leaned back in his chair. "You should call that guy—that friend of yours."

"Which friend?"

"The who would be happy to do this sort of secretarial work for you."

"You're not happy about doing it?"

Willie smiled. "For a man who has a couple grand lying around, I don't see any of it coming across my desk."

"It smells bed."

"What smells bad? My desk?"

"No, the cash."

"Isn't that what the laundry is for?"

"There you go, casting aspersions on my character again."

Willie put his glasses on and returned to his paper. "Call your friend," he said.

"Thanks, Dad," I said.

"And get a job too, you slacker," he said as I left his office.

The friend was a gentleman named Horatio Gomez Bartolomé, though no one—not even his mother—referred to him that way. He was "Huggy Bear" to his friends; he was "That Fuck-nut Huggy Bear" to his enemies; and, well, the ladies added whatever emphasis they wanted, because Horatio Gomez never said no to whatever the ladies wanted. Which had, not surprisingly, gotten him into trouble now and again.

Huggy Bear and I went back to my first week of being a free man. We had met while sneaking onto the set of *Beach Patrol*, a TV show that had gone into world-wide syndication before the first season had finished airing.

Huggy had a thing for one of the female leads.

The simplest way to find Huggy Bear was to figure out where *Beach Patrol* was shooting. He was bound to be rubber-necking from the sidelines.

I called one of those tourist agencies that kept track of the daily hots spots of Hollywood activity and learned that *Beach Patrol* was on-location north of Santa Monica. *Pacific Palisades*, the agent said. *Along the beach.*

I drove down to Ocean Avenue and went north until I hit Santa Monica proper, and then I tucked into the flow of traffic heading onto PCH. The sun dazzled off the water, and playful clouds puffed along the horizon. It was a quintessentially LA weather: not too hot, not too cold, a little breeze off the water. A good DP with a couple of filters could make sun-baked sand look like crystallized sugar and naked bodies glisten like gold.

The big parking lot at the Will Rogers State Park was filled with lots of trucks and fancy-looking trailers. A couple of LA's finest were on hand to make sure traffic kept moving, and I queued into the line endlessly circling the portion of the lot where tourists were allowed to gather. I got lucky and found a spot after a couple of passes. I left my car and wandered over to where a PA was attempting to manage the forty or so fans of the show who wanted to see and be seen.

Beach Patrol was a truly Hollywood creation. It was a police procedural show, but consistently found excuses for its ensemble cast to strip down to form-fitting bathing suits and go running in slow-motion along the beach. Critics hated it because they were either purists or puritans, but the rest of the world ate it up. It was in its sixth or seventh season, and it had spawned a dozen shallow imitators. It was a pipeline for hot young things to go from centerfold to starlet.

A number of the male cast were actually professional surfers or ex-lifeguards, and who could blame them? The hours were better, the threat to life and limb was less, and the company was much more attractive.

I made my way to the front of the crowd at the marked barrier and caught the PA's attention. "Lola's Boy around today?" I asked.

The PA—a kid who looked like he was still trying to grow his first mustache—looked at his clipboard. "I don't—" he started. As he was distracted, a long-haired surfer boy slipped under the sawhorse and made a break for the trailers. "Hey," the PA shouted, abandoning his station to chase after the fan.

I glanced at the portly *Beach Patrol* fan standing next to me. He was wearing a visored hat and had done a terrible job of applying SPF-50 over his sweat-streaked face. "Been here long?" I asked.

"Hey, aren't you—" he started.

"No," I said as I nimbly crossed the barrier and strode off toward the set. SPF Fan squawked behind me, but I didn't look back or run. I merely walked like I knew who I was and where I was going.

It's the first rule in Hollywood, after all. It's on everyone else if they don't recognize you or know what you're doing.

I found Huggy and his coterie camped near the beach-side of the parking lot. They couldn't been seen from the tourist area, and they had an unobstructed view of the action. Huggy Bear was a sparkplug of a man who came up to the middle of my chest. He was narrow in the waist, but thick in the thigh and the neck. He wore a lemon-colored name brand track suit and blindingly white athletic shoes. A shapeless beret covered his short-cropped hair, and sunglasses with enormous designer logos at the temples covered his eyes.

He was sitting in a canvas-backed director's chair, his fingers flying across the keyboard of a blocky laptop computer. On the back of the chair was a stencil that looked like it might have come from a nose cone of a World War II fighter jet.

"View's pretty good," I said as I came up next to his chair. "You can almost see the water from here."

Huggy Bear looked up and did a Tex Avery-worthy double take. His face broke out into a huge grin and he hopped out of his chair. "Bliss!" he cried as he set the laptop down and wrapped me in a spine-cracking embrace.

I returned the hug as best I could with my ribs creaking. Huggy let go of me before all the lights went out in my head, and he turned to the fellows sitting in the other chairs. "Guys! Look who it is!"

His crew looked at me. Expressions didn't change. No light-bulbs clicked on in these heads.

"It's Bliss," Huggy exclaimed. "Butch Bliss!"

"Don't get up," I said to the crew, releasing them from the need to pretend they knew who I was.

"Oh, man. It's been awhile," Huggy said. "What have you been up to?"

"This and that, mostly," I said.

Huggy laughed. "I love that. So authentic." He reached for his laptop, and balancing it on one hand, he pecked out a few words with the other. Mouthing them as he wrote them down. "I'm going to use that. Do you mind if I use it?"

"Go ahead," I said.

Huggy was, like everyone else in LA, working on a screenplay. As far as I knew, he'd never managed to get it in front of anyone with the power to greenlight projects. He kept working on it, and working on it, and working on it . . .

It was a feedback loop in his head. If he finished the script and no one bought it, then it must suck. If he never finished it, then it had to be genius.

It was written for Lolita Brigade—one of the breakout stars of *Beach Patrol* and the object of Huggy Bear's endless infatuation. He had gotten pages of an earlier draft to her, but that was another story for another time. I wasn't sure why she hadn't filed a restraining order on him. Unless—God help us all—she liked his writing.

"She still letting you creep her like this?" I asked, looking over at the row of silver trailers that kept the cast hidden from the public eye.

He grabbed the chair he had been sitting on. "You see this?" he said. "Teaser art."

"Teaser for what?"

"The movie, Butch! The—you know—the movie."

"Oh, *that* movie." I glanced at the others, hoping to get a placard or cue card that would help me. They continued to ignore me.

"Her agent's seen a draft," Huggy Bear gushed. "They think Paramount is interested."

"They *think*?"

He shrugged. "It needs a little work," he said. "It shouldn't take more than a couple of weeks."

"And when did she say this?"

Some of his enthusiasm leaked out when he exhaled. "Six months ago," he admitted.

I clapped him on the shoulder. "You'll get it figured out," I said. "I know you can."

"I'm trying, man. I'm really trying. Lo needs a real role. One that lets the rest of the world see what I see. I know I can do it. I just need—" He shook his head, and then brightened. "Hey, I thought you weren't in the biz."

"I'm not," I said.

"So what are you doing on set?"

"I came to find you," I said.

"You did?" He looked past me and then examined my clothing more closely. "How'd you get on set?" he asked.

"I walked on."

He laughed and looked at his buddies again. "See? What did I tell you about this guy?"

One of the three threw me a look that said *We've heard it so many times that we're ready to run into traffic if he starts again.*

"Did I tell you about that time—" Huggy Bear started, and one of the other guys' head came up with the same expression, except his eyes were bigger.

"Hey, is that Lolita coming out of her trailer?" I asked, interrupting him.

Huggy whirled and stared. "Where? Where?"

The second guy mouthed *Thank you* at me.

I gave him a nod as I put my hand on Huggy Bear's back, gently nudging him away from the lads. "Is that one hers?" I asked.

"The silver one?"

They were all silver.

"No," I said. "The other one."

"Oh, right. Yeah. Yeah." Huggy and I walked away from the canvas chairs, nodding and looking like we were out bird-watching.

No one was coming out of any of the trailers. Once we were far enough away from Huggy's pals that they couldn't readily overhear us, Huggy came to a stop. He stood, rocking back and forth on the balls of his feet. He kept his gaze on the trailers. "She's not on set today," he said quietly.

"You sure?"

He shot me a sidelong glance.

"Her agent never got back to me," he admitted. "It's been . . ."

"Six months," I said. "Yeah, I read between the lines back there."

"Do you know what it's costing me to keep up the pretense of this fucking fan club?"

"Does she know you're doing it, at least?"

"Yeah, I'm sure she does. She has to." He nodded back at the chairs. "You remember that film she was in last summer? The one about the archeologists who found that tomb and the cursed monkey?"

"Monkey? You mean mummy?"

"No, monkey. A fucking cursed monkey. It came back to life and attacked people."

"And?"

"That's it. It was a fucking hand-puppet."

I nodded slowly. "Yeah, I seem to remember something about that. Didn't it go straight to video?"

"No, it went straight to the archive. Opened on three screens in two cities, so the production company could fulfill contractual obligations with her company and the investor group who had put money into it, and then they dug a deep hole and buried it."

I realized the nature of his distress. "How much did you lose?" I asked.

"I don't want to talk about it," he said.

"Jesus, Huggy, you know better. You can't buy your way into a movie star's heart. Not in this town."

He made a noise with his mouth. "It wasn't like that."

I tried to remember the movie. "Didn't she have a bit part in that? Not much more than a cameo, right? Just enoug to put her name on the poster. Why the hell would you invest in something like that?"

"Her boyfriend was the director," Huggy spat. "He told me if *Curse of the Monkey's Paw* did well, he'd talk Lo into doing my script."

I fought to keep a smile off my face. "You're too much of a romantic for this town," I said.

"No, goddamn it. The dream is real, Butch. I'm not going to give it up."

"Nor should you," I said.

We stood and looked at the quartet of movie star trailers, none of which contained the eternal object of Huggy Bear's obsession.

"So, whydja need to see me?" Huggy finally asked.

"I need a favor."

"Sure," he said. "What kind of favor?"

"I need to find out everything you can about a guy named Ralph who was at Tehachapi with me. Eighteen when he came in. Grand theft auto. Got transferred to Lancaster, and probably served out the rest of his sentence there."

"You got a last name?"

"We weren't that close," I said.

"Why he'd get transferred?"

"I may have banged his head too hard against the bars in our cell."

"Our?"

"He got slotted with me."

"What did he do to piss you off?"

I raised my shirt and showed him the pale scar.

"Jesus. What did he do that with?"

"A piece of wire from the bedspring."

"I guess I'd have banged him a couple of times too." He made a face as he realized what he'd said. "Sorry. I didn't mean it like that—"

"I've heard worse," I said.

"Probably seen worse too," he said. I caught him smirking as he looked toward the sun. He broke out laughing a moment later, unable to contain his twelve-year old self. "Damn it, Bliss. Why do you have to set me up like that?"

"I'm the world's last straight man," I said, which only set him off again.

"Can you get me what I need?" I asked when he stopped being tickled by our routine.

"Yeah, yeah," he said. "CDCR is pretty easy to hack. It shouldn't take me long." He reached into the front pocket of his track suit and produced a flat case that he flipped open to reveal a tiny keyboard and screen. "What's your number?"

I looked at him and shrugged.

"You don't have a cell phone?"

"Not today."

"You really are *that* straight."

"I prefer 'rustic,'" I said.

"'Rusty' is more like it."

"Call Willie's Gym," I said. "Over in Venice. Ask for Lorraine."

"Oh, so you have a service, but you don't have a cell phone?"

"She's not a service—"

"Are you banging her?"

I gave him one of the looks we used in the yard, and he put up his hands. "Okay, okay. Sorry." He put his phone back in his pocket. "Yeah, yeah, I'll call. Give me a day or two."

"Great. Thanks, Huggy." I put out my hand, but he wrapped his arms around me again.

"It's been too long, Bliss," he said, his voice muffled against my chest.

"Yeah," I said, tapping my fists on his shoulders. "It has."

CHAPTER 10

I SPENT THE REST OF THE AFTERNOON, WANDERING AROUND MAR Vista and Ocean Park, dropping into pawn shops as I found them. I didn't have a real plan or design; I was fiddling with an idea. Trying to get a sense of the landscape. Letting my brain stew on things. I almost bought a second-hand guitar and a Marshall amp along with a new amplifier for a stereo I didn't have. Somewhere along the way I caved and picked up a worn CD of rock and roll classics. I played it loudly in the car, and the sun kept time as it danced toward the horizon. I ate standing up at a burger stand near the beach, and as I walked back to the car in the fading breath of the magic hour—that last bit of good movie-magic light—I decided to try the Red Eagle again.

Rats come out after nightfall, after all.

The lot was half full when I arrived, and I parked the BMW next to a silver Charger. There was a line of motorcycles along the curb—a couple of customs, two Harleys, and one with a decked out sidecar. A pair of weak lights illuminated the door—the Eagle doing its best to be inviting—and I walked into a place that was very different from the breath of stale air the other day.

The jukebox was playing metal favorites from the '80s, and most of the crowd was gathered around the pool tables. My friend from the other day was on his same stool, and I was willing to bet he was wearing the same shirt. The same hospitality ambassador was behind the bar, and if she recognized me, she gave no sign. I ordered two beers, shoved one toward my stool-bound pal, and leaned against the bar.

The interesting group was the party of five playing at the table closest to the bar. They looked like they had all lived in the same village up in the ice and snow. The tall guy was regal looking and had enigmatic tats running up his arms and around his neck. The short guy shaved his head so there'd be no question how short he was, He wore ripped jeans and a t-shirt that looked like someone had vacuum-sealed it to his chest. The two ladies—shockingly blonde and willowy—were taller than the bald guy, which was undoubtedly a constant source of erotic irritation for him. One of the pair was braiding the other's hair, and the second one's hands kept wandering in a friendly way. The diminutive one kept sneaking glimpses at them; the tall one regarded them with the bored distain one has for pets.

The last guy of the quintent—the most unassuming looking one in the bunch—was concentrating on the game.

In the back, a trio of dudes in biker leather were playing darts. They didn't talk much and the way they were flipping said they were engaged in serious business.

There were a few other patrons, but they were either like the somnambulist on the stool or like me—someone who had wandered in off the street. They hunched over their half drunk beers, wondering if they should be daring and finish their drinks or just get the fuck out while they could.

As I sipped my first beer and considered whether a second was worth my time, the dart game wrapped up and one of the three players came over to the bar.

The bartender gave him a nod that said she knew what he wanted, and as she went to pour for him and his buddies, he put his hands on the bar and checked out the room. He was long in the face, with a scruff of stubble on his cheeks and chin. He had a shadow on his forehead that the light didn't banish. It was more like a burn mark from lightning than a scar. A distinguishing mark, nonetheless, which was probably why he had been wearing a mask the last time I had seen him.

He had recognized me during his first glance around the room. He hid it well, but his eyes went past me and then came back twice more before he got his beers. When he left the bar with two of the four beers, he detoured past the pool table and paused for a minute to talk to the giant. The giant didn't look in my direction, but there was a brief tightening of his face when Scar spoke to him.

Scar returned to his buddies, passed out the beers, and then came back to the bar for the remaining beers. This time, when he looked at me, I met his gaze. I didn't think I had scared him with my *I know the rules of this yard* look, but when the darts started up again, his throwing sucked. His pals were all over his game.

I was just about to make a dignified exit, when Sleepy-Eye spoke. "I know you," he slurred.

I glanced at him. Most of the beer in the glass I had pushed toward him was gone, and he was nursing the last inch like a professional.

"I'm not that guy," I said.

"Which guy?"

"The one you think I look like."

"No, no." He waved a hand. "It's not like that. It's something else. But I know you."

I felt a wave approaching—a psychic parting of the waters as something massive approached. The giant, who was even taller up close than he was at a distance—slapped a meaty hand on Sleepy-Eye's shoulder and nearly made the drunk dribble in his glass. "Dag." The giant's voice was softer and higher than I expected. Downright pleasant, in fact. No wonder the ladies were eager to please. "Pacing yourself, I see."

Dag lowered his glass and levered a corkscrewing finger at me. "I know this guy."

"Yeah?" The giant was close enough to reach me with his mighty mitts. "Where from?"

"The TV," Dag slurred. "No, wait, man. Bigger. On screen. Yeah. I saw him in a movie or something."

"Really?" The giant gave me a look that said *I'm not a starfucker but I know how to be polite.* "You an actor?"

"Who isn't in this town?" I said.

"Me," the giant said, dropping the starry-eyed look for something colder. When I waited a beat too long, he smiled—showing impressive dental work—and stuck out a hand. "I'm shitting you, man. We're all in showbiz, aren't we?"

I shook hands. He didn't try to crunch my knuckles, but there was enough tension there to let me know that he could crush a couple of walnuts without any trouble. Or my nut sack. "Tore," he said.

"Banger!" Dag said suddenly. "That's who you are. You're Bobby Banger."

I shook my head. "No, you've—"

There was no light of recognition in Tore's eyes. Thankfully.

The beer in Dag had pickled his brain to a point where he was seeing connections that weren't there. "No, man. I've seen one of your films. At the Blue." He cackled and nearly slipped off his stool. "On the big screen!"

The Blue was a run-down little theater in West Hollywood that had built a devoted little audience around adult films. When I had been in the business, the studios had read the lay of the land and were scrambling toward VHS distribution as fast as they could set up a tape duplication farm. There were a few holdouts, however, auteurs who weren't ready to let go of the dream of making a film that someone could point to and say, "That's art, man." The Blue was their patron. As long as someone kept printing skin flicks, the Blue would keep showing them. I didn't even remember which of my movies had—

"That one about the muscle cars," Dag said, a fount of knowledge that kept bubbling over. "What was it called? *Hot Chicks and Hot Rods*?

Ah, yes. *Hot Tarts and Hot Wheels*. I had been Stud in the Trunk. One of the three Hot Tarts discovered me shortly after they had reached their hideout in the desert and we had—

Anyway, it had been Bobby's breakout film. He was in, like, a half dozen sequences. The only reason I had gotten a shot at screen time had been because he had pulled a muscle in his calf earlier that day. The producer told him to ice his leg and be back first thing in the morning. Since they had the crew and the talent on-hand, they shot some extra footage. It was never explained why I had been in the trunk of the car. It didn't matter, really. No one watched those films for the intricately nuanced plot.

"Feature film, eh?" Tore was impressed. "Wow."

"It was more of a boutique production," I said, somewhat mortified that I had fallen into that bottomless well of needy validation. Any actor that says they have no ego is lying. Trust me.

Tore gave me a knowing wink. He looked at the bartender, who was clearly more enamored with him than me. "Can I get another round, Inge?" He thrust his well-defined chin at me. "And pour one for this guy, too."

"That's—that's very kind of you," I said.

He shrugged. "You bought Dag a round. That's a point in your favor."

I glanced at Dag, who was lost in his celluloid recollection. "Kind of like the assholes and puppies test?"

"Yeah," he said, a grin tugging at the corner of his mouth. "Kind of like." He hooked a thumb toward the table. "You want to join us? Free could use a partner with a sense of humor."

I looked over at the gang around the table. Short Stuff was practicing his death stare and the other guy—Free? Really?—had a vacant stare that was more unerving than Short Stuff's hard eye. It was the ones who didn't look like they were all there that you had to worry about.

"Sure," I said. "What's the expected ratio between jokes and putting balls in pockets?"

"Whatever lets me win and keeps the ladies laughing. Can you handle that?"

I checked out the ladies in question. The hairdresser had finished braiding the other woman's hair, and they were watching Tore and me with a hint of feral anticipation.

I knew what Mr. Chow would say. I know what Tattoo Bob would say too. Hell, I knew what my own sense of self-preservation was knocking on the back of my skull about.

"Yeah," I said. "I can do that."

"Come on, then," Tore said, putting his hand on my shoulder and giving me a squeeze that made my bones ache. "Let's go make some new friends."

Dag started cackling as we walked away from the bar, and I hoped he was still thinking about *Hot Tarts and Hot Wheels* and not about the hot water I had just eased into.

I assumed "Free" was short for something like Frederick or Freehold, but no, his parents named him in memory of the hazy dream America offered to all immigrants. He—like Tore and Sven—had grown up among the tall trees of Idaho. They had wandered south after deciding they were done freezing their balls off during the long winters. He split the difference in height, disposition, and brooding temperament between Sven and Tore in a way that would make a casting director swoon. Sven had the patience of a howler monkey and Tore seemed like he could pretend to be a tree for so long that moss would grow on him.

The ladies—Margit and Ragnhild—were SoCal born and breed, though it was difficult to figure out how they managed to get a couple decades into life without *some* sun. Ragnhild's hair really was as pale as it looked from over by the bar, and I couldn't fault Margit's fascination with it. They were both as blue-eyed as the sea on a sunny day, though there was a chill in Ragnhild's eyes that said she knew how to bite.

The four of us—Tore, Sven, Free, and I—were there for their amusement, and we played doubles. Tore and Sven—tall and short, fire and ice, hard and harder—against Free and me. Free thought pool was a game of angles and inertia; I knew it was an exercise in finesse and control. We were evenly paired, and I did my best to prance for the ladies during Free's interminable mental calculations.

"Are you still making movies?" Margit asked as Free took up a cue and started examining the table.

"Me? No. I haven't done that for a while," I said.

She pouted and plucked at the lip of her wine glass.

"What are you doing instead?" Tore asked. He was standing beside Ragnhild, and she was pressing her shoulder against the inside of his thigh. He was watching Free pace around the table, but I knew he tracking everything I did and said.

"This and that," I said, going with one of my well-practiced answers. It didn't land as well as I would have hoped, and so I fumbled for another answer. "I like to keep my options open."

You are killing it tonight, Mr. Chow rumbled in my head.

This crowd is a bunch of free spirits, I countered. *They appreciate the simplicity of the unfettered and uncomplicated life.*

Free frowned at the table. As near as any of us could tell, he was trying to calculate how to sink the yellow one in the pocket nearest me and then bank the cue ball to nudge the seven ball into the pocket on other side of the table. The complicated part was all the striped balls that were in the way.

The shot was tough, and Free was going to weigh his options until he was sure he could make it. Unfortunately, Free's opinion about his skills was off by a factor of three, at least.

Next to the pocket where the seven was supposed to go, Sven vibrated. It was his natural state: hyperactive and perpetually ready to blow his stack. The others ignored him, and after a few more beers, I was more able to do the same. Not entirely. A dime in CDCR baked lizard brain survival mechanism too deep.

'You do much driving?" Tore asked, nonplussed about my evasive answer to his previous question.

"Some," I said. "Short-term jobs. Mostly construction. Hauling boxes around. Shifting palettes from one warehouse to another. Out and back in a day. You know how it is."

Tore gave me an absent nod. I watched Ragnhild's hand snake between his legs. Her fingers scratched along the back of his calf.

Free finally went for the shot. The cue ball dumped around the green-striped fourteen, potted the one into the pocket near me and then dribbled across the table to kiss the seven on the wrong side and fall into the pocket.

Sven let out a bark of laughter, like chunks of concrete hitting the pavement.

Free banged his cue against the table. "It's fucking crooked," he fumed. "I've been telling you all night. There's a fucking lean on this—"

"It's your aim that's fucked," Sven said.

"My aim is fine, asshole," Free shot back.

A vein pulsed in Sven's forehead. "What did you call me?"

Ragnhild's hand tightened around Tore's leg. He was pressed against her back. Her eyes were bright and her lips were parted.

"Think these two will be done by the time I get back from taking a leak?" I asked Margit.

She stared at me. A flicker of surprise passed through her eyes when I held out my pool cue. Tentatively, she took it from me and I smiled at Sven, who was not pleased his windup had been interrupted.

I nodded at the striped fourteen ball, which was a couple of inches from one of the side pockets. "He set you up," I said.

"Can you knock it in and maybe something else by the time I get back?"

A flicker of a smile ghosted across Free's face. Yeah, he saw the math. I knew he did.

"I come back and there's only one ball in, you're buying the next round," I challenged Sven.

The top of his head gleamed. He was giving me all sorts of hard eye.

I walked off toward the bathrooms at the back. I wasn't worried about him coming at me on the floor. If he did, it'd be in the stalls. I didn't have to go that badly, and I could wait for a minute or two to see if he did.

Nobody followed me. After doing one of Mr. Chow's more idiosyncratic tai chi moves a couple of times, I did the business I had to do, washed my hands, and returned to the table.

Sven had run the rest of the stripes, and when I walked up to the table, he dropped the eight ball in the corner pocket with a self-satisfied smirk. "Your round, asshole," he said.

And so it went for a few hours, the beer lowering a soft-filtered haze over us. We slipped into that new-pal glow, which would last until we all staggered out to the parking lot.

CHAPTER 11

My car wasn't level, and at first, I thought it was my own tilt. While I stood near my car, staring dumbly at the flat passenger side tire, I tried to remember when Scar had left. The dart game broke up after awhile, and he had left while Ragnhild had been asking about the movie stars I knew.

There were only three cars left in the lot and two bikes parked near the curb. Lots of open space. Lots of shadows along the building. Was Scar lurking nearby, waiting for his chance? A chill started up my spine. I had stayed too long. My new friends notwithstanding, I wasn't sure they would have my back.

"You okay to drive?"

I glanced over at Sven and Free. They were standing next to a dirty pickup with out-of-state plates. Beyond them, I saw Tore holding the door for Ragnhild—all gentlemanly and shit. Margit had already climbed into his sleek sedan. Tore looked over at me as he shut the door after Ragnhild.

A brown or grey sedan was parked across the street—it was hard to tell the color in the weak glow from a streetlight that seemed awfully far away from the lot.

"I'm good," I said to Sven and Free. I waved a hand at my car. "My car, however, has had too much to drink."

Sven ambled over, his thumbs tucked into his belt. He surveyed the damage. "Well, ain't that the shits," he said.

"Ain't it," I echoed.

Free, curious what we were so interested in, wandered over too. "Damn kids," he offered.

"Yeah," I echoed politely. "Those damn kids."

"You got a spare?" he asked.

"Sure," I said. "In the trunk." I didn't move toward the car.

Free was the one who was vibrating now. Sven was calm. Over the course of the evening, I had come to understand the source of Sven's agitation: he didn't like not knowing what was going to happen next. Playing pool was stressful for him. Hell, waking up was probably stressful for him. For some reason, he wasn't wound tight at the moment.

Free, on the other hand, was busy thinking. Running odds. Doing calculations and projections in his head. Still trying to find the optimal path to a problem he had.

I had a pretty good idea what his problem was.

The headlights of Tore's car came on, and he wheeled it around in a big circle. The passenger side window came down as the car slowed to a stop, gravel crunching under the wheels. Ragnhild's face was a composition of shadows and delight, her mouth curled in a laviscious way. "Everything okay?" she breathed in a way that strongly implied there was a right and wrong answer. She was hoping to hear the wrong answer.

"I've got a flat," I said. "It's okay. I've got a spare."

She smiled, and I was reminded of how cats like to play with mice after they've caught them.

Sven pulled a gravity knife from his pocket and flipped it open. With a grunt, he stabbed the blade into the back passenger tire, worked it back and forth before he pulled it out. "You got two spares?" he asked.

I had it wrong. Sven had come out to the lot while I had been taking a piss. My car—a new BMW—had stood out. He was the one who had spiked my tire.

"Yeah, I don't think I have two spares." Free was rubbing at a spot behind his left ear. *Yeah*, I thought, *that's a good spot.*

"Don't play too long," Ragnhild said. "It's a school night." She laughed, a throaty chuckle that would turn heads and make conversation stutter to a halt.

Free looked at her, and that's when I closed the distance between us and smacked him on the side of the head. He squawked and staggered. I stayed close and got a grip on his shirt. He was loose in my hands and I hustled him at Sven who was still standing next to my car. Free pinwheeled his arms when I shoved him, and Sven had to make a quick decision in order to avoid accidentally stabbing his friend.

He danced out of the way as Free ran into my car, his arms flopping. Sven's head was a bobbing dot of light as he came at me. I dropped to a crouch, digging at the gravel with an open hand. I hurled a handful of stones at Sven as he slashed at me. He cursed and clawed at his face. I slammed my hands on either side of his wrist, and the knife went skittering off.

I didn't want to be this close to the sweaty-headed anger machine, but I had had to deal with the knife. Sven roared and threw out his arms. I tried to avoid his meager bear hug, but he was quicker than I anticipated. He wasn't big enough to squeeze me to death, but all he wanted to do was make contact. Holding him off was like trying to wrestle a bag of hornets. I lost my footing, and we went down. I was doing a pretty good job of blocking his fists and elbows until Free joined in the fun. He returned my smack with a boot to the head, and for a moment, I lost track of everything.

When the world came back, they were both having a go at me. I curled up as best I could, grunting and flinching as they took turns tattooing my side and back with their feet. They weren't trying to break my ribs or mess up my face. It was a polite beating among new friends. *Welcome to the club! Have some bruised ribs! It's okay. All the new kids get kicked around a bit. We do it because we like you.*

I started to see red and blue streaks of light, and wondered if I had taken one blow too many to the head, but then I heard a roar of gravel and smelled a gust of car exhaust. The next moment, Sven and Free were gone, and the lights settled down.

Still flickering, but not because of damage to my head or brain.

I felt like a bag of oranges that had been bounced down an escalator. There was definitely blood on my face. I spat, and ran my tongue around the inside of my mouth. Blood in my mouth too.

I'd probably piss blood in the morning. It'd been a while since I'd been on the receiving end of the *Hey, new buddy, here are some cool party favors from your pals!* treatment.

I rolled onto my side and squinted toward the brown or grey sedan—I still couldn't tell—that was idling in the lot. A bank of police lights flashed in its interior. Someone got out of the car. They bent over, and I focused on their face.

"You know," Detective Lorenzo said, "I could have saved you the effort if you had returned my calls."

"Don't get blood on anything," Lorenzo said, ten or thirty minutes later.

I mumbled something terribly ungrateful.

"You want to talk about what you were doing here tonight?" he asked.

"Not really," I said.

"You want a lecture?"

I turned my head painfully and tried to throw some eye daggers at him. Judging by his expression, they were so dull they bounced right off.

"You want to tell me about Bunko?"

"Who?" I managed.

"Okay," he said. His fingers did a *rat-a-tat-tat* on the steering wheel of his car.

We weren't in the Red Eagle parking lot. After watching me drag myself around the parking lot for awhile, Lorenzo had deigned to help me get into the passenger seat of his car. While I struggled with the seatbelt, he went into the bar and got a plastic bag of ice. I rested the bag against the part of me that hurt the most, and when the pain slithered away, I moved the bag to another spot. I had a feeling the ice was going to melt well before I ran out of spots.

We had moved to the lot of an all-night restaurant, one of those chains beloved by long-haul truckers, addicts in denial, and impoverished students. Lorenzo had made no move toward going in, and my stomach wasn't happy about sitting in the car. The lights in the parking lot were big and yellow and there were more of them than necessary to illuminate the lot.

"How about the EZ Quickie?" he asked. "You remember anything you forgot to tell me the other day?"

"I'm not sure I know what day of the week it is right now," I said.

"It's Friday," he said. "Barely."

"You crack the case yet?"

"Would I be talking to you if I had?"

I nodded. "This going to mess up your weekend plans?"

"No. You?"

"I didn't have any," I confessed.

"Must be nice," he breathed.

"Though, I'll probably stick close to home and watch one of those televised sporting events between two teams in colorful costumes. And a ball. Or a quince. Or whatever it is they call those things they fling around while riding scaly lizards."

"Wow. Your brain is really scrambled."

"You have no idea. Maybe I should go home and lie down."

He nodded. "Maybe you should."

A silence followed, finally punctuated by Lorenzo who nodded toward the street beyond the lot. "It's that way," he said. "I think."

I didn't look. I put my head back and re-adjusted the now liquid bag of ice. "Maybe I'll just rest here awhile first," I said.

"Don't get blood on anything."

I found a weak smile. "That's good," I said as I closed my eyes. "Repetition of a line helps establish a routine. You should teach that to Nelson."

He didn't say anything.

"Where is your partner, by the way?"

His silence was unnerving. I cracked open an eye and peered at him. He was still finger-drumming and his gaze was roaming around the sodium-lamped parking lot. I finally took note of his attire. He wasn't wearing a suit. "Are you off the clock, Detective Lorenzo?" I asked.

He stirred in his seat. He was wearing his seatbelt, even though the car was turned off, and he idly plucked at the strap across his chest. I thought of Free and Sven and how nervous energy shows itself.

"You are off the clock," I said. "No wonder you don't want me to bleed on anything. This is your personal car, isn't it?" I looked at the box of lights shoved into the corner of the dash, and wondered where he got the flashers.

"I read the report on the Thai Garden shooting," he said. "Witnesses say Bunko came in and met a guy who was already there. A white man. About your height. Same hair color. Same smart ass personality."

"I'm mildly offended you think I'm that sort of Hollywood douchebag."

"They had cameras," Lorenzo said. "There's footage."

"I'm sure it's grainy and blurry. The kind that defense attorneys love. You can raise all kinds of questions with shitty surveillance footage," I said.

He made a tiny motion with his head.

"It's not your case, is it? You've got the EZ Quickie, and until you can put me at the restaurant, Bunko's death is on someone else's desk. Sure, you read the report, but you need a good excuse to look at the restaurant footage, don't you?"

"You're going to be on that tape," Lorenzo said.

I rested my head against the seat. I recalled how I sat across from Bunko, which was probably the only reason I was still alive. "What are you going to see?" I asked. "The back of my head? That's hardly convincing."

"It doesn't have to be."

I gave him a tired smile. "Are you trying to rattle me, Detective Lorenzo? Get me to do the right thing? Help an honest cop bring some real bad guys to justice?"

"Something like that," he said.

"Can we skip the 'like that' and talk about why you were following me in your—" I raised my head and peered at the interior of the car. "Is this your wife's car?"

"This is not my wife's car."

"You sure? It's awfully nice and clean."

"It's my car," he said, a touch of anger in his voice.

"How many miles you got on it? It still has that smell—you know, the 'new car' smell, even though what the fuck is that smell, really?"

"It's my goddamn car!"

"Okay," I said. "Okay. I'm sorry. Don't get all worked up." I waited a beat. "Here's a different question: what were you doing at the Red Eagle tonight, in your 'not quite new' car?"

Lorenzo didn't say anything, but his fingers kept moving on the steering wheel.

My mind drifted to my last conversation with Bunko. Gang wars, and the endless shifting of territories as gentrification pushed aside old rivalries. I thought about Mr. Chow and the alleged reasons he had gone to jail. About the people he had left behind: his family, his associates, his rivals. The government agency that wanted to put him away, but couldn't do any better than tax evasion. Mr. Chow hadn't fought the charges. He did his time until the cancer came for him.

Was there unfinished business between Mr. Chow and some third party? Did his wife know? Did Jackie know? I thought about coincidences. I thought about seeing connections that weren't there. Or maybe they were, and you didn't have a good idea of what the big picture really was.

"You know the guys who held up the EZ Quicke aren't the same guys who held up the other markets," I said.

Lorenzo's fingers stopped moving.

"The other robberies were done by Mexicans. Why was the EZ Quickie different?"

Lorenzo reached over and turned the key in the ignition.

"You weren't following me tonight," I said, connecting the dots. "You were watching someone else."

The car started, and he slid the gear stick into 'Reverse.' "Put your seat belt on," he groused at me, and it was the last thing he said to me that night.

CHAPTER 12

I WOKE UP ON MY OWN BED, WHICH—GIVEN HOW MY EVENING had gone—was quite an accomplishment. I had kicked off my shoes and undone my pants, but that was all I had managed before face-planting on top of the comforter. There were stains on my pillow case that weren't going to come out, but pillow cases were easy to replace. My face—and the rest of me, for that matter—wasn't as easily replaced.

I dragged myself into the bathroom. I flicked on the light, wished I hadn't, and held on to the edge of the vanity sink until the pinwheels of blazing stars went away. I cracked one eye and took a look at what had dragged itself upright.

It wasn't as bad as it felt, which was good.

Moving with all the enthusiasm of a sloth in sub-zero temperatures, I peeled my shirt off. It stuck in a couple of places, which wasn't fun. I tossed it on the floor, adding it to the pile of stuff Butch had to replace because he had done a stupid thing.

My chest and sides looked like a watercolor canvas of a sunset over Catalina. Purples and reds and oranges, all swirling together in an abstract haze. My skin was hot and tender in a lot of places, and when I twisted to look at my back, I saw more of the same watercoloring. I did slow breathing exercises to open my chest, and managed to unlock some of the hard spots in my abdomen.

Next was a shower. As I was dripping all over the bath mat, I heard a clatter of noise from the kitchen. I didn't panic—that would have taken more adrenaline than I could muster—but I kept listening as I gingerly reached for a towel. I heard a different noise, which my brain processed as voices in conversation. Then the aroma of fresh coffee and bacon slipped under the door and teased me.

I let myself be teased.

Mrs. Chow was sitting at the bar in the kitchen, one sandaled foot wiggling in time to music playing from her phone. On the counter next to her was a carafe of fresh coffee and a heaping plate of bacon. Tony was fussing over a pan on the stove.

Tony—the son who had gone to culinary school.

Mrs. Chow sensed me standing in the door to the bedroom. She turned her head and stared at me for a moment, carefully examining the color chart on my chest. "Put on a shirt and come eat, Butchy Boy," she said, patting the stool next to her. There was none of the usual dismissive arrogance in her voice.

Tony glanced over his shoulder. Of all the Chow men, he looked the most like his father. The same angular face and arched eyebrows. The same downturned shape of the mouth. "Eggs are almost ready," he said. For a split second, it was Mr. Chow standing there in my kitchen—a white apron tied around his waist, a spatula in his hand. *A man is not his best before breakfast*, he said. *Nor is he any good after dinner. The best plans are those that are executed after eggs and coffee, but before noodles and a cocktail.*

Mr. Chow wouldn't have gone to the bar last night. He didn't say as much, but I could read disappointment in his gaze.

"I'll get a shirt," I mumbled, and I disappeared into the bedroom.

Mrs. Chow and Tony watched me eat. I found my appetite under the bed while I was looking for a shirt, and I attacked Tony's egg white omelette with cheese and mushrooms like I hadn't eaten in weeks. There was toast to go along with the mountain of bacon, and Tony had brought over a small jar of the house jam from Three Hares—his bistro over in Santa Monica—and I slathered it liberally on each piece of toast.

Tony's restaurant did lunch (and the occasional cocktail hour, if you were friends of the management), and there were only a dozen tables in the small dining room. He didn't advertise, and the only indicator the small craftsman house housed a fantastic restaurant was the small sign next to the front door on the covered porch. The only reason he took reservations was because to not do so would have caused riots on the front lawn.

All of which is to say that Tony Chow cooking breakfast at my bungalow was no small thing, more so because I knew everything served up this morning hadn't come from my refrigerator. This meal almost made me forget about getting the shit kicked out of me the night before. Almost. Eventually, I stopped cramming bacon into my mouth and slumped in my chair. I made a feeble gesture with my hand as a token of appreciation to the cook.

What brought me to tears was watching Tony clean up.

"You realize he's going to ruin me for anyone else," I said to Mrs. Chow.

"He isn't going to do this for you every morning," Mrs. Chow said. She was still nibbling on the first piece of bacon she had taken from the plate.

"Let me dream for a moment more, would you?"

"You were passed out on the lawn last night," Mrs. Chow said. "After that nice man dropped you off."

"I was?" I had no recollection of that.

She nodded. "It was very undignified. I almost told him to drag you one street over. Leave you on Mrs. Gallegan's lawn."

"That would have been less undignified?"

"Not my problem when you are on Mrs. Gallegan's lawn."

I watched her daintily break off a piece of bacon and raise it to her lips. The delicate and precise motions of a woman who knew the value of her hands.

"How did I get into my bed?"

She wouldn't open a beer. I couldn't imagine her dragging me across the lawn.

"Some things will always be a mystery," she said.

Tony finished loading the dishwasher and took off his apron. He folded it neatly and put in on the counter. "Mother and I are concerned," he said.

"About what?"

"The family is taking care of Gavin's medical bills. Beyond what the health insurance covers," he said.

"Jackie offers health insurance?"

"If you need to see someone about . . . about whatever happened last night—"

"I'll be fine," I said.

"—if you need to see someone," Tony continued as if I hadn't said anything, "we'll take care of it, but . . ."

"But what?"

Tony looked at his mother, who was feigning fascination with a piece of bacon.

"We—the family—can't get involved if you . . . if you break the law."

"What do you think happened last night?" I asked.

Mrs. Chow broke off another tiny piece of bacon.

"Maybe I should talk to Jackie," I said.

Tony looked at his mother, who gave him an enigmatic stare. "Jackie's, uh, Jackie's real busy at the moment," Tony said.

"Is he?" Watching Mrs. Chow eat was like watching a nature documentary. "Any chance I could get on his appointment calendar later this week?"

Tony shrugged. "I'm—I don't know, Butch."

"Of course not," I said. I offered him a smile that said I didn't fault him being the messenger. "I suppose he'll reach out when he's got time."

"Yeah," Tony said, nodding. "I'm sure he will."

"I guess I'll stay out"—I looked at Mrs. Chow again—"I'll stay out of jail until he's free," I said.

Tony rapped his knuckles on the counter like he was signaling the close of arguments at a court case. "I'm going to head back to the restaurant," he said. "You want a ride somewhere?"

"Sure," I said.

We weren't going to talk about why my car wasn't in the driveway this morning. Not in front of the Chow matriarch, at least. Or maybe Tony wanted to talk about something else. Either way, I wasn't going to say no.

Tony drove much more aggressively than he cooked, and I tried not to wince every time he slammed on the brake. The seat belt kept pressing against my bruised chest. We stayed on the surface streets, winding our way west through Mar Vista. He hadn't asked where he could drop me off, and I didn't offer. I was curious where he was taking us.

After several blocks of rapid stops and starts, Tony started talking. "Regardless of what everyone thinks, my father was a small businessman. He came to America after the Korean War and managed to talk the bank into giving him a loan so that he could open the first store. Do you know which one that was? The one over on 7th. That was the first store." Tony's eyes flicked to his mirrors a split second before he changed lanes. "He was robbed six times the first year. But he never gave up. He had three stores before he married my mother. She always said she was attracted to his determination. As a wedding gift, he bought her a nail salon. She thought that was the most romantic thing she'd ever seen."

Tony glanced at me as if he dared me to find that funny. I didn't. Mr. Chow's deeply ingrained romanticism had saved the life of a naive kid from Colorado who had been clueless as to how the world really worked.

"My first job was stocking the shelves at the store on Venice Blvd. The one in Palms. It took me two years to convince him to let me work the register. I was so proud to have that job. I was going to be just like him: owning my own chain of stores." He shook his head at the memory of his younger self.

"Three guys came into the store one afternoon," he continued. "They had shotguns and masks. They were members of one of those Mexican gangs. They weren't much older than me, and probably just as scared. They wanted the cash. Took some beer, and the tape out of the security system. This was . . . fifteen years ago? Something like that. We had a single camera set-up, recording straight to a VCR under the counter. When the tape was full, we'd rewind it and hit record again. I doubt the cops would have gotten anything useful off that tape.

"Anyway, they told me to lie on the floor and count to a thousand before I called the cops. I didn't wait that long. I called Dad as soon as they were gone. He was there in ten minutes. At first he was angry at me—as if it had been my fault. Yelling. Cursing. Telling me this was why he never wanted to let me work in the stores. He wasn't going to lose a son to some stupid gangbanger looking for a fast score." Tony shrugged. "Whatever. It was part of living and working in LA. One of those rites of passage we thought we needed, you know?"

I nodded. "Yeah," I said. "I do."

We all had our rites of passage. Marking our way through adulthood. Gathering scars and stories that we could tell when we got old. *This is my history. This is how I was a part of the world.*

Tony kept talking. "When those idiots came back—oh, they came back, as soon as they figured out that Dad wasn't going to do anything. When they came back, I showed them the shotgun I had bought. It was bigger than the ones they had. They nearly pissed themselves and ran so fast. I was high on that feeling the rest of the day. That night? God, Dad was pissed. I've never seen him so angry. But I stood up to him. I told him if he didn't show these punks who was in charge, they were just going to keep coming back. You had to show them that you weren't going to be pushed around."

Tony paused and ran his tongue along his bottom lip.

"He fired me," he said, his voice softening. "Said he never wanted to see me behind the counter again. I was—He made me feel ashamed for what I had done. I didn't know what to do. I thought—I—that's when I left." He laughed. "I ran away, got as far from the family as I could. Lost myself in New York City. Jesus, Butch. No one wanted a dumb kid like me: filled with unresolved daddy issues, itching for a fight, needing to prove himself. I took any job I could get. Ended up washing dishes in shitty diners covered in years of grease and cigarette smoke. There was a cook at one of those places, who took pity on me. Needed a charity case or something. Who knows.

"Anyway, he taught me how to prep. Showed me how to boil an egg, because I couldn't even do that right. He's the guy who saw something in me no one else did. Pushed me to go to culinary school. It took me three years before I got accepted. Most of my co-workers thought I'd be out in a semester. But I didn't flunk out. I finished school. I got a job as a prep cook at one of those hotels that wouldn't even hire me as a dishwasher. I worked my way up. Sous chef. Line cook. Executive chef. Finally opened my own restaurant. I made something of myself.

"And when Dad got out of prison, Angel called me. Said that he was dying, and that I should come home. 'He doesn't know why you left,' she said. 'And all he wants is for his family to be around him during these last few months.'"

Tony shook his head.

"It look longer than a few months," he said.

"Yeah," I said. "Time gets elusive around that man."

"Do you know why I stayed?" Tony glanced over at me. "Why I opened the restaurant out here?"

I shook my head.

"My investors back in New York were gangsters," he said. "I guess I sort of knew it at the time, but I didn't care. It was my own place. I had made it. But it was a lie. The restaurant was laundering cash for the organization my investors were a part of." His smile was brittle. "When I told them I was going to take a few weeks off to visit the family in LA, they didn't object. My executive chef said he could handle it. I didn't see any reason why he couldn't. It wasn't like we were that busy."

He laughed at his own naiveté.

"God, I was so blind to it. We weren't turning tables as quickly as the books said we were. I'd look out and see the dining room half-empty, and yet, my accountant would tell me we'd had a record week. We were ordering stock like we were packed every night, but half of the orders must have been going somewhere else. Or . . . I don't even know."

Tony kept having a conversation with himself during the next few blocks, but it was all happening without him moving his lips. I watched the scenery roll by, and let him find a way to tell me what he wanted to share.

"About a week or so after I came back, a couple of FBI guys caught up with me at a coffee shop. I wasn't seeing Dad as much as I thought I would, and I was sort of wandering around, not sure what I was supposed to be doing. Anyway, I had been going to the same coffee shop every morning for a few weeks. They had found my pattern. Strolled in while I was in line and suggested we sit down and chat."

"They like doing that," I said. "Popping up unexpectedly. Makes you wonder how long they've been watching you."

"Yeah, it was exactly like that. Anyway, they wanted to talk about my restaurant in New York. Showed me some documents that had been filed in SDNY. Told me that I didn't have a job back in New York. Said they wanted to ask me some questions about my investors and their associates. I told them to fuck off, which they expected, of course, and they backed off, but not before telling me that they had never closed the investigation on my father.

"I knew there had been rumors about stuff that Dad had done. The FBI had sent him to jail for income tax evasion, after all, but I never understood why he hadn't fought it. The family lawyers should have been able to tie the case up in court for years. They could have given the Feds some bad press. But he didn't. He went to jail. He . . . " Tony trailed off, leaving me to finish his sentence for him.

"He let you down," I said. "He got mad when you stood up for yourself, and later, when he got bullied, he didn't stand up for himself. He didn't take a stand for the family."

Tony nodded. "He went to jail, and there was no one to run the stores. Mom had a couple of the nail salons—I think she had just opened the one in East Hollywood. She didn't have the time to run the stores too. There were six of them, and the managers kept calling the house. Asking about invoicing, about payroll, about restocking the shelves. Mom didn't know. Angel was—Mom wasn't going to let Angel manage a bunch of convenience stores. Not when there was the possibility of gang members targeting them.

"Jackie had his custom shop—the one on Exposition—and he knew how to run a business. But Jackie didn't want to run the family business any more than I did. That's why he opened the shop in the first place. It was his thing. Not Dad's. But he had no choice now. Dad's businesses were going to get overrun if he didn't step up. So he did. Marco had just gotten his CPA, and so he knew how to take care of the books. He got them on to some accounting package that took care of most of it. Actually, the two of them were pretty good at managing the stores. It didn't take long for everything to be running smoothly again."

"And your dad never cracked," I said. "He didn't tell them anything. He didn't admit to running the cash. He didn't squeal on who he was working for."

A thought occurred to me. "Shit, Tony, were the stores supposed to go away?" I ran with the idea. "He didn't want Jackie taking over operations, did he? He wanted everything to dry up and blow away. He wanted the stores out of business."

"But Jackie took over," Tony said. "He and Marco made it look all neat and legal."

"Which doesn't mean that it is," I said. "The Feds still think there's a laundering operation going on. And here you are, working for some east coast organization that is moving money through your business. Kind of the same thing that the Feds think your father was doing. Wow. I imagine they had a lot of questions."

"I'm sure they did," Tony said.

"Did you tell Jackie about your visit with the Feds?" I asked.

Tony made a face and wouldn't meet my gaze.

"Jesus, Tony. Why didn't you tell him?"

Tony wrestled with himself for a minute. "It's not just the laundering pipeline," he said. "It's worse than that. When Dad went to jail, the pipeline shut down. Apparently it was laundering a couple hundred thousand a month. Upwards of a half million sometimes. That's a lot of cash. The Feds think it's still out there."

"Do the Feds have their hooks in you?" I asked.

Tony shook his head. "Fuck no. I got a small business loan at an absolutely murderous rate, and I'm busting my ass to make the payments on it. Three Hares is clean. It's all mine. I don't take a dime from Jackie or Mom. Angel doesn't either."

"Have you told her about this?"

"God, no. And she can never know."

"Why not?"

"Because she'll want to save them. Come on, Butch. You know Angel. She'll want to protect the family."

"And you don't?"

He laughed bitterly. "I ran away, remember?"

"Then why did you come back?" I asked. "Why did you stay?"

He looked at me, his eyes hot. "They're still family," he said.

I looked away, cursing the knot in my belly. I know what he meant, even though I wasn't blood.

Mr. Chow knew how to hook orphans. Charity cases, every one of us.

CHAPTER 13

ANGEL WAS ON THE PHONE WHEN TONY AND I ARRIVED. CITING an "unexpected disaster that had just walked in," she got off the phone and glared at Tony briefly before turning her full attention on me.

"What are you two doing here?" she asked.

"Are you representing him?" Tony asked, jerking a thumb at me.

"Maybe," she said.

"You look nice today," I said. Russet colored blouse under a dark blazer. Hair loose about her shoulders. Simple necklace and earrings.

She gave me a patronizing smile. "What's going on?" she asked.

"Show her," Tony said.

"I don't think that's necessary," I said.

Tony walked over to the coffee machine. "Butch got the shit kicked out of him last night," he said.

"Hang on—" I started.

He looked over his shoulder at me. "If you're not going to tell her, I will."

"Wait a second," Angel said. "What?"

"It wasn't that big of a deal," I said.

"He was dumped on the front lawn at Mom's," Tony said.

"It's not what it looked like," I said.

"It's totally what it looked like," Tony said.

"Slow down, you two." Angel put up her hands, cutting us off. "This is like a bad sitcom."

"Show her," Tony said as he explored the options for coffee.

I sighed and raised my shirt so Angel could see the mottled bruises on my stomach.

"Oh my god." Angel shot out of her chair. "Butch! What happened?"

"I slipped while trying to change the tire on my car," I said, lowering my shirt. She came around her desk, and I put up a hand to ward her off. "I'm okay. It's not as bad as it looks."

"It looks horrible," she said.

"It's not that bad," I reiterated.

"How the hell do you make coffee in this thing?" Tony interjected. He waved a hand at the ugly machine.

"I . . ." Angel looked at her brother and shook her head. "I don't know. I get coffee from the shop across the street."

"Then why do you have this—whatever this is?"

"In case"—she looked at me and her eyes widened in annoyance—"in case a client wants a cup of coffee."

"And you trust this machine to make coffee?" Tony rattled the pot on the warming plate.

"No, I—would you leave it alone?"

Tony heard the tone in her voice and put up his hands, letting her know he wasn't touching anything.

"What is going on?" she asked again.

"You should ask your brother. It was his idea to come here."

She put her hands on her hips. "I'm asking you. And don't put me off, Butch, or so help me, I will give you more bruises."

"I had a flat," I said. "While I was changing the tire, a couple of guys wanted to help."

"And they beat you up instead?"

"Well, I may have hit one of them."

Angel looked like someone had surprised her with a live pony. "You hit one of them? What the hell were you thinking?"

"I was thinking the other guy was going to stab me if I let his pal get his hands on me."

"Someone had a knife?"

"Yeah, someone did. How do you think my tire got a flat?"

"Oh my god, Butch. You are—I swear—you are, like, the worst witness a lawyer could ever have as a client."

"So you are his lawyer," Tony interjected.

Angel shut him up with a raised hand. "Butch," she said. "Stop. Take a deep breath—"

"I will if you will," I said.

She gave me a murderous glare. "Tell me everything," she said, forcing calm into her voice. "Don't be . . . so like yourself when you do, okay?"

"Okay," I said. "Remember the guy I knew at Tehachapi?"

"Your roommate."

"Cellmate," I said.

"Whatever." Angel dismissed the distinction.

"What about this guy?" Tony asked, keeping the conversation on track.

"His name was Ralph, and he was a dumb kid who ended up in the system for boosting cars. He wasn't smart enough to serve lunch in the cafeteria, but he was smart enough to know he needed friends if he was going to avoid being someone's boy. Now, the Mafia Mexicana runs things in CDCR—though the state would like you to think otherwise. Ralph wasn't brown enough to join the local chapter at Tehachapi, and so he went and tried to make nice with the gang that was more his color."

"The white boys," Tony said.

I nodded. "In this case, a bunch of skinheads who call themselves the Double-Z. Because, you know, the letters look like lightning bolts, which—"

"Yes, Butch, we know," Angel interrupted.

"Right. So, the Double-Z needed him to show he had the . . . the 'juice,' I guess—something like that. He decided to prove himself by disposing of a nuisance."

"My father?" Angel asked.

"You'd think so, but no," I said. "In fact, your father had put the Double-Z in a bit of a bind."

"How so?"

"Well, not to get lost in the weeds of CDCR politics, but there was another gang at Tehachapi, one filled with large black dudes. As you can imagine, these guys and the Double-Z rarely saw eye-to-eye, and Zalo—he was the leader of the Mafia Mexicana contingent at T—got a kick out of winding these two gangs up and watching them bang each other in the head with the plastic cafeteria trays. Right? So, that's the environment, and now let's drop in a soft white kid who had no business being there."

"Ralph," Tony said.

I shook my head. "No, me."

Angel frowned. "I thought you were—"

"How many years did I get for those bullshit drug charges?"

Angel shrugged and made a vague motion toward her desk.

"Recommendation was ten to fifteen," I said, saving her the trouble of looking it up. "But the judge didn't like how the DA had turned the trial into an campaign rally. He gave me five."

"But you served ten . . ." Tony didn't see how the math worked.

"Right, I did."

"He got five more for involuntary manslaughter," Angel said, her expression flat.

"What?" Tony was even more confused about how the legal system worked.

I watched Angel's face, wondering how much she knew of what had happened in the shower when Lando Turk had tried to shank me. Wondering what her father might have told her. *They don't respect stupid*, he had told me afterward. *They only respect strength, and that is what I gave you.*

Mr. Chow fell very firmly in the *Boys will be strong and take care of the family* camp. Pain was merely an opportunity for growth. At Tehachapi, Mr. Chow had collected a set of lost children. Me, Tattoo Bob, Dicky Boy, and Lin. We were young, in a place where we didn't belong. We needed a father figure, and Mr. Chow was there to provide the stern steering we needed.

"Anyway, there was a guy named Turk—Lando Turk—who had been causing the Double-Z some trouble, and your father . . ." I paused, debating how much to reveal. *He's dead,* I thought, *but he's still their father.* I glanced at Tony, who was hanging on every word of my story. *Don't take that away from them,* I thought. "Your father . . . warned them that Turk was going to try to get a snitch inside their group."

"A snitch? Who?"

I waved away Tony's question. "Turk tried to recruit this person, in a manner that isn't important," I said. "It didn't go the way he planned and, well . . ." I shrugged.

Angel connected the dots faster than Tony. "But the Double-Z weren't sure about you after that," she said.

"After what?" Tony asked. He still wasn't sure what I had skipped over.

"Involuntary manslaughter," I said. "A dead guy in the shower at prison is bad PR, which necessitates action on the part of the state. A defense of 'But Your Honor, he came at me with a sharpened piece of soap and I was in fear for my life' isn't the best defense if you're already serving time."

"You killed him?"

"Involuntarily," I said, sticking with the legalese. *I wasn't the one who stabbed him* was the more truthful answer. That had been Mr. Chow. He had stabbed Lando six times, in fact. Mr. Chow pointed out that since this was my first, I could be excused a little panic and superfluous perforating.

"What does this have to do with Ralph?"

"Ralph needed a nod from the Double-Z, and he thought killing me would show them he was worthy."

"What happened?" Tony asked.

"He tried twice," I said. "The first time I let it pass, because everyone's a little weird when they first get to prison. The second time . . . well, I suggested he find a different hobby since that one wasn't working out for him. He got transferred to a different facility."

"Butch says one of the two guys at the store that night was this guy," Angel said, closing the loop for Tony.

"Which guy?"

"Ralph," I said.

"Jackie said you were talking to one of the guys," Tony said. "On the tape from the store. You and the guy were wrestling, and that's when the other guy shot up the store."

I decided not to press Tony about talking with Jackie. He was family, after all. I didn't like how Jackie had maneuvered his younger brother to come talk to me. There was a degree of separation there that bugged me.

"Jackie's got a policy about robberies," Tony said. "Don't give the assholes any grief. Just open the register, and let them take what they want. I tell my staff the same thing: if anyone wants to hold up the restaurant, don't be a hero. Just give them the money and let them go without any grief. None of the staff gets paid enough to be brave." Tony glanced at me. "We all know the routine. We do regular drops. We don't keep cash on the premises. We have good security systems; we rely on the tapes if we need to give LAPD any information. Not that they care for less than a couple hundred bucks. It's not worth their time and paperwork. It would have been the same at the store if Butch hadn't been there. But it wasn't the same, was it?"

"It was a coincidence," I said.

"Really?" Tony asked.

"You weren't there," I pointed out. "Ralph didn't realize it was me at first. It was only after . . ."

"Only after what?"

"Only after I told them I wasn't going to give them all my money. That's when he recognized me."

"And why weren't you going to give them all of your money?"

I glanced at Angel. She gave me a *You're on your own here, pal* look. "I asked that they leave me enough to pay for the beer," I said. "Ralph said something about how he should have done the job right, back in prison. And when I said something back, his friend started shooting up the place."

Tony shook his head. "You couldn't let them walk out, could you?"

Angel started to say something, and then stopped. She wouldn't look at me.

"No, I guess I couldn't," I said.

A muscle worked in Tony's jaw. "Yeah," he said quietly. "I guess I can see how you'd think that."

Angel tried to read the signals passing back and forth between us. "What's going on?" she asked, when she decided she wasn't going to able to crack the cipher.

"We're bonding," I said.

Angel rolled her eyes.

"There are a lot of convenience stores on the Westside," Tony said. "Robberies happen all the time. But when one chain gets robbed three times in less than a month?"

"Other chains get robbed too," I pointed out.

"What about the odds of you being in one when it happens?" Tony asked.

"There are always bystanders," I said. "It's not unusual."

"And one of the robbers happens to be a guy you know?"

"I know a lot of people who have a history of doing illegal things like this."

"Winning the lottery isn't impossible either, but do you know anyone who's done it?"

I shrugged. "You got a point here, Tony?"

"What if it wasn't an accident that you ran into Ralph?"

"I haven't seen him in, like, a decade," I said. "I'm not sure how you can call it anything else."

"'There are no accidents,'" Tony said ominously.

"'There are only causalities you don't understand yet,'" I finished for him. "Yeah, I heard that once or twice."

"So what are we missing here?"

I stared at him. "You think something's going on?"

He gave me a *Do you not recall what we talked about in the car?* look.

I gave him a *I think you're stretching it pretty thin to find something here* look back.

Angel put up her hands. "Would you two stop with all that macho staring?"

"We're not staring," I said.

"Just stop whatever you want to call it." Angel put her hands on her desk. "I think Tony's question has some merit."

"Which question?"

"The one asking about whether there's something bigger going on." It was her turn to give me a look.

"You think I know something?" I asked.

"I don't know, Butch. Do you?"

"I know that this family is starting to give me a headache," I said.

Angel smacked her desk with the palm of her hand. "I'm serious," she said.

I spread my hands. "I don't know anything. Seriously."

"What about . . . Whatsername?"

"Who?"

"*That* woman."

"Which woman?"

It was Tony's turn to roll his eyes.

"The one that works for the government."

"Frolic? What about her?"

"Wait. Who's Frolic?" Tony wasn't following our conversation.

"She works for some part of the government," I said. "I don't know her name. I call her 'Frolic.' She finds it amusing."

"Oh, is that all?"

"She's a real piece of work," I said. "She likes using me in a way that gives her all sorts of plausible deniability."

"Really? Wow." Tony wan't sure what he was supposed to think about that.

I wasn't sure either. "It's the sort of twisted love affair that Hollywood loves," I said. "God help me."

"Is she involved in this?"

"If she is, we won't know until she decides to tell me." I looked at Angel. "But I think we should be paranoid enough to consider the possibility that she is."

Angel got up from her chair and wandered toward the window.

"Well, that's great," Tony said. He ran his hand through his hair. "You sure they weren't there to hit you?"

"Me?"

Tony lifted his shoulders. "Why else would they be looking for you?"

"Wait. How did we get to this part?"

"Ralph knew you, and when you recognized him, that's when his pal started shooting."

"At both of us," I pointed out. "Ralph was in the line of fire."

"He panicked," Angel said. "You knew Ralph, and Ralph could identify the other man."

"There you go," I said. "He didn't want to be caught, and if Ralph and I were both dead, who was going to finger him?"

"So the whole thing wasn't an excuse to take you out?" Tony kept gnawing at this.

"No," I said strenuously.

"You sure?"

Angel stared at her brother. "Why are you hung up on this?"

"I'm not," Tony said.

"You've asked him twice, and he said 'no' both times. And I can tell by the thing you're doing with your mouth that you don't believe him."

"What thing—? I do believe him."

"Don't bullshit me, Tony. I know better."

Tony's mouth firmed into a tight line. "There's a kid in the hospital," he said tightly, stepping into her space. "There are bullet holes all over one of our stories. Jackie's staff is freaking out about going to work. All because of this guy. And now the *Times* is saying shit about him being involved in some criminal organization that the stores are fronting. That's stirring up all kinds of stuff. People are starting to—" He broke off. "And you're taking his side?"

Angel's face darkened. "I'm not taking any sides," she said carefully.

"I'm just saying—"

"No, you're not. Not in my office," she said, her voice low and dangerous.

"He's—"

"No. Tony. Stop."

He stared at her for a long minute, and she didn't flinch from his glare. A tiny tremble started in her fingers and she crossed her arms, hiding her hands from view.

"Little cher—" he started.

"Don't you dare," she hissed.

He bit back whatever he was going to say. When he stalked out of the office, he bumped my shoulder roughly as he passed. The door rattled in its frame as he slammed it.

"Was he going to call you a little cherub?" I asked.

"Don't." Angel held up a warning finger.

"Like a baby angel?"

She dropped the finger down into her fist and her mouth tightened.

"Did your mom make you wear wings or . . . ?"

Her frown started to fray. "Butch," she started. She shook her fist several times as she walked over to me, and I held very still as she brought her hand down to my chest. She didn't make contact, and there was a lot of tension in her knuckles. I wrapped my hands around her fist, and she released the breath she had been holding.

"Butch . . . " She didn't remove her hand from mine. "Sometimes . . . you make a girl crazy, you know?"

"I know," I said. I squeezed her hand once and then let go. She opened her fist and let her hand hover near my chest for a moment. All sorts of thoughts were racing through her brain, and she was working hard to corral them. Finally, she exhaled noisily again, and then patted me once before walking away to go stand by the window and look down on the street. "My family makes me crazier," she said.

"Jackie doesn't like me," I said.

"He's never liked you," Angel pointed out. "This is just . . . this is just an excuse."

"And he's got Tony all twisted up."

She sighed. "Tony has some issues." She ran her hand through her hair. "We all knew he was just getting away from the family. I'm proud of him for actually going to cooking school. But he and Dad never . . . they never had a chance to patch things up, and now . . ."

"This theory that these robberies are tied to my past is a stretch."

"I know," she said.

"Your father and I were in the same prison. We interacted with the same guys. If there's someone from those days who wants me dead, there's a good chance they weren't a fan of your father either. Or any of the rest of us."

"Who?"

"The other guys in our . . . group. Our club. Whatever you want to call it."

"Gang?"

"It wasn't a—fine, our *gang*. There was Tattoo Bob, Dicky Boy,

Lin, Wang, and Dougie. And this other guy, what was his name?"
I tried to remember the skinny kid who had been hanging out
with Mr. Chow when I had first arrived at Tehachapi. "Biscuit,"
I said. "Yeah, that was his name."

"Biscuit?"

"I don't remember his given name. We all called him 'Biscuit.'
He got parole, like, what? six months or so after I got there.
Something like that. Anyway, after he was gone, we didn't talk
about him. Parole is like dying, you know. You're just gone, and
no one sees you again. Well, a lot of them come back. So, it's not
quite *dying* but—"

"I get it, Butch," she said.

"Anyway, we kept to ourselves and your father worked out
some deal with Zalo and the Mafia Mexicana. They didn't
harass us. The Double-Z were dicks, but, generally speaking,
that was the sum total of their game plan, anyway." I gave her a
What can you do about white supremacists? shrug.

"And Ralph?"

"I haven't thought about him in years. If he spent all that time
thinking about me, well, that was a waste of his time, in my
opinion, but whatever. He was a punk kid who wasn't in a rush
to hit the very low bar he set for himself. Frankly, I'm surprised
he served his time and got out."

"And last night?" she asked.

"What about last night?"

"Why were you 'changing a tire.'"

I shuffled my feet and thought about making an excuse. "I
went looking for him," I said. "Well, looking for the sort of
people he might hang out with. I ended up at this bar called the
Red Eagle. Bikers. White boys. The sort of crowd that would
adopt him, I guess. I thought I was getting along pretty well,
but when it was all over, a couple of them decided to have a go
at me in the parking lot and . . ."

She wrapping her arms around her waist. Like she didn't trust herself. "Is it bad?" she asked, her eyes straying to my chest.

"Nothing's busted," I said. "It's just some bruises. I've had worse." And had the scars to show for it, too.

"Why did they do it?"

I thought about Scar and seeing him talk with Tore. "I don't know," I said. "Maybe they didn't like . . . I dunno . . ." I thought about Free and Sven and the ladies. An image of Ragnhild swam into my head. Watching from the car, hers eyes glittering with excitement. "Maybe it was the movie thing," I said, pushing aside the memory of the pale-haired witch.

"What movie thing?"

"One of the regulars in the bar—older guy, like '60s biker type—said he recognized me from, you know." I waved a hand in the general direction of my torso.

"He knew your—?" Angel couldn't say it. A slightly blush started to creep up her neck.

"No, it wasn't me," I said. "He thought I was Bobby Banger."

"He thought someone else's . . . *body part* . . . was your . . . ?"

"We did a couple of films together," I said. "I can see how there might be some confusion."

"Oh, some confusion? Like, your fans can't tell the difference between two—I can't believe I'm having this conversation."

"Anyway, yeah, it was awkward all around, and maybe that had something to do with it. I don't know, really. I'm just speculating . . ."

"Okay, so let me see if I have this straight," Angel said. "You went to a biker bar where a bunch of white gang members hung out and someone—can we go out on a limb and say a 'secretly gay biker dude'?—fanboyed all over your . . . *package*, and a couple other guys—not quite as gay as the old feller, apparently—decided that was all too queer for them and stomped you in the parking lot later. All because you had a memorable dick?"

"Sure," I said. "That's probably why it happened."

"Oh, Butch, where did you go wrong?"

"Probably about fifteen years ago when I took that first film role," I said.

"You think?"

"Anyway, my car is still over there."

"Where?"

"At the Red Eagle. I really was trying to change the tire when the fight started."

She gave me an epic eye roll—deservedly so—but I didn't care. Regardless of what she had said to Tony, she *had* picked a side, and I was glad it had been mine.

CHAPTER 14

Since the car was part of a leasing package the family had with a BMW dealership on Wilshire, Angel called them and explained the problem. Her mock outrage at the whole situation—"Can you believe those damn kids slashed both tires!"—was Oscar-worthy.

When she hung up the phone, she said the dealership was going to send a guy over to fix the tires and then drop off the car wherever she wanted. Crime syndicate or no, the family had some pull. They were going to call back in a little while and give her an ETA.

Since there was nothing to do but wait for the call, I wandered downstairs to the taco shop. Mostly to let her get back to work, but also to get out of her line of sight for awhile. We both needed a little space to think.

So as to not be the guy that takes up a table and nurses a beer for an hour, I ordered a couple more tacos. I took a Cerveza over to a window seat, and stared at the building across the street. It was one of those buildings that was too hip for the current clientele. Sort of a *Build it and they will pay the premium when they start moving in to the neighborhood* sort of houses. The heavy metal gate covering the front archway didn't match the colonnades, but there's only so much wishful thinking a market will bear.

The bottle was about half empty when a woman got out of the crappy Dodge sedan parked in front of the house. She strode across the street with a lanky stride that was a joy to watch. She was wearing sensible shoes, jeans, and a couple layers of t-shirts under a well-cut jacket. Her black hair had been straightened and her figure had a pleasant curve to it. The geometric precision of her sunglasses were supposed to make her look harder than she probably was. She came into the taco shop and walked right up to my table and sat down.

"Hi," I said.

"Hi," she said.

"Do we know each other?" I asked.

"We know some of the same people," she said.

"I know a lot of people."

"One less today."

"Ah, yes. I suppose that is the case. I'm sorry for your loss. Were you close?"

"We weren't," she said. She took off her sunglasses. "But it's nice of you to say."

Her eyes were big and dark, and I got a sense that she would have no trouble rolling my body off a pier on a moonless night if it came to that.

"Can I buy you a beer?" I said, indicating the bottle on the table.

"It's too early for me," she said.

For some reason, I felt like I had to justify myself. Maybe it was her eyes. "I've had a busy morning," I said. I picked up the beer and took another swallow.

She made a show of examining the bruises on my face. "Mmmm," she said.

"You're very good at that," I said.

"At what?"

"Derision," I said.

"My mother disapproved of a lot of things," she said.

"Oh, you were that kind of girl?"

"Mmmm," she said again, but there was a different note to it this time. One that tickled the back of my throat and made me want to sit up straighter.

"Were you his source?" she asked.

"Whose? Bunko's?" I wanted to be sure of who were talking about.

"Yeah. Bunko."

I shook my head. "I didn't know him," I said. "We talked once. On the phone."

"He tell you how much he liked noodles?"

I held her stare for a moment, and then I let my gaze wander. She had a tiny silver ring in her left nostril. Her ears were pierced in several places, but she wasn't wearing any earrings. No other jewelry either. Her mascara was neat and precise, and she wore little else in the way of makeup on her dark skin.

"We didn't get that far in our chat," I said, deciding to play along for a little while longer. "How about you? You one of his sources?"

She shook her head lightly. "I earned my own way."

"Journalist?"

She inclined her head.

"The *Times*?"

She snorted and looked out the window.

"Right," I said. "A little too 'establishment' for you. What's the point of being a rebel if you just end up working for the Man?"

She turned her penetrating gaze back to me. It was like being stared at by a raptor. "We had a deal," she said. "I'd write the angry 'people of the streets' material for *The Voice*—all the ideology and outrage fit to print—and he'd use that to rattle the white folk whose investments might be in danger."

"White folk," I said.

"Yeah, lot of that going around." She waved a hand at the street outside the taco shop.

"Well, other than being one of them . . ."

"One of them white folk?"

"Yeah, one of them. Other than that, what can I do for you?"

"I'm not sure," she said, her eyes narrowing.

I took another sip of my beer. "Well, now you've got me all a-tingle with curiosity," I said.

"Yeah," she said. "Me too."

We stared at one another until Miguel called my name, letting me know my order was ready.

"That's mine," I said, nodding toward the counter without taking my eyes off my table companion.

"'Bliss,' huh?"

"Yep."

"Wow."

"I make it work."

"I'm sure you do," she said. She put a business card on the table and then reached for my beer. Her fingers brushed mine as she plucked the bottle out of my grasp. She raised it to her mouth and drained the last inch of beer. She knew I was watching her, and she licked her lips as she put the bottle back down on the table. "Mmmm," she said, making eye contact once more.

She stood up, and ran a damp finger along the table near her card. "Call me when you figure it out," she said.

"Figure what out?"

She walked out with telling me, and I watched her cross the street and climb into her two-door sedan that had spent most of this last decade caught in the tangle of LA traffic. I glanced at the card, seeing her name, but mostly thinking about the way she walked.

Toya Rose, the card said. *Investigative Reporter*, the card also said.

You can't handle this, her walk said.

"Mmmm," I tried. It didn't sound the same when I did it.

"I thought you might have fallen into a well or something," Angel said when I returned to her office.

"Not today."

"The dealership called. The car's not at the Red Eagle."

"It's not?"

"Their service guy said it had been towed by whatever company the Red Eagle had patrolling their lot. I told them to take care of it and put it on the family account."

"Thanks."

"You can tell my mother about it."

"Or not," I said.

Angel tried to keep her mouth from twitching toward a smile. "Or not."

I wandered over to the window and looked down at the street. The dusty sedan was still there. "When will the car be ready?" I asked.

"I should have left you hanging," Angel said.

"Oh, come on. Who is going to drive your mother around?"

She gave me a *That is not a card you want to play with me* look, and I held up my hands in acknowledgement of my gaffe.

"I—I made some noise about it, and . . . and the car should be ready later this afternoon."

"Great," I said.

She looked at me. I looked at her.

"You are not hanging around until then."

"I didn't say I was."

"I have a client coming in. I have work to do."

"Okay. I'll just get a cab over to the dealership then. It's no problem."

"Okay. Great."

"Yup. All great—I mean, all good. That's what I meant. All good."

She nodded and there was an awkward pause between us. I came over to the desk, thought about giving her a hug or a friendly pat on the shoulder, and decided that was all too complicated. I rapped my knuckles against her desk instead. "See you, counselor," I said.

"See you, convict," she said, a hint of a lilt in her voice. "But not too soon," she added hastily.

"Fair enough," I said.

Toya rolled down the window of her car as I crossed the street.

"Two things," I said.

She lowered her sunglasses enough for me to see a raised eyebrow.

"One, I totally looked both ways before I crossed the street."

"So?" she shrugged.

"You didn't. You just walked right off that curb like the cars would stop for you."

Her head titled back slightly. "And the other thing?" She made a tiny motion with her mouth, a little satisfaction showing that I had watched her walk back to her car—exactly as she had wanted me to.

I flipped her business card against my open palm. "I don't have a cell phone, so calling you is a little complicated."

"How so?"

A car passed behind me. I was surprised the driver didn't lay on his horn.

I pointed down the block. "You see that building over there?" I said. "The red one?"

She looked. "Yeah?"

"That's the nearest pay phone."

"So?"

"I was wondering if you'd give me a ride over there."

"A ride?"

"Uh huh."

"So you can call me?"

"That's right."

She showed me her teeth when she smiled. It was a fabulous smile. "Get in, Bliss," she said. "I'll give you that ride."

I went around the car and climbed in. She waited for me to get my seat belt on, and then, with more care and attention to her surroundings than I anticipated, she eased away from the curb.

The car was the first thing about her that wasn't sleek and polished, and I could tell by how hard she was clenching the steering wheel that she wasn't happy I knew this about her.

The car slowed to a stop not far from the blue-topped phone booth. I got out and went into the booth. Fortunately, there was a dial tone when I dropped some change in, and I dialed the number on her business card. It rang a few times, and then she picked up.

"Hello, you've reached the desk of Toya Rose at *The Venice Voice*. I'm sorry I'm not here to take your call, but please leave your name, number, and the reason you're calling, and I'll get back to you as soon as possible. Wait for the beep."

I waited. The machine beeped. I left a message.

Toya had a smug smile on her face when I returned to the car.

"You weren't in," I said.

"Mmmm," she said.

"I left a message."

"Oh, good. What did you say?"

"I wanted to know if you were free for dinner tonight," I said. "About seven or so."

"Seven?"

"Too soon?"

"No, seven is good."

"Great."

We sat in the car. Other cars whooshed by. Her right leg vibrated. I could have easily reached over and put a hand on it.

"What—" She cleared her throat and made a pretense of looking in her mirrors even though we weren't moving. "What should we do until seven?" she asked.

"We could make out in the back," I said.

"Definitely too soon," she said, but there was the slightest hesitation before she said it.

"Well, I suppose we could do some of that—what do you call it?—'investigative reporting.' Maybe get to the bottom of this curiosity we seem to be sharing."

"Yeah? You sure you're up for that?"

"I'm a quick study."

She tongued the inside of her cheek. "I bet you are," she said.

By the time we got to Willie's, I was seriously considering telling her everything. I needed a confidante, someone who wasn't tied to the Chows or my past. Someone interested in figuring out what the hell was going on. Sure, Toya had her own agenda which I was bound to trip over, but I figured I'd see it coming.

The evergreen optimism of the foolhardy, right?

"What's this?" Toya asked as she switched off her car. It rattled for a moment or two before it went still.

"It's a gym," I said.

"I can see that. Why are we here?"

"I need to check my messages."

"This is where you work?"

I shook my head. "No, I just—"

"You don't have a cellphone," she said. "And so you have people call you here?"

"It's not like—"

"Mmmm," she said.

"You're quite good at that."

"At what?"

"Saying a lot without moving your lips."

"Imagine what I can do when I move them," she said.

I looked at her lips and let my imagination run for a minute. She laughed and got out of the car. "Does that work on all the girls?" she asked, looking at me over the sun-baked roof of the car.

"Only the ones that want it too," I said.

"Fair enough," she said. She locked her car and started walking toward the entrance to the gym, assuming I'd follow her. Knowing I would.

Stevie's face lit up when we entered. "B—!" He only got one letter out before his attention was transfixed by Toya. "Hello," he beamed. "Welcome to Willie's—wow!—I mean, welcome to Willie's House of . . . how can I help you today?"

Toya leaned on the front counter and gave Stevie the full force of her attention. "Aren't you a big one," she said, dazzling him with a flash of her deadly smile. He was hooked, ready to bench press an elephant if she asked.

"I do my workouts here," Stevie managed. "It's great at Willie's."

"Gosh, it must be."

"Anyone call for me, Stevie?" I asked, vainly trying to get the big man's attention.

"No need to call ahead," Stevie said. "I'm always here." He was still transfixed by Toya.

"No, Stevie." I snapped my fingers. "Messages."

Toya gave a throaty laugh at Stevie's expression, and then came to my rescue. "Do you know Bliss?" she asked, dropping her sunglasses so she could look at me over their rims.

"Yeah," Stevie said. "I know him." He seemed to notice me for the first time. "Oh, hey, Butch. How's it going?"

"Going well, Stevie."

Dimly, Stevie realized we were standing next to each other. "You two know each other?" he asked.

"Carnally," Toya said.

Stevie frowned. "What?"

"We had lunch together," I explained.

Stevie's face brightened. "I usually have a protein shake and some fruit for lunch," he said. "That way it doesn't interfere with my afternoon workout." He made the individual muscles in his chest pop as he did a quick bicep pose. "It's an arm day today."

"Hey, Butch," Lorraine said, materializing at the desk.

"Lorraine," I said.

Toya was startled by Lorraine's sudden appearance. She had been paying attention to Stevie's muscles—which had delighted him—and she hadn't see the other woman approach. It was an old bit of misdirection that Lorraine and Stevie had finessed without actively working on it. Stevie's job was to impress and distract, allowing Lorraine to sneak up and start her sales pitch while folks were under the thrall of Stevie's impressive set of assets.

"I'm Lorraine," she said, holding out her hand to Toya. "Welcome to Willie's. Would you like a tour?"

"No, I, uh—" Toya collected herself. "Can I ride on his shoulders during it?" she asked, nodding toward Stevie.

"The ceilings are too low upstairs," Lorraine said smoothly.

Toya laughed. "I'm not the first to ask for that, am I?"

"Butch and I tried it," Stevie said.

"You did not," Toya said.

"They did." Lorraine smiled, like our effort had been a source of great amusement.

"Though, to be completely transparent, I didn't even get halfway up the stairs with him on my back," I said.

Stevie laughed. "And I was twenty pounds lighter then, too." He did another bicep pose.

Toya put her hands on the counter. "Could I . . . ?"

"You wanna touch one of them?" Stevie asked.

"Is that too much to ask?"

He crowded against the counter and presented one of his massive arms. "Go ahead," he said.

Lorraine cleared her throat. "You have—a gentleman called for you," she said, looking at me.

"Oh?"

"Said he had some information for you."

"Excellent."

"He gave me a phone number for you to call him back."

Lorraine tried to navigate around Stevie, who was nodding and making encouraging noises as Toya stroked his immense bicep. She finally gave up and waved a hand at the other side of the counter. I leaned over, and spotted the scrap of paper with her neat handwriting on it.

"He also said I sounded way too pretty to be taking messages for a lazy bum like you," Lorraine said.

"That is very observant of him," I said as I picked the note Lorraine had written. "Could I—?" I pointed at the phone.

Lorraine rolled her eyes. Toya smirked as Stevie showed her how his other arm was exactly the same size.

I dialed the number on the note. "It's Bliss," I said when Huggy answered the phone.

"Oh, Bliss. Hey. How you doing?"

"I'm good. How are you, Huggy?"

"Good. Good. You got my note?"

"I did."

"You know, that gal who answered the phone. She sounds really—"

"Did you find anything out for me?" I asked. "The info I asked about?"

"Oh, yeah. I did. I did."

Stevie was telling Toya about his training regime. She was listening intently, her sunglasses in her hand. She was tapping them against her lower lip, which kept distracting Stevie. I turned away before I got sucked in as well. "And?" I asked.

"I wrote it all down somewhere . . ." Huggy said. I could hear the ellipses over the phone line. They were like listening to the wind blow across a dry lake bed.

I sighed. "What do you need, Huggy?" I asked.

I heard him moving around, and when he spoke, his voice was softer. "Meet me tonight," he said. "At the Totem. Ten o'clock. I don't want to . . . you know . . . the Totem, OK?"

"Yeah, okay," I said. "Ten o'clock. The Totem."

"And get a phone, will you? I know you're not paying that girl to be your secretary. Dude, that's not okay. She's got better things to do with her life. I can tell by her voice."

I turned around and looked over at Lorraine. She caught me looking at her and gave me a smile that made my chest creak. "Yeah, she does," I said.

I hung up the phone. Toya looked back and forth between Lorraine and me. "When he does that thing with his eyes," she said, looking at Lorraine but pointing at me with her sunglasses, "does it make you feel all tingly on the inside, or do you feel like barfing up a hairball like a cat or something?"

"Or something," Lorraine said, her smile not wavering.

"All right," Toya said. She leaned over the counter to pat Stevie on the cheek. "You are a marvelous specimen of man flesh," she said. "I could stand here all day and feel you up, but"—she put her sunglasses on and turned away from the counter—"Butch and I have things to see and people to do."

She walked out of the gym. Stevie watched her go. I resisted the impulse. Lorraine shook her head at both of us.

"Or 'something'?" I said.

"She's out of your league, Butch," Lorraine said.

I looked at Stevie, who nodded in agreement. "I got nothing that'll help you, dude," he said. "You're on your own."

"I'm not even—" I held up my hands, admitting defeat.

"And get a phone, would you?" Lorraine added.

I kept my hands up as I made a hasty retreat.

Toya was leaning against the side of her car, staring at nothing in particular. A knowing smile softened her face. "You like her?" she asked.

"Who? Lorraine? Yeah, she's like a kid sister, you know?"

"Your kid sister would take her top off if you asked nicely."

Toya laughed at my expression.

CHAPTER 15

THE OFFICES OF THE THE *VENICE VOICE* WERE LOCATED ON the second floor of a red brick building at the corner of Pacific and Windward Avenues. Letters spelling out the town's name were strung on a heavy wire across Windward, and at night, fat yellow bulbs on the wire frames would light up the letters. You could see the beach from the street corner, but the *Voice's* offices looked out over the alley.

"The rent is cheap," Toya said when she noticed me eyeing the view of the building across the alley. Her editor's office was in the corner of the space the paper rented, and it had the best view, though you'd have to press your nose against the glass to get even a hint of beach. At night, you'd have to squint even harder to see through the glow from the Venice sign.

Her editor and publisher was a curly-haired Berkeley grad who wore the regulation counter-culture costume with pride, but he also had the zeal of a literary dissident who couldn't stand sitting still while everyone else smoked up and dropped out. "Franklin Toggerash," he said when Toya introduced us. "I pay the bills and try to get her to turn her stories in on time."

"Butch Bliss," I said, shaking his hand.

"What's your story, Bliss?" he asked. "I bet there's a story with a name like that."

"Of course there is," I said.

He continued to smile and work my hand, as if I was a pump that would eventually produce enough oil for a couple juicy headlines. I remained steadfast, pretending to be one of the old derricks down near the marina that had finally dried up.

"I'll—uh—I guess I'll hear that story later," he said, finally dropping my hand.

"Sure. Later is fine."

He gestured at the open door of his office. "I'm going to take care of some advertising stuff, okay?"

"Okay," I said.

He gave me a thumbs-up, and then turned those fingers into guns for Toya. "Philzee's invited some VIPs to the gallery tonight. A preview of the preview. Six in the PM."

She groaned. "Frank—" she started.

He bang-banged his fingers. "You know he likes you, Toya," he said. "Get me some gossip, alright? It pays the bills."

Toya put her head back and stared at the ceiling.

"Fine," Frank said. "Six-thirty."

Toya let out a long exhalation that vocalized into a swear word.

"That's my girl," Frank said, backing into his office.

When she ran out of air, she raised both hands, middle fingers extended, and then spun on her heel and stalked across the open office. Her desk was one of four cubicles lumped around a small conference room table, and her desk overflowed with stacks of books and papers. Her computer monitor looked heavier than Stevie's arm, and the swing lamp clipped to the wall of the cubicle emitted a tiny buzz when she turned it on. She flicked the housing a couple of times and the buzzing stopped.

"Find a chair," she muttered. Hers looked like it had come from a closeout sale at an office liquidation sale.

I glanced around. The guy who sat in the cubicle directly opposite her was watching us. He looked like he was prone to taking the afternoon off and hitting the waves with a board. His hair had highlights and his tan was manufactured. His watch was worth more than Toya's car, which wasn't saying much, but as status symbols went, it marked a definite delineation between his side of the room and hers. "How you doing?" I asked.

"I'm good," he said. He gave me a good view of his dental work. Nice and straight, but it lacked that ultra white glow you got when you had your work done over in Beverly Hills.

"Isn't it time to surf, Chaz?" Toya asked.

"Nah," Chaz said. "Tide's out."

He was attuned to the natural rhythm of the water, like a fish.

"Frank tell you about Philzee's preee-view tonight?" He made it sound even skeevier than Toya thought it was.

"Yes, Frank told me about it."

Chaz held up his hands and gave us a *Don't shoot the messenger* face. "Just passing it along," he said. "Being helpful and all."

"Yeah, Chaz. I see that."

I grabbed one of the straight-backed chairs from the conference table and situated it at the front of Toya's cubicle, blocking Chaz's view.

"Well, yeah, okay." Chaz kept going behind me. "You let me know if you—"

"I'll be fine, Chaz," Toya said, putting an end to the conversation. She dropped her sunglasses and her keys on her desk. She leaned back in her chair, and rubbed her temples. "I swear . . ."

"Hey!" Chaz popped up, right at my shoulder. "Who's your friend?" He looked down at me, heaping on the charm. From my angle, I could look up his nose, which wasn't the best view he could have presented. I also took in the body spray he was in the habit of . . . overspraying. I wondered if he confused bees and hummingbirds when he walked down the street.

"He's nobody," Toya said. She reached for her keyboard and starting typing. I could see the document she was working on. *I will strangle this mothefukcer and dump his body in a canal.*

I thought about pointing out the spelling error, but figured she'd notice eventually.

"I'm with the city," I said, leaning away from the blond-haired, hazy-hibiscus scented surfer. "Pest administration and riot control."

"We—they—" Chaz frowned. "There haven't been any riots in Venice," he said.

"Of course not," I said. "I'm that good at my job."

"And, uh, pests, huh. What kind of pests?"

Toya looked up and gave Chaz a smile that could shatter a man's confidence. "Chaz," she said, drawing out the last letter.

He finally got it. "Oh, right. Right. Sorry." Except he wasn't, and there was a bitchy brittleness to his smile as he wandered back to his cubicle.

Toya closed the document she was writing secret fantasies in, and then navigated to a place on her computer where image files were stored. "It was the fortieth anniversary of the paper last year, and Frank wanted a series of stories about the history of Venice and the surrounding area. Something that would make everyone feel good about themselves, bla bla bla and all that bullshit. Well, I didn't feel like doing that, and so I went somewhere else with the story. Frank said he'd run parts of it. If enough people complained, I'd have to go back to puff pieces. No one complained, and we turned it into a regular column."

"Congratulations," I said.

"Thank you." Toya opened one of the images in the folder on her computer. It resolved into an aerial shot of the city. "Do you know what this is?"

"Looks like the Westside," I said. Everything west of Downtown LA, south of the Santa Monica mountains, and north of the marina. I could see the dark ribbon of California State Route 1 where it separated Venice from Mar Vista.

Toya pointed at a section of the map close to the right side of the image. "Did you know that Culver City was a sundown town when it was founded, less than a century ago?"

"A what?"

She looked at me. "A whites-only community," she said. "Blacks were not allowed after 'sundown.'"

"Jesus."

"In fact, on land that originally belonged to the Tongva-Gabrieliño Native Americas, Harry Culver built a sweet little suburb for the white folk who wanted to escape the 'big city' life of Los Angeles, and since it was his money that was doing all the work, he got to make the rules. One of those rules forbid blacks, Hispanics, Latinos, *and* native peoples from owning land in his new town. How about that? A little slice of heaven for European oppressors."

"It's not like that anymore?" I tried.

"Oh, thank goodness, no. No, no, no. The movie industry moved in, and, well, ruined it for everyone. All those liberal degenerates needed cheap labor to do the heavy lifting for their movies. Oh, and managing their households. You needed a nanny, a gardener, a cook, and probably someone to wipe your ass because—hey now—you don't have time for that shit when you're a studio-owned movie star."

Toya gave me a tight smile that made it clear this was her sarcasm voice, in case I hadn't figured it out. Fortunately, I was better at body language than Chaz, so I was keeping up.

"Now, where did all those unwanted and unseen folks live? I'm glad you asked." She tapped the screen where the land hit the ocean. "Meanwhile, over here, we've got swamp land that no one wanted, except for an old romantic named Albert Kinney who had always dreamed of owning a seaside resort town. He and his pals bought the land from the edge of Santa Monica down to the pier, and that's where they built Ocean Park." Her finger drifted toward the dark line that was Interstate 10. "Santa Monica really liked Ocean Park, so much so that they made some love notes on city planning documents, and whoops! Guess what is now part of Santa Monica?"

"I feel like that is a trick question," I said.

Toya patted my knee the way you pet a cocker spaniel that wants to be rewarded for not shitting on the carpet while you've been gone all day.

"Kinney and his pals were forced south," she continued. "Eventually, they fell out with each other—one of them died— and Kinney walked away with the very south end of this stretch of land, which was the nasty, marshy bit. Of course, since he had won it in a coin toss, he wasn't about to complain. Thought he had done all right, in fact.

"Kinney drained the worst spots, made some canals, and named the place after the Italian city that he was always dreaming about. Quaint, picturesque, and a little swampy, but hey, it's all part of the charm. Tourists loved it, and God, did they flock here. Some of them even wanted to buy property, which made Old Man Kinney's day. He went from having nothing but a coin which had won him the land to having people wanting to throw money at him."

Toya paused for a second, a finger raised. "Ah, but not everyone was throwing money," she said. "The black folks weren't. Not because they didn't have any, but because—once again—they weren't welcome. They had to live in Oakwood, which was neither wooded nor oaky. Nor was it very close to the water."

She chose another picture. It showed a series of aging oil derricks. "Did I mention oil was found in Venice? No? Well, welcome to the middle of the twentieth-century. Movie lots, oil derricks, and ferris wheels. All within ten miles of each other. Straight from the center of LA to the sea. All sorts of money coming in. Should have made Kinney a millionaire a couple dozen times over, right?"

The next picture was a shot of a sprawling complex of run-down apartments. There was a park in the foreground, but the equipment looked like it had been hit by an aerial bombardment.

"Well, that wasn't quite how it turned out," she said. "Most of this land was part of LA—on paper—but it was pretty far from the city center. Past the 405, for crying out loud. Who wanted to go out there? Even when the federal government got serious about funding housing projects, it took a long time for very little to trickle down to places like the Mar Vista Gardens."

I nodded, recognizing the place now. A lot of work had been done in that area during the last decade, but it had also gotten a lot of bad press as a stomping ground for one of the notorious street gangs that ruled parts of LA.

"You know what happened next?" Toya asked.

I thought about it for a second. "Crack," I said.

"Bingo," she said. "Drugs have been a huge part of the Venice culture, ever since the hippies stormed the barricades and got everyone high. Part of the turf war over Oakwood involved the drug trade, because, you know, it's right over there." She waved a hand at the side of the office away from the beach. "It got really bad during the early '90s. Someone got shot ever week or two. Parents didn't want their kids walking to and from school. Residents were yelling at the city for more police. The city officials were yelling at LAPD. LAPD was yelling at the federal government. It was a mess. Still is, actually, but—but!"

"But what? Did the LA DA get soft on crime?"

She laughed at that. Head back. Loud and joyous. Chaz looked over, his eyebrows tight, wondering what I had said that had made her laugh that hard.

"No," Toya sighed when she was done. "The LA District Attorney did not get soft on crime.."

"Well, a boy can dream," I said.

She narrowed her eyes. "And what kind of dream is that?" she asked.

I brushed off her question. "So the basic playbook is still the same: find some drugs, round up the usual suspects, throw them into the pokey for a nickel or two."

"The 'pokey'?"

"Yeah, you know—prison."

"I know what the 'pokey' is," she said. We looked at each other for a minute. I had a feeling she knew more about me than she was letting on. She had been sitting outside of Angel's law office for a couple of hours. Maybe she and Bunko were part of the same tinfoil hat league. Maybe she was the one who had told Bunko about the Chows. Maybe he had told her. It didn't matter. I was curious as to how much Toya knew.

"Did you—" She cleared her throat and rocked a fingertip on her desk. "Did you call it the 'pokey' during your trial?" She threw up her hands when I grimaced. "Come on. I'm a journalist. It's my job to know more about people they are comfortable sharing."

"No," I said. "I did not call it the 'pokey' during the trial."

She clucked her tongue. "That's a shame."

"The prosecutor would have been highly offended—more so than he was already. Probably would have asked for five more years during sentencing."

"Might have been worth it for the sound byte," she offered.

"Very little is worth 'it' when it comes to time behind bars," I said.

Her face softened. "Yeah, I imagine so."

I felt a tug of curiosity, but she pulled her armor back up before I could tease at it.

The history lesson continued for another forty minutes or so, and therein I learned about Vista 13—a branch of the Mafia Mexicana which had come out of the Mar Vista Garden community—the Culver City Boyz, and the Venice Shoreline Crips. We covered the turf wars that had made the early part of the decade tough in Oakwood. The race riots in '92, following the Rodney King verdict, hadn't helped.

More recently, law enforcement started caring about what was happening in Oakwood. Not because some magic number had been passed—you can only have so many tragic and pointless deaths in a year's time before the state starts to notice, after all—but because the people who were threatened by all the drugs and violence were white.

We adjourned to the boardwalk for some fresh air and ice cream. I got butter pecan. She got strawberry. She made that "mmmm" noise more than I thought was necessary as she ran her tongue around the perfectly conical shape of her cone.

"Back in the day, even though white people didn't want the land, they made a big deal out of letting the black folk have it." I said, letting her know I had been paying attention in the office.

"And the brown people and the red people," Toya said.

"Them too," I said. "Now, generations later, they want it back."

Toya nodded. "And since they can't run us out, they talk it up. They get their friends to write articles about it. White boys and girls with art degrees from fancy colleges move into the lofts and warehouses. Why? Because they're cheap as shit. And it makes them feel like they're tapping into some kind of 'urban passion' or some such nonsense. After that, the foodies show up, all keen on rediscovering local cuisine—though, if you ask the locals, it was never lost. Then, finally, some tastemaker somewhere says the magic words—'trendy' and 'upmarket'—and boom! Property values skyrocket. All the people who have been living here for generations suddenly can't afford it anymore."

She stopped and gestured at the festive colors of the banners and signs along the Venice beachfront. "Do you know the cheapest way to fight crime?" she said. "Get the city assessor to add a zero to every property value. The tax rate hike will clear out a quarter of the houses within eighteen months. The rest will follow in another year. You wake up one morning and discover *you're* the stranger in the neighborhood."

I bit into my cone, and tried to keep the ice cream from falling off.

Toya shook her head. "God, you can't even eat ice cream right."

"What does all of this have to do with me?" I asked, ignoring her jibe.

She stared at me. "Have you been listening at all to what I've been saying?"

"I have," I said. "And it's been very educational. Thank you. But nothing you've said connects to Bunko, or why he called out the Chows during his write-up. His *last* write-up, remember?"

"You're right," she said.

"I am?"

"You are. Nothing I've said makes that connection."

"Okay, well, what the hell, Toya? I don't understand."

"Well, maybe I wasn't done schooling you." Toya ran her tongue around the edge of cone. The ice cream had been licked down to a perfectly flat plane just below the top of the cone. She showed it to me, and I gave her a *I have seen that done so many times that it doesn't impress me as much as you think it does* look.

She coughed, reading the subtext of my look, and took an aggressive bite out of her cone. A fleck of ice cream nearly escaped, but she caught it in time and pushed it into her mouth. I was looking at a pair of kids with kites and so I missed the whole travesty. Tragedy? Whatever.

"Culver City is apparently trying to make amends or something," she said once she got her ice cream back under control. "They're trying to win the Most Diverse Demographic City Award or some shit. And west of there? What do you think is the fastest growing ethnic population?"

"Asian," I said.

"Indeed. And who has a tidy little empire of convenience stores and nail salons in this region?"

"Hang on," I said. "This is another trick question."

"Did you know that Chow Enterprises, Inc. own at least a half dozen other buildings around the convenience stores? And, in most cases, CEI owns the building the store is in."

"How about that."

"You didn't know."

I shook my head. "The youngest son is an accountant," I said. "Frankly, I'd be a little suspicious if they didn't own more property."

"And their ties to the Hong Kong triads?"

"That I definitely don't know anything about." I polished off my ice cream. "How long has Bunko been chasing the Chow family?"

Toya raised her shoulders. "A while. I dunno. A decade? Probably more."

"Probably," I said. I put my hands on my hips and stared out across the water. The waves was dotted with tiny shapes—surfers who were trying to catch a ride in the slow-rolling surf.

A guy like Bunko didn't worry something like an old dog for more than a decade because he was in love with the human interest angle. He thought the prize was out there: the story of his lifetime. The big one that would justify all the shitty hours of shitty takeout and shitty stakeouts. The one that get the words "Pulitzer Prize Winner" attached to his name.

And yet, it didn't make any sense. I had been out of prison for a couple of years. Mr. Chow had died at home. Life had gone on. Whatever secrets he had, he took them to the grave. The only "empire" to speak of was the one that Jackie had built.

And yet the Feds had run a game on Tony. They made him nervous. Gave him hints. Blinded him with their badges. Got him thinking. Hell, they probably did the same to Bunko. One of them called him late at night, breathed heavily into the phone, and dropped enough hits to stir that fire in Bunko's belly. Awaken that journalist's sense that there was something going on. something worth digging for. Something worth killing for.

"Mmmm," Toya said.

"What?"

"You look like you're thinking," she said.

"I was."

"And?"

"And I think I need to talk to Jackie."

"You should," she said. Then she snorted and covered her mouth. "Sorry," she laughed. "I mean, you could *if* you had a cellphone."

"Goddamn it. Not that again."

She grabbed my arm. "Come on," she said. "Let's get you one right now."

I anticipated having the awkward conversation I always have with someone when we start talking about money. If you need to acquire anything that costs more than a hundred dollars, the scions of capitalism would rather you borrow that money to buy the shiny whatsit. Sure, it's a minor loan and you can totally pay it off at any time, but don't be in a rush about it. It's kinda like free money, right? Sure, there's some interest, but everyone pays interest, so whatever.

"You done?" Toya asked when I paused to take a breath.

"I'm serious. This is why I pay cash," I said.

"Yeah, I got that, but what does that have to do with getting a cellphone?"

She looked at the gray-haired guy in tie dye behind the counter. He shrugged like he had heard it all before.

"They won't sell you a phone," I said. "You *lease* it. It's under contract. You have to pay a monthly fee to connect." I realized I was waving my hands and doing a lot of air quotes. All I was missing was a special hat, lined with aluminum foil. Now I was starting to sound like Bunko.

"Okay, so?" Toya still didn't see the problem.

I gave her a slightly patronizing smile. "They aren't going to let you have that contract without making sure you aren't a credit risk."

"Ah," she said, getting it.

The guy behind the counter nodded. He got it. He pointed at the phone in the plastic case on the convenience store counter. "This one doesn't require a contract," he said.

"It—what?"

"That's what I was trying to tell you before you went off on your—whatever that was," Toya said. "It's pay-as-you-go. You pay more per minute than everyone else, but hey, if you want to keep whistling 'Free Bird,' then you pay for that luxury."

"So, wait. I can just pay cash for this"—I pointed at the phone—"and get some of those"—those being prepaid phone cards—"and I'm good?"

"You're good."

"What happens if I run out of minutes? Does the number go away or something?"

"Oh, honey." Toya tried to keep a straight face. "How do you think they do things in Oakwood?"

I paid the man for the phone, and suddenly gripped with that stupid fear of not having enough—that panic the whole system tries to hook you into—I bought, like, a couple thousand minutes of phone time.

Who the fuck was I going to talk to for a thousand minutes?

CHAPTER 16

"I KNOW WHO I'D TALK TO FOR A THOUSAND MINUTES." HUGGY had to shout to make himself heard over the industrial buzzsaw noises coming from the speakers.

We were sitting in a black leather booth on the mezzanine level of The Totem, a club off Sunset that catered to spine-rattling beats, World War I trench warfare attire, and fishnet stalkings. The only thing missing was the pungent stench of mustard gas, but I heard they waited until midnight to drop canisters.

I smiled and nodded, fighting the migraine that was blooming. After leaving Venice, I had dozed in a cab while the driver had fought traffic over to the BMW dealership. I suffered through a bunch of passive-agressive sighing from Lucas, the poor bastard who was the Chow family account manager. After which, to further improve my mood, I had driven up to Sunset and stop-started my way toward West Hollywood. After an hour and a dozen blocks, I had given up and parked in a pay lot. Ate standing up at a food truck and then touristed along the Walk of Fame for awhile. The stars were still there—they would always be there—but the rest of the landscape kept changing.

This had been an unexpectedly difficult part of coming out of prison. A decade had passed. Nothing had stayed the same. Christ, I missed grunge entirely, for crying out loud. I didn't even know what I was supposed to feel about the industrial demolition noises coming out of the speakers.

Huggy noticed the tension in my expression. "It's not my thing," he said, nodding at the pair of leather-clad nuns in vintage gas masks standing near the railing. They had modified their masks with pale green lights so we could see their dark and decorative make-up. "Lolita comes here." He jerked a thumb toward the leather nuns. "It's the masks," he said. "Makes her feel like she's doing something kinky."

I gave him a somewhat queasy look.

"What?"

"There's a fine line between research for a character study and outright stalking."

Huggy spread his hands to encompass the club. "This is Hollywood, baby. There is no line."

I took a long drink from my beer, wishing it were something stronger. The leather nuns pantomimed making out with each other. The masks got in the way, or maybe that was part of the point. Performance art, and all.

Huggy laughed and pounded the table, making our beers dance. "Did you get a phone?" he asked.

When I nodded, he gestured for me to give it to him. I dug the phone out of my pocket and handed it over. He grimaced like I had handed him a petrified dog turd. "What the fuck is this?"

"It's a mobile phone," I said.

"I know that. But—Jesus, Bliss."

"It's a phone, Huggy. It's not a personal assistant."

He made a noise like a wounded animal. "You're going to get scurvy texting with this," he complained.

"I don't think that's how scurvy works," I said.

He showed me the minuscule display. "You have to push the number, like, four times to get all the letters."

"My last phone had a big dial on it, and it took twenty seconds for the thing to spin. We had to hand-crank the generator in the basement to power the damn thing."

Huggy gave me a *Your old man routine is older than your phone* look as he dug his device out of a pocket. "What's your number?" he said. I told him, and his thumbs danced over the glowing buttons on his phone.

My phone lit up and buzzed on the table. "That's me," he said. I looked at him.

"Pick it up," he said.

"I'm right here."

He grabbed my phone, answered it, talked to himself for a second, and then hung up. "I'm putting my number in your phone," he said. He moved his thumbs much more slowly over the keypad on my device. "There. I'm in your contacts."

Bear, the contact read.

"Give everyone a code name," he told me. "That way, no one knows who you are talking to."

"Why would anyone care?"

He gave me a *Did that question really come out of your mouth?* look.

I slipped my phone back into my pocket.

My beer was half empty. I was going to finish it, but I wasn't going to get another. "What did you find out?" I asked.

"About Ralph?"

I nodded. "Yeah, about Ralph."

"His juvie record is sealed, so I couldn't get into that, but I could see when—and how often—he went to Hillgate Hall." Huggy shook his head in admiration. "He started young."

"We've all got to be ambitious about something," I said.

"So, yeah, he got five to seven for grand theft out in Bakersfield. Probably would have been out in three for good behavior."

"It was three years more than he could do," I said.

"He spent four months at Tehachapi. Then he got sent to Lancaster. There was some notation about the transfer— medical, psychological, I dunno, something like that."

"A little of both," I said.

"He did his five in Lancaster." Huggy leaned forward. "Get this: he was back in the system within the year."

"Was he now?" I wasn't all that surprised. Guys like Ralph didn't like being on the outside. They couldn't figure out how to stay out of trouble. The world offered too many choices, and they never bothered to learn impulse control.

"LA County, and then back to Lancaster. Did five more there. Got out last summer. He's got another year of parole."

I nodded. Parole was good. Parole meant he was sticking around. He had to check in with his case manager on a regular basis. Had to have a job. Show he was a productive member of society and all that.

"You get a last known address?"

"Does Lolita Brigade wear a—"

I stopped him. "Don't," I said. "I don't need to know that you know . . . whatever it is you were about to tell me."

"It's in her bio," Huggy complained.

"Do you have Ralph's address?"

"Yeah, I got his address. I'll text it to you."

I started to argue, but his fingers were quicker than my mouth. My pocket vibrated soon after he snapped his phone shut.

"Thanks," I said. I'd figure out how to read his message later.

He peered around the club, trying to identify people in the gloom. "She'll be here soon, I bet," he said, a hopeful kink forming in his forehead.

I clapped him on the shoulder. "Yeah, I'm sure she will." I left enough cash to pay for another round or two and slipped out after finishing my beer.

When I pulled into the driveway at the house, the headlights caught a flash of brown fur near the bungalow. Baby Baby paused near the corner of the house. With the air of a stage actor in the spotlight who knew the audience was raptly paying attention to his every gesture, the Pekinese lifted his leg and peed on the foundation of the bungalow.

He barked at me once as he trotted back to the main house. Head up. Tail wagging. Proud of his accomplishment.

Like he didn't do it three or four times a day.

A dot of orange light glowed on the deck. Mrs. Chow was smoking a cigarette while her dog did his regular business on the side of the bungalow.

"Evening," I said.

She went into the house without saying a word. Baby Baby didn't bark again either.

When I went to bed an hour later, I pulled the covers up to my chin, and did my best to imagine I was back in my cell at Tehachapi. Six by six. Bars on the door. There, in that tiny room, I was safe.

Baby Baby woke me up eight hours later, barking like I was a thief in my own house. In my dream, I was being stalked by one of the leather nuns from the club. She was chasing me through an abandoned castle. I felt like I was trapped in a remake of Jesús Franco's *Les Chatouilleuses*, but with more gas masks.

I showered, made coffee, and stared out the window at Mrs. Chow's house. Baby Baby sat on the deck. Watching me. Waiting for me to leave so he could pee on the bungalow again.

Last summer, I had taken a job that required ready cash, and I had been packing it up when Mrs. Chow dropped by. She had left the door open behind her, and the dog had come running. He jumped up on the couch and started wrestling with the duffel bag that contained the money. Before I could stop him, he had gotten it open, whereupon he had climbed in the bag and peed all over the cash.

I never did get the smell out of the money.

Since then, I had taken to storing my money on the top shelf in the bedroom closet. In a metal box that locked. It was a dog proof as I could make it. And yes, a bank would have been better, but once you put the money in the bank, then people and institutions—like the IRS, for example—know you have it.

I had done my time. I didn't owe anyone anything. That was my excuse, but yeah, standing there, having a staring contest with a small dog whose happy place was making my cash smell fusty, it sounded like a pretty pathetic excuse.

With a sigh, I dumped the half-drunk cup of coffee in the sink and gathered up my wallet and keys. Oh, and my phone.

Baby Baby barked at me the whole time I was in the yard, and it was only after I started up the BMW and revved its engine unnecessarily that he shut up. I let the car idle as I poked at my new phone. Yes, there was a way to send text messages, and I had one from *Bear*. I had to scroll down several times to read all of Ralph's address.

I found my contacts. There were two. *Bear* and *Toya*. I recalled Huggy's rule about cell phone contacts, and while I was trying to change Toya's display name, I accidentally dialed her.

"Hello?" She sounded like I had woken her.

"Ah, yeah, hi. It's me," I said.

"It's early," she grumbled.

"Sorry. I was trying to figure how to use this phone and must have dialed your number."

"Jesus Christ, Bliss."

"Sorry," I said again. "Hey, look. I'm going to get some coffee. You want some?"

"Mmmm," she said.

"Uh, how do you want it?"

"I want it in my mouth right now," she said.

"Um . . ."

She gave me a throaty chuckle and hung up.

I put the phone down and slipped the car into reverse. I could call her again when I got to Perks A Lot. She sounded like she needed a little time to wake up. Probably having the same sort of weird Euro sex dream that I had been having.

☆

I got in line at Perks a Lot behind a pickup and a minivan. As I was fumbling with my phone, deciding whether to call Toya back now or when I got to the front of the line, the guy driving the pickup leaned out of his window. He was talking with whoever was working, and I got a glimpse of his profile.

It was Free.

I dropped my phone and kicked it around the car as I tried to back away from the minivan. There was another car behind me, and the driver laid on his horn as I nearly backed into him. I put the BMW in drive and yanked the wheel to the right, nudging around the bumper of the minivan. The driver behind me kept honking.

Free looked back. I was impossible not to notice, bouncing and fussing in the queue behind him. His head darted back into the cab of his truck, and with a squeal of rubber, his truck accelerated away from the shack. I kicked the pedal in my car, felt all the horses under hood wake up, and slewed out of the line after him. He bounced out of the parking lot, heading east, and I was right behind him.

Two blocks later, I noticed red and blue bubble lights in my rearview mirror.

Free's truck wove indiscriminately through traffic. I stayed on him, but kept splitting my attention between the cars ahead of me and the cop car behind me. As a result, he pulled farther ahead. We came to a 405 on-ramp, and he took it, his truck grumbling as he accelerated up to the elevated freeway.

I stayed on the surface street. The 405 was bound to be a parking lot at this time of day. The cop behind me had probably already called the pursuit in. By the time we reached the next exit, it would be swarmed by an entire fleet of black and whites. And once the cops got involved, I'd have no chance talk to Free. I had to lose the guy on my ass.

I cut through a residential neighborhood, scaring the shit out of a morning dog-walker who had just stepped off the curb. They and their dog did their outrage dance in the street, which nearly got them killed when the police car came careening around the corner. I took a hard right down an alley, felt the undercarriage of the BMW scrape a few times, and then I cut through a church parking lot. The other side of the street was light industrial—warehouses and alleys—and I was nearly clipped by a delivery truck as I darted across the road.

I hauled ass around a line of warehouses, hoping there would be a lot of open space in the back where I could let the car go. The BMW didn't have as many horses as my old Mustang, but it was one of those status symbols that had way more engine than was necessary for its class.

The engine roared as I floored it. I spared a glance in my rearview. The flashing lights were still there, but I had some breathing room now. *He's calling his pals*, I thought. *Time to disappear.* I hauled the wheel to the left, and I felt the momentary sting of a hanging chain as the car snapped through the barrier separating two lots. I slid around a stack of palettes and spotted a narrow alley between two warehouses. I gunned the engine, fluttered the brake, and pretended I did this sort of thing all the time.

I nailed the slot, and when I got my breath back, I put my foot down on the accelerator. The walls—*too close, way too close*—flashed by, and I hoped to God no one walked out of a building, hoping for a cigarette break.

Red and blue in the mirror. They were still back there.

Movement in front of me. Ahead, the alley opened up, and from my right, a panel van backed into the alley.

I slammed my palm against the wheel, sounding the BMW's horn. Trying to get the driver's attention. I didn't slow down.

He heard me, even though he couldn't see me. The van stopped. Its tail lights flashed.

Behind me: red and blue, red and blue.

The van's tail lights flashed again. It started to edge forward, disappearing from view. I eyed the gap between the back bumper of the van and the wall opposite. *It'll be wide enough*, I prayed.

There was a terrible scraping noise along the right side of the BMW. The wheel jerked in my hand, and I fought it. Something held on to the car for a second and then let go. I heard metal banging off concrete.

But I was through.

I shot out of the alley like I was on fire. I careened across an empty lot, got into traffic heading north, and as soon as I found a big box store parking lot, I squeezed the BMW into a parking space. I was out of the car before the last growl left the engine. Head down. Walking quickly. Trying to look in every direction at once without being obvious.

There was no sign of the cop car. I had left him behind in the alley.

It took a half hour for my hands to stop shaking.

CHAPTER 17

I SPENT AN HOUR WANDERING AROUND A NATURAL FOOD STORE, breathing in all the eucalyptus-scented free radicals. When I returned to the car, my phone—which I had left behind in my mad dash to vacate the premises—was politely alerting me to several missed calls. They were all from Toya.

If she left messages, I had no idea how to retrieve them. I called her back, and she answered right away. "How long does it take to get coffee?" She sounded both more awake and less pleased to be so.

"I ran into an old friend," I said.

"You don't have any friends," she said.

"Now, that's mean."

"I'm feeling pretty mean," she snapped.

"I probably shouldn't bring you any coffee then."

"Fail before you start: that's a good way to make a girl happy."

I stopped talking. Nothing I could say was going to make things better. She had brought her own outrage to this call. It was better that I didn't get sucked into it.

"Look," she said after a minute, "I'll just drink the shitty stuff at the office."

"You okay, Toya?"

"It's—I'm fine."

I considered telling her about my meeting with Huggy. I thought about asking her how the gallery event had gone last night. Should I tell her about Free?

"I have—I have a deadline today, so . . ."

"Sure," I said.

"We'll talk later," she said.

"Okay."

"Yeah . . . okay."

She hung up. I felt like I had missed something, but I also felt like I didn't have all the pieces to the puzzle I was trying to put together.

In a dark room.

While blindfolded.

You're playing with a serious handicap, Mr. Chow said.

I'm not even sure what game I'm playing, I said.

Or if you should be playing.

I tapped the steering wheel, sounding out my thoughts. Why had Mr. Chow gone to prison? Why had he left the stores unmanaged? Why were the Feds trying to spook Tony?

What's the game? I asked myself.

Mr. Chow didn't say anything.

My fingers stopped their beat. *What's the game?* I asked myself again.

No, that wasn't quite right. *Who are the players?* That was the question I needed to ask. Mr. Chow was right. I shouldn't be at this table, playing this game, but if I was, then I should know who else was sitting there, and why.

I drove out of the lot, found a major cross-street, and headed east. Toward Palms, where Jackie had his custom auto shop.

The auto body shop was located on Exposition, a couple of blocks from where the 10 curved and ran alongside the 187. The area was a riotous tangle of light industrial and cheap single-dwelling housing. Half of the body shop's lot was enclosed by a heavy fence topped with barbed wire, and across the street was the concrete foundations of the freeway.

There were three bays in the shop, doing basic custom work: rims, detailing, frame modifications. The more custom stuff was done out back, in a second building. A pair of cheap imports were up on the risers this morning. One was getting detail work done on its undercarriage. The other one looked like it had been hit by a giant cheese grater.

I nodded at one of the guys working. "Hey, Tré."

He looked up when he heard his name. He ambled over, wiping his greasy hands with a rag that was even greasier. "What's up, Bliss?" He held out a fist for me to bump.

We bumped.

"Jackie around?" I asked.

He mashed his wide lips together. "Nah. Haven't seen him. Usually doesn't come in on Saturdays."

Was it? I had lost track of the week. "How's business," I asked, pretending to be interested in his answer.

"Good. Good."

We nodded at nothing for a minute or two. "You hear about those robberies?" I asked.

"Naw. Which ones?"

"Jackie's stores. The one on Rose, and . . . I don't know . . . one of the other ones."

"Yeah, right. I did hear something about that. Wasn't it a couple of weeks ago?"

"About right."

"Yeah, yeah. I remember that. Let's see. Who was it? It was— yeah, Goldie's brother's girlfriend knows a girl who lives in the same building as the kid who was working that night."

"Really?"

"I know, man. Shit is too close to home, you know what I mean?"

"I do, Tré. I do."

We nodded some more.

"You want me to tell Jackie you stopped by?"

"Nah," I said. "Don't worry about it. It's not that important."

He wrinkled his nose. "Okay."

"What?"

"Nothing. I—just—aren't you like living with his mom or something?"

"It's not like—no, I'm not living with his mom."

"Yeah, okay. But you know her, right? I mean, you're, like, part of the family and shit."

"More like 'and shit' than anything else, but yeah, I know the family."

"You can't call him?" A mild bloom of curiosity was rising in his eyes.

"We're not that close," I said, offering him a disarming smile.

"Yeah, sure." Tré rubbed the side of his neck. "Maybe try the tea house," he said. "Next to Camellia."

Mrs. Chow's nail salons were named after flowers. Camellia was the one in West Hollywood. It shared a ground floor with a quaint little tea shop owned by the family. I thought of what Toya had said yesterday: *In most cases, CEI owns the building the store is in.*

It occurred to me I had no idea what was upstairs in that building. *Why hadn't Angel rented office space there?* I wondered.

"Yeah, the tea place," I said. "Yeah, okay. I'll try there. Thanks, Tré."

"No problem, Butch." We fist-bumped again and he wandered back to work.

I had no better luck at Camellia or the tea shop. The rest of the building was accessed by a lobby that was locked. I peered through the window. There was a nice looking fake fern on a metal stand, an elevator, and a board listing the building's tenants. I couldn't read any of the names on the board.

He'll be at the house tomorrow, Mr. Chow said. *Why are you trying so hard?*

I don't like waiting, I said.

He laughed. *That's all we did in the yard,* he said. *We waited for the sun to fall. We waited for someone to die. We waited for the weather to change.*

He wasn't wrong. Prison is boring, for the most part. Learning how to survive boredom is the hardest part. It should be a skill that transfers to the outside world.

Except the outside world is noisy. It's constantly in your face. *Pay attention to me! Look at me!* It's a lot harder to wait when you're under constant assault by noise and flashing lights and giant billboards that threaten to block out the sky.

I fiddled with my phone and found the address Huggy had given me. I was close, relatively speaking, and since my schedule was open, I figured I'd go see if I could find Ralph.

I wound up in a neighborhood that was in that ugly molting stage of gentrification. Boxy apartment buildings that were as artfully designed as a shipping warehouse were stacked on top of one another. Anything larger than a feral cat would have trouble squeezing between buildings. Ralph's apartment was on the ground floor, facing the street, and the metal security door might as well have been a screen door, for all the security it provided. The blinds in the single window were sun-damaged, and several of them had broken ends.

I circled the block a few times. You can never get too uptight about looking for parking in LA. You either pull up front, give the valet your keys and part with some cash, or you get into a Zen headspace about cruising for a spot. You practice patience. You drift like a leaf on the wind. You let the current of life wash over you. You imagine you are the fat salmon, waiting in the slow-moving eddy. Waiting for a fly to land on the water right above you. Waiting for an opportunity to come to you.

I had been white-knuckling the wheel since the chase with the cops yesterday. Not because I thought they were still looking for me, but because I hadn't let that tension go. I was still fighting upstream. I hadn't become the fat salmon.

I needed to breathe. I needed to let go of the anger building inside me. I needed to find that quiet spot, where the water was deep and slow. I needed to wait for the fly to land on the water.

After about twenty minutes of pretending to be a sleepy fish, a spot opened up across the street from Ralph's. I slid into it and, maintaining my mental calm, settled in to wait.

An hour passed.

The door of Ralph's apartment opened and a young woman came out. She was dressed in men's sweatpants and a pink hoodie that had a fanciful logo on it. The bits of her hair that stuck out of the hood looked like bleached seaweed. She wore dark glasses and furry ankle-boots. She hustled up the block, and I thought about getting out of the car and following her on foot, but then I realized she wasn't going far. Not in that outfit. Even in LA.

I was right. She went to the convenience store at the end of the block. She disappeared inside, and came out again in a few minutes. As she hurried back to the apartment, gusts of smoke trailed behind her. *Cigarette run*, I thought.

She ground the cigarette out beneath her boot on the walk in front of her door. She fumbled with her keys, dropped the pack of cigarettes she had bought, and then dropped the keys as she bent to retrieve the cigarettes. Her sweatpants had trouble staying on her hips. Eventually, she got the cigarettes into the pouch of the hoodie and the key into the lock.

The door shut behind her. I waited a few minutes. The blinds rattled. A building over, a calico cat squeezed out from between the buildings. I waited a few more minutes.

The parking spots in front of the building were reserved. Most of them were empty. She had walked to the store for cigarettes. She didn't strike me as the type who liked walking.

Ralph had the car, and he wasn't home.

Zen Master waiting bullshit probably wasn't going to bring him home any faster.

☆

My phone rang a half hour later.

"Hey, it's me," Toya said when I answered.

"Hey, you," I said.

"I hit my deadline," she said.

"Congratulations."

"Yeah, well, it happens a lot, so, you know . . ."

I didn't say anything.

"What are you doing?" she asked.

"Sitting in my car," I said. "Which isn't moving."

"Welcome to Los Angeles," she said. "How long are you going to be doing that?"

I glanced at the clock on the dash. "A while, I suppose."

"Pretty exciting?"

"Not especially."

She exhaled noisily. "Look, I—I was a bit of a bitch when we talked earlier and—"

"You don't have to apologize," I said.

She laughed. "I wasn't."

"Oh, okay."

"But I was thinking that maybe our conversation hadn't been the best part of your day and . . ."

"And you thought we could have a non-apology conversation?"

"Yeah, one of those."

"Okay." I waited. I was in the zone, after all.

"What *are* you doing?" she asked.

"Watching the front door of an apartment," I said.

"Gee. Now I'm reconsidering having made this call."

"I was hoping to drop in and see an old friend," I said.

"You don't have any friends," she reminded me.

"An old roommate."

"Mmmm," she said.

I glanced at the clock again. It hadn't moved.

"What are you doing?" I asked.

"Well, for reasons I'm not going to bother you with, I didn't make that suck-up preview last night at Philzee's gallery, so I have to go the actual preview tonight, or Frank will have words with me."

"You don't want that."

"I mean, I would probably survive another insufferable monologue about the parasitic relationship that is pleasuring our constituency so that we can harangue them about the stupid shit they're allowing to happen in their communities. However, after the third or fourth time, the talk gets a little tiresome. Plus it gets longer every time."

"So instead, you'll suffer an evening of sycophants and snobs."

"Someone has too."

"I think you secretly enjoy it."

She made a hiccuping noise. "I dare you to say that to me in person," she said. "Say, about six? At the office?"

The clock on the dash kept taunting me. Was I really going to sit in my car all afternoon, waiting for Ralph to come home? I knew where he lived. I could come back any time.

My Zen Master resolve wavered.

"What if I'm early?" I asked.

"How early?"

"About thirty minutes from now."

She laughed. "Yeah, fine. We can go shopping and you can buy me a drink."

CHAPTER 18

Toya wanted to go to the Santa Monica Promenade. I took a left, a right at the beach onto Pacific Avenue, and headed north. Toya had the window down and was tapping her fingers on the door frame. There was something on her mind. I figured she'd get to it when she was ready.

"There a good story about what happened to your car?" she asked at one point, referring to the long scratches along the passenger side.

"A good story?" I shook my head. "More of a dumb mistake than anything else."

She nodded absently. "That's not going to buff out," she said.

I decided not to mention the back bumper, the edge of which had been peeled away from the car. A hammer wasn't going to fix that either.

We rolled through traffic until we reached the large parking garage at the southern end of the Promenade.

The Promenade is a year-round walking mall, because that is how perpetually persistent the weather is in Santa Monica. A light breeze floated in off the ocean, and a handful of fluffy clouds were playing hide and seek across the blue sky. We crossed Santa Monica Boulevard with a gaggle of tourists and flowed into the ecosystem of the Promenade. Brand name shops winked and beckoned at us. Dread-headed dudes, a-fog in patchouli and lavender, hawked and haggled herbal supplements and tie-die bandanas from mobile carts. Young couples strolled with dogs instead of kids. Roaming bands of white-legged tourists gawked and stumbled along the pedestrian roadway, while tanned women in lycra shorts and crop tops whizzed around them on roller skates.

"I did some research on you," Toya said.

"Must have been a slow afternoon," I said.

"There was a thing recently. Some snake guy and some starlet."

"She wasn't a starlet. Her mother's the actress. She was getting a biology degree at UCLA. Studying habitat loss and global extinction events."

"Really?"

"What?"

"Nothing. I didn't think—never mind."

"Surprised that she had a couple of brain cells?"

"Yeah, okay. Sure. I mean, what with the rest of your . . ."

"Dossier?" I suggested.

She smiled. "Sure. *Oeuvre* sounds pretentious. It's certainly not a *curriculum vitae*—"

"A what?"

"It's academic speak for resumé."

"What's wrong with 'resumé.'"

"It's French. 'CV' is Latin, and therefore twice as pretentious."

"I thought 'oeuvre' was pretentious."

"Well, maybe. I don't know. Jean-Luc Godard is the only person who can get away it, frankly."

"Which?"

"Look—never mind."

I stopped walking. "You're hung up on the porn thing."

"What? No!"

"You are. You think it's stupid and shallow, and that the people involved are all degenerates and idiots."

"I do not."

"Really?"

"Look, it's not my . . . it's not my thing, so I'm not one to judge."

"Uh huh."

Her mouth snapped shut and her eyes narrowed. "Don't get sanctimonious on me," she said.

"Back at ya," I said.

She fumed for a minute, and I decided to not be a jerk about it. "What do rocket science and porn have in common?"

Toya frowned. "What?" she said, finally deciding to play along.

"It's important to know your coefficients of friction."

She laughed at that, and the tension between us dissolved.

"Come on," she said, grabbing my arm. "I don't want to get caught up in all that."

You brought it up, I thought, but I let it go. In my experience, trying to hold the high ground—such as it was—in conversations like this never turned out the way anyone hoped.

"Look at them," she said a few minutes later, nodding at the crowds around us. "This is what Venice is going to look like in a few years."

"It doesn't already?"

She acquiesced that point. "Gentrification is the disease no one wants to talk about in local communities," she said. "It's displacing families. And I'm not saying it's only happening in LA, or that white people are the ones doing it. It's happening among black and brown communities too. Money comes in. Money buys the cheap land that is undervalued. Money wants a return on its investment." She shrugged. "Pressure gets applied. City councils start making decisions driven by money, by the new residents . . . "

We stopped to watch an older gentleman in tails do magic tricks for kids. They were mesmerized by his bow tie and his ability to make a balloon animal appear out of thin air.

"Money changes everything," Toya said as the magician finished his act. Without an ounce of shame, he shoved his collection hat at the kids' parents. "It comes to town, and nothing is ever the same again. If you don't have it, you have to leave." She waved a hand in the direction we had come, indicating Ocean Park, Venice, Marina Del Mar, and all points farther south. "And when you go, you leave something behind. It's not much, but it's a little bit of who you were. It's a little part of your heritage. Of your community. You can't get it back. It's lost forever.

"This isn't a new thing, of course," she continued. "For centuries, tribes subjugated other tribes when they conquered them. Frontier settlers shoved the Native Americans out of their ancestral lands. White people brought blacks and Chinese to this country to do all the nasty work they didn't want to do. When the work was done, other white folk moved in. *Thank you very much; now get the fuck out.*"

She turned on me, her hands on her hips. "Twenty years ago, the word used to describe Oakwood was 'ghetto.' The streets weren't paved. Half the houses didn't have sewer lines. Then the Civil Rights Movement came along, and folks felt bad about how they'd been treating some classes of people. The federal government passed some laws, and city governments did some hand-waving and the bare minimum. Swell of them, don'tcha think? But nothing changed. Sure, we got paved roads and running water, but access to all the things that white folk enjoyed on a daily basis? Not so much. And now?" She let out a hard laugh. "Now, it's a fucking war zone because Mexicans and blacks both want the same shitty piece of land that some white dude 'gave' them a hundred years ago. Who wants to live there? A lot of folk, apparently. And even if they do manage to grab a piece, they can't afford the payments. They're all nine hundred square foot houses that weren't meant to last twenty years, and that was sixty years ago."

Her eyes were bright and fierce. "It's all changing, Butch," she said. "And even the assholes who get shot and bleed out on the street corners can't afford to live there. Money is bulldozing whole blocks and putting up huge mansions with big fucking fences. Gated communities. Private security forces. Little fortresses against the rest of the world. Hey, some gangbangers shot each other on *that* corner over there a year ago, and sure we're all secretly thrilled to be *that* close to blood and death, but we don't want our kids getting hit by some wild spray from a Mac-10, you know?"

"But many of those families—the ones whose parents bought that land back then—they aren't leaving, are they?" I said. "They're digging in."

She threw up her hands. "What the fuck for? I mean, I get it. But come on, money always wins. It's a lost cause."

She started walking again, her stride long and angry. "And it's not just Vista 13 or the Southies or whatever name the Hungarians are calling themselves this week. Everyone wants to be in the right zip code when it gets hot. Every group of immigrants wants to be there when the American Dream comes shooting out of the ground like a freshly tapped oil well. Chinese. Vietnamese. Czech. Russian. Whatever. They all want their little version of home. We have Koreatown, don't we? Well, where's Thai Town? Or Czech Town?"

"If you can call it home, you can put up walls," I said. "You can be safe."

"Yeah," she said, coming to a stop. "That's what it is, isn't it? They all want someplace they can call 'home,' and they're pissed it keeps getting taken away from them."

I thought about what she had been saying. I thought about what she had said yesterday. I thought about the Chows and the two dudes who had come into the convenience store.

"You think someone is making a move against the Chow empire," I said.

"I think someone *thinks* the Chows have an empire, and because it exists, they want it," she said.

"Okay, whatever. The distinction is sort of irrelevant, isn't it?"

She nodded. "It is."

"Okay, I'll bite. Who is it?"

"Vikings."

"What?"

"Honest to God, Bliss. I'm not kidding. I think it's a bunch of neo-Viking wannabes who are moving in on Chow. White dudes without money but with twice as much attitude about being white." She threw up her hands. "And do you know what really pisses them off?"

"They think the other folk—the ones who aren't white—they think they have money," I said. "And they think they can take it."

She gave me a sad, knowing smile. "I take back everything I said about you yesterday," she said. "You do get there eventually."

"Wait, what?"

Her lips turned up at the corners. "See?" And she was off again, walking with purpose and fire.

After a half hour of watching Toya shop for dresses, I may have let my attention wander. She snapped her fingers to pull me back to the present. "You need a jacket," she said. "And a better shirt."

"I like this shirt," I said.

"Great. Keep it for when you have someone sleep over, but I can't have you wearing that." She shook her head as she racked through a dozen more dresses. "I am going to look amazing, and you looking like a beach bum is going to harsh my glow."

I glanced over at the woman who worked at the boutique we were in. She gave me a tiny nod and a tinier frown. She didn't want to annoy paying customers, and while she might still be undecided if Toya was actually going to buy something or if she was just going to fondle all the fabrics, she did know a fashion disaster when she saw one.

"Yeah, all right," I said.

Toya motioned for me to be on my way. "And do not go to one of the chain stores," she admonished me.

I did my best.

It didn't take long, and when I was done, I wandered into a bookstore while waiting for Toya to finish. They had a decent non-fiction section, and I stumbled on a book about Vikings. I paid for it and found a bench outside that wasn't in direct sunlight and passed the time, reading about the ancient lies families told one another.

A prison family is different from a flesh and blood family, but only because it is thrust upon you. In either case, the hierarchy was important. If you wanted to elevate yourself above your station, you played all the games. You were nice to other family members. You nodded along and said rude things about the people who weren't family.

Groups of families made treaties and pacts between each other. Coalitions would form. Rules would get codified. In prison, those rules were handed down by the Man or the System. While these structures were supposed to keep you safe, they were actually there to dehumanize you. To remind you that you weren't free. That someone else was in charge of everything you did.

The side effect of these rules was the strength it gave to found families. Everyone on the inside had a common enemy, and it wasn't the other guys who were trapped behind those ten-foot concrete walls with you.

The California Department of Corrections and Rehabilitation was happy to put out press releases claiming they controlled the prisons, but on the inside, the Mafia Mexicana was in charge. Those of us who weren't members, either by race or disposition, made smaller families in order to stay alive. In some prisons, these families were strictly defined by racial lines. In others, the groups reflected the same power dynamics in the outside world. Tehachapi was far away from anything, and that distance made for some fluidity in the familial arrangements.

One of those families at Tehachapi was the Double-Zs. White nationalist dickbags who preached the Aryan Nation rhetoric, though without the snappy uniforms and goose-stepping dance moves. I hadn't paid much attention to whether they had a presence outside of the system, but why wouldn't they? Folks who did their time and got released lost access to their concrete family. They weren't going to shrug off those bonds they made in prison. *Oh, well, those kids were nice and all, but I'm different now. I should find some new friends.*

Finding new friends was hard. Finding like-minded people who had suffered the same systemic indignities as you? That was easy. There are always malcontents who feel they have suffered unjustly under the thumb of the Man. It wasn't hard to imagine Ralph's trajectory during his time at LAC, the state prison in Lancaster. Of course he found a family, and once he was out, he stayed with what he knew.

I thought about seeing Scar at the Red Eagle. In my head, I replayed his conversation with Tore. There had been a deference in Scar's body language. The slight dip of the head. Eyes on the floor. Nodding when Tore spoke to him.

If you wanted to stay in your little family, you respected the hierarchy. It didn't matter if it was a family of blood or convenience or inclination. You toed the line. You showed respect. That was how families stayed together.

Toya came out of the shop across the boulevard, carrying a pair of bags. She was wearing a light brown jacket, a teal silk shirt that hung loose over the low waistline of a pair of jeans that looked like they had been lacquered on. She stopped before me and struck a pose: hip cocked, shoulders back, one arm up so she could hold the bags against her back.

"Usually I insist a guy buys me a drink or two before I let him look at me like that," she said.

"Usually I have a drink or two before I look at a woman like this," I admitted.

"Look at us," she said. "Breaking all the rules."

"Indeed." I nodded toward the bags in her hand. "I thought you were buying a dress."

"I did."

"And?" I gestured at the clothes she was wearing.

"Since I was going to expense the dress, I figured I might as well get a few more things," she said. "Frank won't mind."

"He will," I said. "But I suspect that won't stop him from writing a check."

"Probably not," she mused. She nodded toward the book in my hand. "What did you find?"

I showed her. "It's a collection of Norse mythology."

"Yeah?"

"Yeah. I knew about Odin and Thor and Ragnarok—that big fuck-all fight they have at the end of the world—but there's a lot more, you know?"

"I do," she said. "I like Sif—she's a tough lady."

"And the Valkyries."

"Right. But, let's be honest, it's all male gaze wish-fulfilment with them. I mean, come on. They show up to carry fallen heroes off the battlefield and take them to Valhalla, where they get to drink and fuck for all eternity."

"It's a pretty good incentive to die in battle," I said.

"Well, sure. If that's all you've got."

"Better to win and take all the gold."

"And the women," she said. "And the property. And . . ."

"Yeah," I said with a nod. "That much hasn't changed."

"Nope," she said.

Toya picked a place with a hyphenated name and a design aesthetic that was meant to suggest we were eating out in the woods. The hostess tried to seat us near the front, but Toya shook her head and asked for something in the back. The hostess, who knew how this town worked, redirected smoothly and showed us to a small table near the bar. The place was already filling up with the pre-happy hour crowd, and we had to sit close and lean closer to hear one another. Neither of us minded.

A member of the wait staff brought menus, which led to a comedic moment when everyone realized the table wasn't large enough for one—much less two—of the menu broadsheets. Toya asked for waters for both of us, and shooed the waiter off.

"Are we ordering food?" she asked, eying the menu. She held it up so I could only see the back, which listed cocktails and overly expensive wines. I looked at Toya instead, which was what she wanted anyway.

"There going to be food at this gala thingie?"

"It's a gallery opening," she said. "Not a gala."

"Which means what in regards to food?"

"Less is more," she said. "Philzee is in a minimalist phase."

"Philzee?"

She gave me a *Don't ruin a perfectly fine moment by making me explain some douchebag's affectations* look. "Did you get a jacket?" she asked. Her foot nudged mine under the table as she kicked the paper bag that contained my new clothes and my book.

"I did. And a shirt. Some socks too."

"Briefs?" She eyed me over the top of the menu.

"This is where I tell you that I typically go commando, right?"

She wrinkled her lips. "Please don't—even if you do."

"I don't, and I didn't," I said. "They were ridiculously overpriced."

She gestured around us. "It's the Promenade, for crying out loud. What did you expect?"

"And yet, you bought two entire outfits," I said.

"Frank did," she corrected.

"Indeed."

"And a new bra and some panties," she said.

I stared at her.

"What?" she asked innocently.

"Your writing must be amazing," I said. "For Frank to put up with you."

"Or I'm incredible in the sack," she pointed out.

"No reason why you can't be both," I said.

She actually blushed. Her mouth worked around some words, but she didn't ruin the moment. I spent it thinking about the undergarments she had bought, because that was what I was supposed to be thinking about, and I didn't want to disappoint.

The waiter wandered into our periphery. "What's your poison?" Toya asked, flipping down the menu and looking intently at me, as if we hadn't been talking about other things a few seconds ago.

"Bourbon," I said.

"That's very All-American of you."

"I also like apple pie, football, and puppies."

"And fucking," she said. "Don't forget that."

"I rarely do," I managed.

She smiled at the waiter whose eyes were ping-ponging between us. "Can you have the bartender make us something with bourbon that will help him help me out of these pants in about an hour? Oh, and we'll also have the gorgonzola and bacon wagyu sliders and the coconut prawn street tacos."

The waiter scurried off to pass along her order. The food sounded nice, but I was developing a strong thirst.

CHAPTER 19

AN OLDER MAN IN A BLUE SHIRT WAS EMPTYING THE TRASH AT the *Venice Voice* offices when we returned from our shopping trip. "Evening, Gabe," Toya sang out as she waltzed into the common area with the cubicles. The cleaning man nodded and waved at her. He had a portable radio on his cart, and it was tuned to a local station. Toya—who had been fortified by food, shopping, and sexy talk—danced across the room and twisted the volume knob on the radio. "I love this song," she shouted over the brassy sound spitting out of the tiny speaker.

She spun, swayed, and rocked her hips as she came across the room to where I was standing, burdened with the bags from our trip. "'Your love has set my soul on fire,'" she sang as she bumped her hips against mine. Her mouth was close, and her eyes were fixed on my chin. I felt one of her hands snake around my hip. "'Burnin' out of control.'"

I leaned forward, closing the already small gap between us. Her lips brushed mine. "'You taught me the ways of desire,'" she whispered. Her fingers found mine, and bags were liberated from my loose fingers. She nipped at my lips as she darted away. "Get dressed," she tossed over her shoulder as she danced toward Frank's office.

She shut the door. The song hit its chorus. I looked at Gabe. He looked at me. Moving at his own pace, he wandered over to his cart and turned the volume down on his radio. "Miss Toya is very spirited," he said.

I nodded, unsure of how to respond. I raised the one bag I had left. "Is there, ah, somewhere I can change?"

He went around his cart and started pushing it toward the door. "I'm done here," he said. "You'll be fine."

"Thanks, uh, yeah, thanks, Gabe."

He nodded as he pushed through the door and left. I thought I heard him laughing, but it may have been someone on the radio.

I looked over at Frank's office. I thought about what was happening on the other side of the closed door—*something with bourbon that will help him help me out of these pants in about an hour?*—and thought it best to stick with my own wardrobe for the time being.

Philzee's gallery was on the second floor in a building across the street. We walked over from the office, and it was like doing the fashion runway at a spring show in Paris. Toya wore a red dress that seemed like it had been spun from spider silk. It clung to her body. It shimmered when she moved. It threatened to tear when she breathed. Her shoes—stiletto heels and a color that matched the dress perfectly—were an inch taller than practical, but they accentuated her *This body will shake the foundation of your world* swagger. She had pulled her hair back and up, fashioning a swoop and sweep of darkness, like something teased into being by wild-eyed ravens. You couldn't help but wonder what she had done—and with who—last night.

No one noticed me, even though I had—in her words—cleaned up pretty good for a white guy. You take your compliments where you can get them. I learned that while making movies. That wasn't one of the life lessons you learned in prison.

She went up the stairs ahead of me, and it was both the shortest and longest climb in recent memory.

A thin woman, wearing a pale blue dress that had been fashionable a few years ago and would have fit better had she been ten pounds heavier, was in charge of greeting people as they arrived. There was a hollowness to her face that spoke of too many office visits, where the lighting was terrible and the side-effects of the chemotherapy sessions was worse. "Toya," the woman said, when the fiery fury I was pursuing reached the top of the stairs. "Look at you!"

"Nancy!" Toya gave the other woman a hug that wouldn't have crushed the wings on a ladybug. "You look radiant."

A little bit of color flushed into Nancy's face. "I've been responding well to the treatments," she mock-whispered. "Plus I've met—" She gave Toya a conspiratorial wink.

Toya laughed. "Good for you, girl," she said. "That's what I've been saying. Doctors can only do so much for a body. You need other therapies to make your soul whole again."

"Indeed," Nancy giggled. She eyed me. "And who's this?"

"This is Bliss," Toya said.

Nancy giggled again, and Toya joined her. I smiled politely, already having guessed the role I was to play this evening. "He looks like a movie star," Nancy whispered in a voice that people on the street could hear. "Have I seen any of his movies?"

I answered before Toya could. "No, ma'am," I said. "It's been awhile, and they were all for direct-to-video markets."

"Oh," Nancy said. "Like art house . . . ?"

"Home fitness markets, mostly," I said.

Toya let out a snort of laughter. "We must mingle, dear," she said, offering Nancy an air kiss. "And I am going to tear him away from you now, because if I don't, he will succumb to your charm and I will never see him again."

"I doubt that very much," Nancy said. "But it is lovely of you to say so." Our exchange had brought some color to her face. I let her fondle my bicep and gave her an air kiss as Toya led me into the gallery.

"She and her husband used to own this space," Toya said quietly as we wandered down a hall decorated with a gamut of watercolors and abstract oils. Spotlights focused attention on the paintings—attention that was drawn away by Toya's dress, which sparkled and flashed indignantly under the lights. "But he died in a sailing accident a decade or so ago, and then she came down with some kind of cancer."

She glanced over her shoulder. "They caught it early, but it took a lot out of her. She needed help with the gallery and brought in some investors. When the cancer came back last year, she decided to sell the rest of her share. They keep her around, because it's good for her spirit and it maintains the illusion of a legacy, of a continuous history with this place." Her face hardened for a moment. "That illusion is important to a lot of people," she said.

At the end of the hall, we entered the gallery proper. It was an open space, with white walls, a white floor, and a white ceiling. Large windows on the west side of the building looked toward the water. Black-edged partitions broke up the space, and around each of these, there were clusters of guests who were already deep in earnest discussion about the art.

A poster on an easel near the door announced that we were in the presence of "The Art of Emptiness." Fine print said the art was done by "emerging talents of a new generation of abstract minimalists, who promised to reveal the liminality of the infinite." The lower half of the poster was filled with a Pop Art pixelation of the gallery's namesake.

"Philzee," I read.

"More emphasis on the 'zee,'" Toya corrected.

"Will he have Nancy throw me out if I get it wrong?" I asked.

"She'll gladly try."

A tall man in a white suit with a white shirt and a white tie appeared to step out of a nearby wall. His shaven head gleamed in the gallery light, and the frames of his eyeglasses and the ceramic rings on his left hand were also white. "Ah, Toya Rose, the braying voice of the establishment," he said, flashing a smile that was as fake as his attire, but no less blinding in its purity. He opened his arms as if he expected a big hug.

"Ah, Philzee, the brazen patron of the beleaguered arts," Toya replied, likewise spreading her arms, but making no move to go in for the squeeze.

His smile tightened a fraction, but he covered well by bringing his hands together. His gaze flickered in my direction.

"This is your gallery?" I did what Toya hadn't. I swept the white wizard up in a bear hug. "I'm such a fan of modern art. People like you are angels."

It felt like I was hugging a giant popsicle. I waited until he started to squirm—proof of life, you know—before I let go.

"Hmm. Yes. Yes. Well, thank you." He wanted to adjust his suit, which wasn't necessary. I knew how to hug without wrinkling expensive fabrics. Another useful lesson learned from Hollywood. "I'm, ah, I'm delighted you could attend our modest opening, Mister . . . ?"

"Bliss," I said.

His eyes were large behind his fashionable eyewear, which—if I were to judge, and I certainly felt in the mood—were cosmetic and not prescriptive. "Yes, I see. And . . . ?"

"Bliss is good," I said, smiling and nodding. He was one of those who wanted everything to be on a first name basis, even though the name we were supposed to call him was an atrocity committed on the English language.

I was flustering him, and as he turned his pearly smile on Toya, I caught a brief glimpse of a deep cavern of suppressed resentment. "Well, my dear, I'm glad you could find the time to attend our preview," he said. "Are you here in an official capacity . . . ?"

"Of course, darling," she said. "Bliss and I have dinner reservations later this evening, and I thought we could drop by for a bit before we went into the city. See what new talent you've dug up."

Philzee managed to maintain his composure. I was impressed. She had kicked him three or four times in half as many sentences. "I'm sure even your jaded eye will find something of beauty in tonight's collection," he said smoothly. He wasn't going to let her prick him, not this early in the evening. No stains on that suit. Nosiree.

She opened her mouth to savage him again, but I touched her elbow and interrupted her. "Let's take a look," I said. "I want to hear all your thoughts."

She gave me a frosty glare, but let it melt away with one of her fabulous smiles that was mostly meant for Philzee. "Of course," she said. She dipped a knee toward Philzee, a minor acknowledgement of his hospitality. "Congratulations on the show."

He inclined his head. "I look forward to your commentary in next week's column. I'm sure I won't be the only one hanging on every word."

She blew him a kiss and let me lead her away. "Motherfucker will be lucky if I write a single inch," she said as soon as we were out of earshot.

"Play nice," I said, patting her arm. My grip was firm on her elbow. I was gaining a better understanding of Frank's burden as publisher of the weekly newspaper. "Let's not forget you need Frank to write you a nice big check for your shopping trip this afternoon."

She growled in her throat. "Frank wants a glowing review. I'll bang out five hundred words excoriating all of this bullshit. He'll throw it back at me, telling me he can't run it. I'll threaten to quit if he so much as touches a comma. He'll yell at me. I'll stamp my foot. Maybe I'll cry in front of him this time. But he'll cave and run it. And we'll get hate mail and fan mail in equal parts for the next few weeks. Frank'll give Philzee an op-ed slot to offer a 'measured' response. The hate mail will continue for a week or two more. And then everything will go back to normal."

She gestured at the canvases on the walls. "Meanwhile, the controversy will drive traffic to the gallery. Everything will be sold by the end of the month."

Toya glanced back at the door, where Nancy was greeting people. "And she'll get none of it. Not a goddamned dime."

She slipped out of my grip. "I need a drink," she said. There was an open bar over by the windows, and Toya marched off in that direction.

I was distracted. The painting in front of me was a white landscape, broken up with tiny abstractions done in slightly less white shades of white. It was a piece that might have revealed a variety of secrets under a variety of lighting. But that wasn't what had caught my attention. On a tiny card next to the painting, the artist's name was listed. "Margit Oppegard." There was also a picture of the artist.

The last time I had seen that face was in the back window of a German sedan as it was leaving the parking lot of the Red Eagle.

CHAPTER 20

I LOOKED AROUND THE GALLERY FOR MARGIT. SHE WASN'T THE only artist at the opening, and I anticipated the local art-lovers would be clustered around the stars of the evening. Margit wasn't a tall woman, in my recollection, which meant I'd have to mingle to find her.

Or . . .

Or I could just make eye contact with Tore, who was a head taller than everyone else in the room.

When he spotted me, a smile ghosted across his face, and for a moment, it felt like all the spotlights in the room were suddenly trained on me. The feeling passed as the coldness returned to his eyes. He walked toward me, the crowd parting in front of him like he was the carved figurehead on a Viking longship.

He was dressed in a light grey silk suit, with a pale lavender shirt and a slightly darker lavender tie. His hair was slicked back, and this was apparently an important enough event that he had shaved. He looked like a movie star, but he was trying for that marquee gleam. Couldn't fault him for trying.

"Well, well," he said. "Look who's more cultured than he appears."

"I'm here by accident," I said.

"Aren't we all," he said. He was trying to be aloof, but his fingers were fidgeting. Like he wanted to strangle something.

"Big night for Margit," I said. Out of the corner of my eye, I caught sight of a shaved head. This time on a man who wasn't secretly yearning for a call-back from a fantasy trilogy's casting director. "The whole crew here?" I asked, trying not to look at Sven, who was leaning against one of the black-framed partitions.

"It's a family affair," Tore said. "One must show support for one's family."

"Of course," I said.

I felt my focus sharpening. The rest of the room was dropping away. I was sliding into the schoolyard dance. Tore's nostrils flared. He was feeling it too.

Ragnhild floated into view. She was wearing a sheathed dress that made her look like a stalagmite with tits. Somehow, even with all the hard edges, she made it work. "Boys," she said, her voice like a flick of a knife. "Let's not get blood in the snow. It'll ruin the aesthetic." There was a gleam in her eye that said she wanted exactly the opposite.

Sven slipped behind the partition, and a tiny part of my brain filed that detail away for later. *He listens to her*, my brain noted. And not in a fawning way, but because he was afraid of her.

I didn't blame him. She spooked me.

Tore gave me another burst of his *Holy on high* smile. Radiant light shooting down from the mountain top.

And then, like the dazzling mythological fire that saved a lost tribe from an eternity of darkness, Toya shattered the frigid ice shelf forming between the two knuckle-draggers shoved into suits. "I'd climb that mountain," she said, giving Tore the full power of her gaze. She ignored Ragnhild, whose proximity to Tore clearly suggested ownership.

An expression she couldn't quite control slipped through Ragnhild's perfect mask. She got even icier, and her gaze could cut glass.

Tore stared at Toya with a hot intensity that made my knuckles crack.

Toya wrapped herself around me, and put her mouth close to my ear. "I want to watch when you two strip naked and slather oil all over each other." Her voice was loud enough for Tore and Ragnhild to hear.

Ragnhild's mask cracked, and the look on her face was equal parts fury and revulsion. She swirled in front of Tore before he could move and put a hand on his chest. She said something to the big man, and his eyes unfocused for a moment. He looked down at the ice queen. A current passed between them, and he nodded. "Aye," he said. "For family."

He let himself be led away, though his gaze was the last to go. I stuck with him to the hard-eyed end. Toya, feeling the tension pulsing in my shoulders, cooled me off by blowing in my ear.

"Let it go, tiger," she whispered.

She had a pale cocktail in a fancy glass in her hand. I took it from her and drank it down. She didn't stop me.

"I feel like there is a much better story buried in here than this shitty gallery opening," she said, tapping a finger against my chest. "And I want to hear it, sweetness, but I need to work for a little while. Can you manage to keep it in your pants without me having to rescue you?"

"Yeah," I said. "I can manage."

"Good." She took hold of my chin and turned my head so I could look her in the eye. "Bar is over there," she said, directing me with a nod. "Maybe you should go stand next to it and make polite conversation with people you don't know for a bit."

I focused on her face. "How polite?"

"Tell them how much you like the art. That's what they want to hear, anyway."

I looked at Margit's painting. It was called "Sympathetic Allusions of an Antediluvian Ancestry, No. 14."

"Good thing I took that correspondence course on modern art history," I said.

"There you go." She patted my chest. "You'll have my job in no time."

☆

During the next hour or so, stretched and tanned socialites tried to chat me up. I alternated between being effusive about the art or being entirely indifferent. It didn't seem to matter to the ladies. They were flexible in their thinking, and several suggested they were flexible in other ways too.

Philzee appeared in a puff of white smoke, tried to engage me in a verbal battle of wits, and disappeared in a huff when I asked if he could show me a card trick or two.

Sven came by for a shot of vodka and downed it while daggering me with his *You don't know cold until you've looked into my soul* dead-eyed stare.

I gave him a *I shat something harder than you last week* look.

After Sven stalked off, I asked the guy behind the bar which of us had looked meaner. The bartender, aware I had an open tab and that Sven hadn't tipped, said I definitely looked meaner.

We both watched Toya walk away after she swooped in for a cocktail. Distantly, I told the bartender to put her drink on my tab. He reminded me that she had started a tab with my name on it already.

I told him he wasn't getting paid enough to put up with us. He didn't disagree.

Eventually, hollow-eyed Nancy approached. Her elbows were hard against the counter, and her body shook a little as she tried to catch her breath.

I nodded at Chuck—we were on a first name basis now—and he poured Nancy a measure of white wine into a glass.

"Thank you," she said. She raised the glass and took a small sip. Her skin was nearly translucent under the track lighting. "Do you appreciate art, Mr. Bliss?" she asked.

"I have, once or twice," I said. "Sometimes quite accidentally."

She laughed. "It's meant to remind us of what we don't have," she said. "Or it show us something grander than ourselves."

"Or sometimes it's just a picture of a pipe," I said. "Or a can of soup."

She laughed again. "You are smarter than you look," she said.

"And you are cattier than you let on," I replied.

She shrugged. Her eyes tracked the absence of color and taste that was Philzee. "He wants to be important. A taste-maker. I wanted there to be art in the world. Cancer wanted more of me than I was ready to give. A deal was struck. I may let my bitterness show now and again."

"Someone told me recently that was the purpose of art."

"How's that?"

"If we don't have something to be bitter about, then we're not paying attention."

Her eyes narrowed as she sipped from her wine glass. "You're not an actor," she said.

"No, ma'am. I am not."

"You're something else entirely." She looked at me with an appraiser's eye. Seeing beneath the slap-dash layers of paint. Looking at the delicate marks left by the spirit that had put brush to canvas. "Or you may be nothing at all."

"Oh?"

"No one owns you, do they, Bliss?"

"That's right," I said. "I have paid all the debts foisted on me."

She turned and looked out at the crowd and the paintings. "Let me ask you then, as a man who lacks nothing and who knows the value of his own desire: what do you see when you look around this room? Do you see the art on the walls or do you see something else?"

I looked and saw Toya—a fire blazing on a plain of shadowed ice. I thought about the song that had been playing at the office. I thought of her hips, and of my hands on them.

Beside me, Nancy made a noise in her throat. "Mmmm," she said knowingly.

☆

Toya fumbled with her keys in the lock of the office door. She giggled, dropped the keys, and then bumped my shoulder when I bent to pick them up for her. I wrapped my arm around her thighs to keep from falling over. She leaned against me, and I almost picked her up when I stood. Throwing her over my shoulder to carry her off to my cave.

Together, somehow, we managed to get the door unlocked.

The office was dark, but Toya navigated the table in the cubicle area without hitting anything. I banged into one of the chairs and nearly fell over it.

She giggled again, and I chased after the noise. We bumped into the wall, our bodies pressed together. Her breath was hot on my neck. Her hands tugged at my jacket. I ran my hand up and down on her dress, raising sparks.

"Not here," she whispered. Clumsily, she found my hand. We brushed along the wall until we reached the door to Frank's office. It wasn't locked, and when she opened it, the yellow glow of the Venice sign bled into the hall.

"Here," she said, sweeping a stack of paperwork off Frank's desk. She kicked off one of her heels and reached for me. I crushed her against the desk, and she gasped with delight. Her hands moved with more delicacy than mine. I felt the fabric of her dress tear. She bit me at the base of my neck. I gasped as her hands were rough against my tender chest. She wrapped her legs around me.

Her dress twinkled in the light from the sign. Her eyes were filled with words she was too busy to say. My hands told her what to do, and she didn't argue.

The desk made more noise than we did—and oh, we were noisy—but it held.

CHAPTER 21

I ESCORTED TOYA TO HER CAR. OUR HANDS BRUSHED ONCE OR twice as we walked. When we reached her car, she unlocked it and I put the bag with all of her crumpled clothing on the back seat. A breeze off the beach teased her hair and she toyed with it for a moment before giving up.

We hadn't talked much after trying to break the furniture, but not because we were embarrassed. There was a lot of mental packing and unpacking to be done. A ferocious collision between two people like that leaves marks, and you have to decide whether you want to keep those marks or hide them. We had to decide how we felt. How we were going to feel tomorrow. If we were going to talk about it. Or maybe we would just never speak of it again. Keep it as a secret treasure.

"I'll call you tomorrow," I said.

"Mmm," she said.

She brushed her lips against mine before she got into her car.

The alley felt very empty after she was gone. Distantly, I heard the susurration of the surf. A gull screamed somewhere, and there was a tinge of horror to the sound. As if the bird was surprised to give voice during the night, and it was frightened by what its cry might summon.

I went to find my car.

It was where I had left it, though all four tires were flat.

The sound of the gull's shriek came back to me, and a shiver crawled its way up my spine. I fumbled for my phone as I circled my car, examining the slashed tires. I found Toya's number and hit the button to dial her.

She answered almost immediately. "Miss me already?" she purred.

"Check your mirrors," I said brusquely. "Anyone following you?"

"What—?"

I heard him coming, and slipped out of the way before Sven could brain me with the claw hammer in his hand. The metal rod bounced off the BMW, and his backswing was wild. I backed up and my heel hit something hard. I lost my balance, and my phone jumped out of my hand. It skittered away, taking with it the tiny sound of Toya's voice, shouting my name.

Sven's face was a mask of menace, a grinning death's head. His breath whistled through his clenched teeth as he came at me again. I was several inches taller, which meant my reach was longer, but that claw hammer evened things up, even as it gave him fewer options.

I slapped at his wrist as he came at me, and the hammer went past my shoulder. I bumped him—hard—and he flew back against my car, rocking it. The car alarm went off, a shrieking howl that startled every rodent and night bird for blocks. The noise covered Scar's approach too, because I had no sense he was behind me until he sunk a fist into one of my kidneys.

It was my turn to stagger against the car. Sven tried to hit me on the side of the head with the hammer, but I got my arm up to take the hit on my forearm. If anything was going to get broken, I'd prefer the forearm to the skull, thank you very much.

The pain was intense. I rolled against Sven, forgetting everything Mr. Chow had taught us about being supple reeds. I was a stubborn bull, his domain challenged. I was an old silverback, facing down a young male who thought he could take one of my harem. I was an old boxer, who knew he was outclassed by speed and youth. I swung my fists. I stomped my feet. I tried to hit with the hard part of my head.

This sort of fighting was Sven's domain, however, and he was younger and fitter than me. He dropped the claw hammer and responded to my flat-footed assault with the flickering quickness of a forest predator. For every glancing blow I landed, he peppered me with shots that were going to leave fist-shaped bruises all over my body.

I tried to put some distance between us, but all I managed to do was lumber into Scar. Scar bounced me back toward Sven. This was the smaller man's fight; Scar was there to make sure I didn't wander off. I knew I couldn't take Sven, and so the second time I managed to get away from the furious fists, I lunged for Scar. Divide and conquer. Maybe I would have a chance that way.

Scar and I did a giddy dance, circling the car and bouncing off the hood and the side. We slid off the trunk, and I got lucky. I landed on top, and I got in a few good shots to the face, turning his grin bloody and messy. He bucked me off, and I rolled across the pavement. Breathing was hard, thinking was harder, and as I tried to get my shit together, the night lit up with red and blue lights. And people stared yelling.

I blinked a few times, and found myself on my back. Lying on the beach. I was close to the water, and the sky was brighter than it should have been. A single gull wavered on a thermal high overhead, and I watched it try to hold its position.

It will shit on you if you don't move, Mr. Chow said.

Mr. Chow was lying on the beach next to me, dressed in the thin bathrobe he always wore during his last month. His skull was the wrong size for his body, and his skin was tight across his face and loose around his neck. The foamy edge of the surf crept up and licked the top of his bald head.

Maybe it will shit on you, I said, rolling my head back so I could stare at the bird instead.

I will kill it with a thought if it does, Mr. Chow said. *And the bird knows this. They are smart that way.*

I fell down, I said.

You do that often, he said. *Some say that it is a sign that you are getting old.*

I'm not getting old.

Then you are clumsy, he said. *It is better to be old.*

It's also better to be alive than dead, I said.

That depends on the life you have, he said.

I thought about the pressure of Toya's tongue. Her hips grinding against me. *That it does,* I said.

I also thought about the conversation Nancy and I had had at the gallery opening. *Your wife likes to remind me that I owe you,* I said.

Debts are like family, he said. *They are easy to accumulate and difficult to rid oneself of.*

Which am I? I asked.

He didn't say anything, and I laboriously turned my head to look at him. He was even more translucent than the last time I had looked. *You never gave Jackie a choice,* I said.

Of course I did, he replied.

Much like you did for me? I asked.

Do you regret the path you are on?

No, I said.

Then why do you fuss about what I wanted or did?

I thought about the look in Tony's eyes when we had talked in the car. That haunted look of abandonment. Debts versus family. Easy to accumulate. Difficult to get rid of.

This is the problem with similes. Things get compared to each other, but no one stops to consider which came first.

Hours later, the cop managing the lockup at Venice PD banged on the bars of my cell. I cracked open an eye and thought about sitting up. It was more than I wanted to do right then, but the cop kept banging. "You've got a visitor," he said.

I found the will to rise. "What?" I croaked.

He unlocked the door to my cell and held it open. "Let's go, convict," he said. "Don't keep the man waiting."

I moved like a slab of beef on roller skates, and the uniform led me to a small interrogation room. It had a lemon fresh smell, and the table was actually handmade. Chairs weren't bad either, though my tailbone hurt when I sat down.

Detective Lorenzo was wearing a nice suit too. I said as much as I put my arms on the table and leaned against them.

"Headache?" he asked.

"Little bit of one, yeah," I said.

"You need some aspirin or something?"

"I'd prefer whiskey."

He shook his head.

"How about some bacon and eggs?" I asked. "Maybe from that nice diner we were at the other night?"

"You get the shit kicked out of you a lot," he said.

"It's not a trend—"

"Shot at a lot too," he added.

I raised a finger. "It's been a trying week," I said.

"I bet."

He regarded me for a moment. "Disagreement between friends?" he asked.

"Did we look all that friendly?"

He shrugged. "I wasn't there."

I nodded. "Yeah, you showed up late the last time too," I said.

He leaned forward incrementally. "You sure?"

"Yeah," I said. "I'm sure."

"They can't hold him," Lorenzo said. "Any more than they can hold you."

"I know."

"Drunk and disorderly, maybe. Assault, if one of you wants to press charges."

"I'm not pressing charges."

Lorenzo's lips firmed into a tight line. "Neither is he."

I raised my head. "When did they kick him loose?"

"About twenty minutes ago."

"Shit," I sighed. "Of course they did. They always hang on to the guy with the record."

"Oh, he has one too," Lorenzo said. His lips shifted into a tiny smile. "Just not as colorful as yours. You're a celebrity, don't you know? They like to make a spectacle of celebrity fuck-ups around here."

"So nice of you to stop by and tell them otherwise," I said.

"Maybe." He let that word hang there for a minute.

"What do you want, Detective Lorenzo?"

"I have an FBI task force crawling up my ass."

"Sounds uncomfortable. But better you than me."

"Oh, they want to be all up in yours. They really do."

I shrugged. "So why aren't they?"

He chewed on his tongue for a minute. "What's going on with the Chows?" he asked.

"I have no idea," I said. "I really don't."

He looked away, trying to hide the glint of frustration in his eyes.

"Why are the Vikings moving in?" I asked.

"Who?"

"The Vik—the Double Z—I don't know. Whatever name they call themselves."

"How about 'The Sons of Freedom'?" Lorenzo said.

"Fine. The Sons of Freedom. Are they making a move?"

"I was hoping you could tell me."

I showed him my empty hands. "I was just getting beer that night," I said. "That's all."

"And yet, I got a dead reporter, a kid in the hospital with a gut wound, and two guys duking it out in an alley in Venice."

"Well, it's LA," I said. "Sounds great if you're playing Hollywood Bingo."

He sighed and reached into his pocket for a business card. He put it on the table and slid it over. "Call me," he said. "When you want to talk about it. And soon, before more people die."

I nodded as he left. I considered leaving the business card, but I swept it up and shoved it into a pocket. The door opened when I banged on it, and the Venice PD guy stopped me when I started back toward the cell. "We're done," he said, pointing me toward the front of the building.

If I hadn't been so tired and so sore, I would have wondered why Lorenzo had kicked me loose, but I shuffled down the hall. You don't ask too many questions when the police are shoving you toward the exit. These are the times when it is best to follow directions.

Someone was waiting for me in the lobby.

"Come on," Frank said. "I'll give you a ride."

I didn't volunteer anything during the drive back to the *Venice Voice*, and he was patient as I slowly navigated the stairs to the second floor. The lights were on in the offices, and when we got to his corner room, there were more people than either he or I expected to see.

"Chaz!"

The blond surfer looked up from where he was lying on the old couch tucked into the corner of Frank's office. "'Sup, boss," he said.

"What the hell are you doing here?" Frank demanded.

Chaz wiggled his fingers in that age-old symbol of the wave-riders. "Caught a squeal on the scanner. Thought I should come down and see if there was any action."

I stared at Toya, who was standing by the window, her arms wrapped around her waist. She was wearing a faded pair of jeans and a hooded sweatshirt with a tiny school logo on the breast. "You okay?" I croaked.

She nodded. The look in her eyes was hurting me more than my ribs. I let my gaze wander, and I noticed the desk had been tidied. The paperwork we had scattered was back on the desk. I looked away, in case someone noticed my attention, and latched on to the couch. *Why hadn't we—?*

"Okay," Frank said. "Someone want to tell me what the hell is going on?"

I wandered over to the couch and waved at Chaz to move his legs. He did, with a suppleness that made me ache to watch. How long was it going to be before I could bend at the waist like that again? I fell more than sat, and the couch wasn't very welcoming. Part of me started to think that maybe the desk had been—

I shushed that noisy voice.

"Okay," I said, focusing my thoughts on the task at hand. "I guess it starts in prison, more than a decade ago . . ."

Frank, a half-squint / half-hang dog expression on his face, had been glaring at Toya during the latter half of my story. When I finished, he huffed in a big breath. "How long have you been doing research for Bunko?" he asked.

"It wasn't like that," Toya said.

"No?" Frank added a raised eyebrow to his expression.

"He would call me after one of my columns ran. He wanted to talk about it. He—he wanted to talk about a lot of things."

"You didn't think he was cruising for information?"

"You don't think I was doing the same with him?"

Chaz made eye contact with me, and gave me *She's got a fair point* tilt of his head.

"Was he working on something?"

"He was always working on something."

"That's not an answer," Frank said.

"I don't have the answer you want, so anything I say is going to piss you off," Toya shot back.

Frank shrugged like what she said was probably true. He turned his attention to me. "Do you work for the Chows?"

"I do not," I said.

"You drive Mrs. Chow around," Toya said, not letting me off the hook.

I glanced at her. "Occasionally," I admitted.

"She doesn't have a car of her own?"

I conceded that point.

"Does she pay you?"

"She doesn't."

"How about that car? That's a new BMW. Has it got 15,000 miles on it yet?"

"No," I said.

"How did you pay for that?"

"It's leased."

"Who pays for the lease?"

I didn't answer.

She wasn't done. "Where you do live?"

"Okay," I said, cutting to the quick. "I am the recipient of some largesse on the part of the family."

Frank's other eyebrow went up. "Largesse?" he said.

"Yeah, it means—"

"I know what it means, thank you very much. I went to Berkeley, where I learned fancy words like that. I also learned how to spot a line of bullshit."

"I don't work for them," I reiterated.

Frank pursed his lips and looked at his staff. "He doesn't work for them," he said.

Toya rolled her eyes. Chaz hadn't stopped smirking.

"Look," I said. "No one asks me to carry envelopes. No one asks me to deliver messages to other business owners. I'm not directed to lurk in the background and look menacing when I take Mrs. Chow shopping. Well, okay. There is one market in Koreatown where it can get pretty fierce in the produce aisle, but—"

"This doesn't seem like a strange arrangement to you?"

"No," I said. "It's pretty cut-and-dried."

Frank sighed. He ran a hand through his tangled hair. "It's—" he started. He made a face like he was tasting something sour.

Chaz said it for him. "Everyone is going to think you're sleeping with her."

"Well, I'm not."

"You know, that's not how this works," he said.

"How what works?"

"This"—Chaz tried to be polite—"this sort of *arrangement*."

"Well, I guess I'm a pioneer then." I looked back and forth at the three of them. "What do you want me to say? I'm an ex-con. Before that, I made stag movies. You know what that looks like on a job application?"

Frank squinted as he thought about that, and then tried to *not* think about it. "Why didn't you go back to making movies?"

"I dunno. After a decade of prison, it didn't have that same— what do you call it?—*frisson* it once had."

"Now you're just trying to impress me with your vocabulary," Frank said.

"It's not every day I get interrogated by a Berkeley graduate," I said. "It's a good thing I got that diploma from mailing in all those cereal box tops."

Chaz perked up. "Seriously? From a cereal box?"

"You have to know how to lick stamps, Chaz," Toya said.

Chaz grinned. "Oh, I'm a good licker, T," he said.

Frank gave me a look that fell somewhere between blaming me for the back and forth between his staff and begging me to put him out of his misery. "Let's back up a minute," he said, changing the converation. "You used to work in the . . ." His mouth worked around the words a bit before he managed to get them out. ". . . the adult film entertainment industry. And then you went to prison, where you did your time. You didn't get an early release. You didn't get parole. You just did the time."

I nodded.

"Why?"

"Why what?"

"Why didn't you seek parole?"

I shifted on the couch. "You aren't free if you're on parole. You're merely on a longer leash. I wanted to be done with the system."

"Jesus," Frank sighed. He glanced over at Toya. "He's a goddamn Emersonian existentialist."

She made a motion with her shoulders that said she didn't have any problem with that. He turned his gaze to Chaz, who was looking at me and nodding. "Don't—" he said, levering a finger at me. "Don't give him any ideas."

"Who? Chaz?"

Chaz, hearing his name, perked up. "What?"

"Don't," Frank said, holding his finger very still.

"I'm not a very good role model," I said. "Nor do I have any designs to be."

"You just want to be left alone, is that it?" Frank asked. "You and your freedom from the tyranny of the Man and his oppressive systems?"

"I'd be all right with that," I said.

"World doesn't work like that, son," Frank said.

"I guess that makes me a pioneer *and* a rebel, doesn't it?"

Frank threw up his hands and raised his face toward the ceiling, silently imploring some divine agent to take him. When no one answered his plea, he returned to the mundane world. He noticed the fierce intensity of Toya's gaze, and he looked to the object of her attention.

I had been avoiding her gaze, fearing I would fall into the hot depths of her eyes. We'd start sending messages back and forth across the room, messages that both Frank and Chaz would be able to read pretty easily. We wouldn't be subtle.

I thought about staring at a corner of the room, but feared that would be too obvious. I looked at my hands, but that felt guilty too, and so I wound up looking straight ahead, which meant I was staring at the desk. Frank, who had gone to Berkeley after all, finally noticed the disarray. The stacks weren't the way they had been when he had left earlier in the day. He nudged some of the paperwork around, looked at Toya, looked at me, and his expensive education led him to a conclusion he really didn't want to reach.

"You—" He stared at Toya. She tried to look like she didn't know what he was thinking, but he knew her well enough to know how terrible she was at faking innocence. He glared at me. I was looking at my hands, which was exactly what a guilty man would do. "Goddamn it," he roared. "This is my office. You don't—Goddamn it!" He picked up a stack of paperwork and threw it theatrically. "Get out of my office. Get out!"

Chaz was startled by Frank's outburst. He didn't understand what had just happened, but to the credit of his well-practiced *Sun, Surf, and Free Love!* persona, he figured it out pretty quick. He startled chortling, which only made Frank angrier. He got red in the face and threw more paperwork, and the three of us vacated his office as quickly as possible.

In the hall, Chaz leaned against the wall, still caught up in the delight of what had happened. Toya stood nearby, both embarrassed and angry. Chaz finally got a handle on his delight, and he held out a closed fist. "Rock on, sister," he said. "I thought I was the only one who brought friends up here."

Understanding dawned on Toya's face. "You didn't—"

Chaz winked at her and did an air bump with his fist. Still smiling, he wandered off, leaving Toya and I dumbfounded.

"Toya!" Frank shouted from his office. "Get me the bleach! And a mop!"

Don't go, Toya mouthed at me.

I spread my hands, letting her know I wasn't going to abandon her.

CHAPTER 22

THE SUN SLIPPED INTO A POSITION WHERE IT COULD SPEAR MY eyeball, and Baby Baby started up his morning ritual of barking out military marches. I was sprawled in my own bed, which was a good place to be, but when I reached over to tug up the blanket, my hand found another body.

"What the hell is that noise?" Toya grumbled. She squirmed closer, and put her leg over mine. I was suddenly aware of how naked we were.

"That's—" I coughed lightly, trying to shake off the fog of sleep that clung to my brain. "That's my landlady's dog."

Toya nodded sleepily. Then, like it had for me, reality hit. "Oh, shit," she whispered. "Mrs. Chow's dog?"

I nodded. "Yeah," I said. "Every morning."

She sat up, her wide-eyed stare taking in my tastefully minimalist bedroom. "Oh, shit," she said again. "This is your place."

"Yeah," I said. I was piecing together the remnants of last night. She drove me here last night after we had left the *Venice Voice* offices. There had been some kissing in the car. I had lured her to the door of my bungalow. We had tumbled through the front door. Onto the couch. Off the couch. And—

"Bliss—" She looked around for her clothes. "Shit, how did I let you talk me into staying here?"

"I think I said something along the lines of 'here, let me help you out of that,'" I said.

She got out of bed, dragging the blanket with her in a sudden bout of modesty. It left me in a rather natural state. She got

halfway to the bedroom door before she realized the opportunity she was missing. I grabbed for a pillow and tried to
cover myself as she turned to get a good look. Her laughter—
full-throated and slightly manic—lingered as she left the room.

I rolled out of bed and grabbed a pair of sweat pants.
Marginally clothed, I went after her.

She was shoving her feet into her shoes when I came into the
living room. She had found her sweatshirt and pants. Part of
her bra was hanging out of the front pouch of her sweatshirt. It
was a light teal in color. Matched her panties, as I recalled. Both
had looked great against her dark skin. "I've got to run," she
said, heading for the door.

"Okay." I followed her out.

The cheerful sun hovered over the roof of the house. Toya's
car was in the driveway, and Baby Baby bounced toward it as
Toya walked swiftly across the yard. He barked at her a few
times—so much nonsense in such a tiny body—and I snapped
my fingers at him. He barked at me too, as if he wasn't going to
be intimidated by a lumbering giant. You gotta admire a dog
with so little sense.

Toya threw herself into her car. It didn't start right away, but
when the engine did catch, she threw it into reverse without
checking if the dog was under her tires. He wasn't, sadly, and
he stood—stiff-legged—in the driveway after she was gone and
barked his head off.

Some of last night's shadows lingered on the deck, hiding
from the sun, and I didn't notice Mrs. Chow standing next to
the sliding glass door until Toya had left.

"Morning," I said casually, as if running around half-naked
when an overnight guest fled the scene was something I did
every morning.

Mrs. Chow exhaled a plume of smoke from the cigarette in
her hand. "Where's your car?" she asked, arching an eyebrow
toward the empty drive.

I shaded my eyes with a hand. "Huh," I said. "It looks like it isn't here. How about that?"

"Lucas will be delivering a new car in a half hour," she said.

"Wow. He really does try to please, doesn't he?"

"When the car arrives, you and I are going to drive over to Camellia and have a talk with Jackie."

"Works for me," I said.

"This does not *work* for me," Mrs. Chow said. Her whole body dripped with disapproval.

I met her gaze. "Yeah, well, you get what you pay for these days," I said.

I went into the bungalow before she could ruin my exit line.

The car Lucas dropped off was silver, and mercifully, he didn't ask about the other car when I dropped him off at the dealership. Other than a brief moment where she told Lucas to call me directly if there were further issues, Mrs. Chow was an alabaster statue in the front seat during the drive to Camellia.

The gal in the tea shop ushered us into a back room. A fancy tea service was brought in a minute later. I made nice and arranged place settings. I put the tray of petit fours close at hand for Mrs. Chow before I started steeping the three different kinds of tea that had been provided. I wasn't a master by any stretch, but—okay, yes, so I knew how she liked her tea because I had prepared it often enough for her when we visited the salon. That didn't make me an employee.

I could see myself saying "largesse" in Frank's office, just as I could see the expression on everyone else's face when I said it. Sometimes things are exactly what they look like. Denial is a powerful drug, after all. It keeps a lot of the world from falling apart.

Jackie showed up after the tea had steeped and been poured. Unlike the rest of the family, who tended toward willowy, he was a heavyset man with a bodybuilder's neck and the hands of a butcher. He spoke quietly, as if he was trying to use as little air as possible, even though his lungs were larger than mine. He wore designer knockoffs—jeans, sneakers, watch—and he always smelled like he had tried all the perfume samples in this month's issue of the trendiest fashion magazine.

There was one thing that Jackie and I both agreed on: we did not like the other. In that way, we saw eye-to-eye.

He paused when he saw me, and I realized his mother had not told him I was attending this impromptu meeting. "What do you want, Mother?" he hissed in a stage whisper that carried across the room. "I am very busy."

"Butch is agitating the people at the BMW dealership," she said. She delicately plucked a tiny cake from the tray and nibbled off the corner.

"Most of that will buff right out," I said. "I mean, once you get the car back from impound."

She arched an eyebrow.

"So don't let him have a car," Jackie said.

"Oh, and a couple of tires," I added. Jackie glared at me, and I made a deal of counting on my fingers. "Hang on. Two from the other night, and yeah, all four from last night. That makes six." I looked innocently at him. "You can take it out of my paycheck, I guess."

He blinked once, like a predator deciding what to do with a stupid wildebeest who had gotten stuck in a muddy riverbank.

"What is this?" He directed his question at his mother.

"Why is a man at the *LA Times* writing news stories about the family?" she asked.

"Was," I said. "He *was* writing them."

Mrs. Chow gave me a stare similar to the one I had gotten from Jackie. I could see where he learned it, though he was a long way from mastering it. "And why is this man not writing these stories anymore?" she asked.

"He was shot a few days ago," I said.

"And why would someone shoot this man?" This time she looked at Jackie when she asked her question.

Jackie slammed a hand down on the table, making all the saucers rattle. "Mother," he exclaimed.

She was not moved by his outburst.

"Are you suggesting—"

"I'm not suggesting anything," she said, her voice like a door slamming shut. "I'm merely asking a question."

"I don't know why this man was shot," Jackie said. "He wrote about gang violence. Maybe one of the people he maligned wanted revenge."

"A victim of the very conflict he wrote about?"

"Exactly."

Mrs. Chow, having nibbled all the corners of the petit four, put the rest of it in her mouth. She chewed. She swallowed. She sipped from her tea and put the cup down. Turned it slightly on the saucer so that it lined up with a geometry only she could see.

Jackie breathed noisily. His leg vibrated under the table.

"Pity," Mrs. Chow said finally. "A man should not be remembered as a victim of the injustice he was trying to correct. Such sacrifice makes martyrs. The world has enough martyrs. Your father, may he be comforted by the spirits of our better selves, did not like martyrs. They bring ideology with them. They create followers. Problems that might have gone away on their own suddenly require solutions. Finding solutions means changing the way things are done, which, in turn, exposes weaknesses and creates opportunities for others."

"I know, Mother," Jackie said flatly. "Fathers tend to burden their children with all sorts of meaningless platitudes."

I shifted in my seat. As minute as my motions were, they weren't lost on Mrs. Chow. "You disagree?" she asked.

"Your husband, may he be eternally nuzzled by baby goats, was a manipulative narcissist, who never did anything that didn't advance his own designs," I said. "He might not have liked martyrs, but he liked to think of himself as one."

Mrs. Chow's expression was so cold the temperature of my tea dropped several degrees.

I had always wondered why she tolerated my presence. Sure, she had complained when he gave me the bungalow, but she hadn't thrown me out. She harassed me about being a bum, but she always expected me to be around so I could drive her places. Hell, she had the BMW dealership add a car to the family lease for me. I had figured it for some kind of long-term passive aggressive nonsense between parents and their first-born child, but I wasn't going to psychoanalyze the situation beyond that.

Yeah, okay, so I was a bit of a bum. Whatever. It wasn't a capital offense or anything. This was LA, after all. I wasn't the first person to accept some *largesse* from others and not think too much about it. Wouldn't be the last either.

I reached over and grabbed a petit four and popped it in my mouth. Giving myself time to think. Mrs. Chow sipped her tea. Jackie was vibrating so hard he could probably buff out the scratches on my old BMW with his bare hands.

I swallowed the petit four and decided to shake up this meeting. "Why is there an FBI Task Force investigating the family?" I asked.

Mrs. Chow didn't blink. She merely looked at her son.

Jackie fumed. "There isn't a task force," he ground out.

"No?" I reached for another petit four. "I'm sure Tony just made up all that shit about the Feds having a surprise sit-down to get some attention from the family. I'm not sure why he told me and not you, but hey, can you blame him for liking me better?"

Jackie went still and his gaze was hard and flat, like the dead eyes of a shark. *God, he loathes me*, I thought. He saw me as someone who had replaced him in the eyes of his father. With Dad gone, that wound would never heal. It was going to fester forever.

Jackie's gaze flicked away, like a fly darting off before you could swat it.

"Why is the Federal Bureau of Investigation talking to my son?" Mrs. Chow asked.

She was looking at Jackie when she asked the question, and I found her choice of words interesting. "You should ask Tony about that," I said.

I hesitated a second, debating if I had read her body language correctly. *Fuck it,* I thought. *Might as well find out, one way or another.*

"Jackie doesn't know shit about this," I said.

He came out of his chair so fast it toppled over. Mrs. Chow stopped him with a harshly barked phrase in Mandarin. He froze, quivering, and when he replied, it was in Mandarin too.

They went at it for a bit. I refilled my lukewarm tea from the pot. Had a couple of petit fours. Mentally rearranged my sock drawer (which wasn't very large).

Jackie cut the conversion off with a thunder of words. He stormed out, slamming the door behind him.

Mrs. Chow delicately picked up her tea cup, took a larger than normal sip, and put the cup back down again. I watched her fiddle with its alignment on the saucer. "My son wants to kill you," she said, as pleasantly as if she was commenting on the faint floral aftertaste of the tea.

"And were you trying to talk him out it?" I asked.

She shrugged lightly.

"No? Were you arguing about the best way he could go about accomplishing this deed?" I tried.

She shrugged again.

"Well, I'm out of guesses," I said.

"His desire will bring unwanted attention to the family," she said.

"I think it's a little late for that."

She ran a delicate finger along the rim of her teacup.

She was an alabaster statue again. I couldn't read anything from her expression. "Are you expecting me to help Jackie out by—I don't know—stepping in front of a bus or something. Or are you waiting for me to suggest an alternate solution . . ."

"I haven't decided," she said

The look she gave me dropped the temperature in the room five more degrees.

Fucking hell. This family . . .

CHAPTER 23

THIS WASN'T THE FIRST TIME SOMEONE WANTED TO KILL ME. IT wouldn't be the last. In prison, the solution was to strike first, but this approach was frowned upon outside the steel and concrete world of state-managed rehabilitation. It was supposed to be one of the perks, actually. In the outside world, you could get a good night's sleep without worrying about getting shanked while you snoozed.

Anyway, I drove around for awhile after that meeting, waiting for all of my conflicting thoughts about killing and being killed to go away. Somehow—and I didn't think about it too much—I wound up at Ralph's apartment. A silver Pontiac Grand Prix was parked in the slot reserved for Ralph's address, and I double-parked behind it.

The metal grate on the door was locked, and when I squeezed the handle on the door, the grate didn't shift. It was more secure than it looked. There was a small door in it that you could open to knock on the door. I did and waited.

Eventually, the dead bolt clacked and the door opened an inch. There wasn't much light coming from inside the apartment, and I couldn't tell who answered the door.

"Ralph home?" I asked.

"Who?"

It was the girlfriend. Her voice was a decade rougher than I expected, which said something about her nicotine habit.

"Scrawny little fucker about *this* high," I said, holding a hand up to my mid-chest. "Likes muscle cars like that one over there. Has terrible taste in friends. That sound like Ralph?"

She slammed the door shut.

Oh, well. It wasn't like I expected to be invited in. Plan B, then.

I walked backward until I was in full view of the window. I stood there, looking my best, and waited for the blinds to twitch. It didn't take long.

I cracked my knuckles and waited. Occasionally, I'd glance up and down the block, as if wondering what was taking the cops so long to show up. After about ten minutes, I got tired of waiting and I wandered over to Ralph's car.

It was one of those late '80s models that had been redesigned for track racing, but which hadn't taken off in the commercial market. Well, not as a family car, at least. This one had the bubble-shaped back window and the integrated trunk spoiler. I wondered if the title was clean or if Ralph had boosted it. *If the cops ever show up, I could ask them,* I thought.

I glanced back at Ralph's window, giving him one more chance, and then I popped the trunk on the BMW. It took me a minute to figure out where the spare tire was hidden. I was disappointed to discover that the tool kit only came with a short metal rod with a squared knob at the end.

I held up the rod so Ralph and his girlfriend would see what I had. I bounced it lightly off the roof of the Grand Prix. It left a mark. I peered at the scratch. Rubbed it with my thumb.

Yep, that was definitely a scratch.

The blinds twitched and swayed.

I ran a hand along the slope of the hood. It had a nice shape. Be a shame to put a dent in it like—

Oh, whoops. How clumsy of me.

As I raised my arm to hit the car again, I heard someone yell.

I looked over at Ralph's apartment. Someone was wrestling with the metal grate. It opened and—*surprise!*—a scrawny little fucker about *that* high came tumbling out.

"Hey, Ralph," I said. "Been a bit. How you doing?"

He held up his hands, entreating me to stop abusing his baby. "C-c-c-could you—could you step a-a-a-way from the car?"

I nodded toward the door. "You going to invite me in?"

"Oh, man. I d-d-d-don't—do I have to?"

I gave him a sober nod. "You do," I said. "If we stay out here, I'm going to keep beating on your car. If we go in, maybe we can talk like civilized people. Wouldn't you prefer that?"

He nodded vigorously.

I juggled the iron rod and watched him clench his teeth. "Okay," I said. "Let's step inside."

I indicated he should lead, and he scampered back toward the open door. I gave him some space and tried to get a look at the room before I walked in. It was dim, and it looked like a badly decorated living room in a shitty apartment. He was standing over by a couch that was slowly collapsing into a bundle of sticks and cheap fabric.

I didn't see his girlfriend.

She was waiting in the kitchen area with her hood up on her sweatshirt, as if that made her invisible. As soon as I came through the door, she came at me, waving the golf club like an extra in some post-apocalyptic disaster film. Luckily, the ceiling fan made the overhead clearance even worse, and all she managed to do was bounce the club off the blades.

I took the club away before she went low and tried a chip shot with one of my balls. I shoved her toward the couch, and she and Ralph tumbled into its embrace, landing like sacks of bricks on a pile of rocks.

I waved the golf club at them. The head was bent.

"Nice hospitality," I said.

Ralph's girlfriend clutched at his sleeve. "Who is this guy?" she demanded. "What have you done?"

"I ain't done nothin'," he said. There was a tonelessness to it, like it was the default noise that came out of his mouth. How many times had he said it over the years?

I pulled up my shirt and showed his girlfriend the knot of scar tissue. "Actually, he did this," I said. "You remember doing this, Ralph?"

He shook his head, but the way the blood ran out of his face said otherwise.

"Is this . . . ?" his girlfriend asked.

Ralph kept shaking his head.

She looked at me. "You're that . . ."

"His worst fucking nightmare?" I shrugged. "It's not a cliché if it's true, right?"

She came off the couch like a cat that had been tossed in a fish tank. One of her fists careened across my face. I yanked the cords on her hoodie tight, cutting off her air, and dropped her on the floor. I put a foot down hard on her hip, letting her know that things could get worse in a second. "Cool it, frisky," I snapped.

I touched my cheek, and there was blood on my fingertips.

I looked at Ralph. He tried to make himself smaller on the couch, but there was nowhere to go without unzipping one of the cushions and crawling inside.

The girlfriend was still feeling a bit frisky. She tried to bite my leg, and I knelt, putting my knee on her chest, and pinned her arms beneath my other leg. I outweighed her by a considerable amount, and when I leaned forward, she got a good sense of how much weight that was. She calmed down, though she glared at me from the depths of her hoodie. I dragged her left arm free and looked at the sparkly thing on her finger.

It was an engagement ring. Silver band. Little ornamentation. Single diamond solitaire. At least a full carat.

"Jesus Christ," I said.

I got off her and prodded her toward the couch with the golf club. She went without any more trouble, and she curled up next to Ralph. They both gave me a *Are you going to eat us while we're still alive?* look.

"You give that to her?" I asked, pointing at the girlfriend's ring.

"It's mine," she shrieked before he could fumble out an answer. "We're in love." She balled her hand into a fist and covered it with her other hand. Greedily hiding the shiny from a man she thought was going to rob her.

"Of course you are," I said.

I looked around for somewhere to sit down, and there wasn't anything but a TV on a cheap stand and a cat tower near the window. A tiny dinette with a pair of chairs was all the way over by the kitchen, and I didn't feel like going that far from the door. And so I stood, legs spread. Back muscles tight. Golf club swinging idly in one hand.

They watched me, the fear starting to leak away from their eyes. Ralph looked like a kid who knew his father was about to tan his hide good for something that had nothing to do with him. The girlfriend had a feral wariness about her. Even money she'd try to jump me again.

I was suddenly very tired. I wasn't sure I had it in me to knock them around. What was the point?

"Are you working?" I asked.

"Wh-wh-what?"

"You got a job?" I clarified.

He nodded.

"Is it a good job?"

He paused, glanced at his girlfriend, and then nodded again.

I pointed the golf club at her. "What's your name?"

"Suzzana," she said. "With two 'z's."

"Sure," I said. "Why not?"

She narrowed her eyes and pulled back her lips from her teeth.

I wondered if she was going to slit his throat some night. She seemed quite capable.

"Who was your pal that night?" I asked.

"W-w-which night?"

I smacked his leg with the golf club. He howled more than necessary, and she babbled at me to stop hurting the man she loved. It wasn't even country club playhouse quality acting.

"Come on, Ralph," I said. "Don't drag this out. Who was the guy who came into the store with you that night?"

"K-k-kristoff," Ralph stuttered.

"Kristoff? He go by 'Kris' or 'Krist'?"

Ralph shook his head.

"All right. 'Kristoff' it is." I rapped the golf club on the bottom of his shoe, which made him pull his leg back. Like I had teased a slug with some salt. "You ever go to a place called the Red Eagle?" I asked.

He thought about it for too long and finally nodded.

"Kristoff go there?"

This nod came more quickly.

"The rest of the gang hang out there too?"

Another nod. He was getting the hang of it.

"One of them a little firecracker of a dude with a shaved head?"

Ralph frowned. "Sven," he muttered.

"Not a fan of Sven?"

Suzzana's lips curled and she looked like she wanted to spit.

"Is Sven in charge?"

Ralph shook his head.

"You meet the guy in charge?" I asked the question, even though I had a pretty good idea of the answer.

Ralph's head bobbed, verifying what I already suspected.

"All right," I said. "Let's talk about the robbery."

Suzzana sat up like someone had lit a firecracker under her ass. "What robbery?" she hissed, turning on Ralph.

"It-it-it-it's—I ain't done nothin'," Ralph tried.

She slapped him on the shoulder. "You promised," she squawked.

He tried to deny it once more, but she slapped him again. "All right, all right," he said, looking like he was about to break into tears. "I-I-it was just the one time."

She turned all that feral energy on him, hard slaps against his head and shoulder. As much as I thought he deserved it, I was losing control of the conversation. I stepped forward and rang Suzzana's kneecap with the golf club. "Eyes on me," I said. "You can manhandle him later, but right now, it's all about what I want, okay?"

She settled down, but there was space between them on the couch.

I focused on Ralph. "What do you mean 'one time'?" I asked. "Two other stores had been robbed before that."

Ralph hunched his shoulders, anticipating another burst of fury from Suzzana. She managed to restrain herself, though she spent more energy watching the golf club than looking at Ralph.

"I don't know nothin' about the other stores," Ralph said. "But we only did the one. That was the plan. That was all we were supposed to do."

"Whose plan was it?" I demanded.

"I don't know, man," he said. "I j-j-just drove. Kristoff wanted me to come in with him."

"What about later?" I asked.

"W-w-what do you mean?"

"Were you following me? Did you know I was meeting the writer?"

He tucked his chin down, trying to make it impossible for me to see his eyes.

"You know what I'm talking about, don't you?" I said.

He started to shiver. Or maybe he was trying to shake his head, but his chin was buried so far into his chest that moving his head moved his entire body.

"Whose idea was it to take a run at the restaurant?" I asked.

His voice was muffled. "Kristoff, man," he whined. "It was Kristoff's idea."

"But you drove, didn't you?"

He stopped shivering. It was as close as I was going to get to an answer.

I understood the timeline now. I had gone to the Red Eagle earlier that day. I had had a beer and shot the shit with the old biker dude who thought Bobby Banger's junk was my junk. After that, I had gone to the library and had sat there for an hour or so, reading the paper. If the waitress had called someone after I had come in, they might have picked me up while I was reading Bunko's articles. After that, I had walked down the block like some fucking tourist. Led them right to the restaurant. Bunko shows up, and man, Kristoff gets a hard-on of an idea.

I turned and put the head of the golf club through the TV screen. "Sorry about that," I said as I left.

Violence never solves anything, Mr. Chow used to say to us. *It makes you feel good, but it doesn't make your problems go away.*

Wrecking the TV had been satisfying, but by the time I got back to my car, that endorphin rush was gone. All that was left was the same urge I had felt before. That *Hit 'em first* feeling.

I wasn't in a good head space. I needed to find a way out before it got any worse.

CHAPTER 24

I CALLED TOYA. SHE DIDN'T PICK UP.

I called Huggy, even though I didn't really know what I was going to talk to him about. It didn't matter. He didn't answer.

That was it for my phone's contact list. The only other number I had was the one on Detective Lorenzo's business card, and I didn't feel like calling him.

Driving aimlessly in LA is never therapeutic, regardless of what you see in the movies. You had to go all the way out to the desert to get those long stretches of empty road, where you could pose all introspectively against the deepening blue backdrop of night falling. No one mentions the two hours of bumper-to-bumper traffic you had to suffer through to get to that stretch of highway.

I headed west, trying to get out of my own way. When I passed the Brentwood Country Club, I realized I was going to make an impromptu visit to Angel's. She had a condo in a new gated community near Westridge, and when I drove by, the gate was surprisingly open. I rolled in, knowing that my car wouldn't be out of place on the twisted streets that curved back and forth along the base of the hill. Driving in her community was like playing Snakes and Ladders without the ladders.

I found her place eventually, and was surprised to see a car in the driveway. It wasn't a Range Rover, but it was in the same family of sports utility vehicles—the kind that weren't very aerodynamic and were rarely driven off-road.

I parked my car across the street and sat there for awhile, trying to figure out what I was feeling.

I wasn't surprised. I should have expected to find a car there.

The last time I had been at Angel's, there had been a different car in the driveway—a silver Porsche that had belonged to a lawyer named Nathan. Nathan and I hadn't gotten along very well, and not just because he was a lawyer. He was also a spineless weasel, and his relationship with Angel hadn't lasted. Since then, Angel had been busy graduating from law school and setting up her own practice. I had just assumed that she'd been too busy to make new friends.

Silly me.

I had met the new guy. He had a name. What was it? Oh, yes. Darnell. That was it. I peered at the windows on the second floor, where the living room and kitchen were located. She had nice curtains in the windows, which kept curious eyes like mine from seeing what was going on inside.

My stomach knotted itself several times over. What was I supposed to feel? What was I *allowed* to feel?

I remembered the pair of earrings I had bought at the pawn shop, and my hand strayed toward the center console before I realized they weren't in this car. They were in the car I had been driving yesterday. *Just as well,* I thought.

Mrs. Chow had once told me she'd lop off body parts if I so much as glanced at Angel. She hadn't been talking about hands or feet. I had laughed. Angel had laughed when I told her about it. Without saying anything to each other, we had agreed to treat her mother's words as a suggestion more than a warning, and we hadn't curbed the natural attraction between us.

Except . . . *there's always someone else's car at her house when you come by, isn't there?* I thought.

When seized by doubt, double the workout. That's was Dicky Boy's solution to everything. *You gotta purge the toxins,* he said. *Purify the body and the mind will follow.*

Or something like that.

Regardless, it was Dicky Boy's advice that got me to the gym. I spent an hour with the rope and the bag, and then did another hour working through the entire sun salutation routine we did in the yard. Twice. By the end of it all, my body was slick with sweat, my brain was numb, and I ached in the right places. A hot shower took care of the rest of my consternation, and by the time I came out of the locker, I felt much more calm and—

"Oh, hi," Greta said. She was standing at the top of the stairs. She was wearing comfortable jeans, sneakers, and a fabric vest over a soft t-shirt. She had a clipboard in one hand and a tape measure in the other. A pencil was tucked behind her ear. Her red hair was loosely pulled back from her face, and there was a smudge of dust on her forehead.

"Hi," I said.

"How was your workout?"

"Revelatory," I said.

"Nice."

"Yeah." I switched my bag to my other hand and tried to be casual as I leaned against the hand rail. "You?"

She gestured toward one side of the landing. "I've been taking measurements."

"Measurements?"

"Yeah. For the coffee and juice bar."

"Oh, right."

"Willie asked me to, you know, provide—"

"Yeah, coffee and juice. I heard."

"I didn't realize you worked here."

"No," I said. "I'm just—the staff and I are close." I looked past her and spotted Stevie at the front desk. He saw me and raised a fist. I did the same.

He gave me another fist raise, and I started to match it, but stopped, knowing we were going to keep doing it for an hour if I didn't.

Greta watched us, an eyebrow raised.

"Real close," I said.

"Okay." She hesitated, fought with herself a minute, and then decided to rush into the breach. "Anna said—did you stop by the shack yesterday?"

"Yesterday? Yeah, I might have."

"She said you jumped out of line."

"Did I?"

"Yeah, you did." Greta was watching me closely. "Any reason why?"

"I, uh, had forgotten something at home," I said. "My wallet. Yeah, that's it. I had forgotten my wallet."

"It wasn't because I wasn't there?"

"What? N—" I caught myself before the word came all the way out. "Yes," I corrected. "That's it. Sorry. I had been hoping to see you and—wow! This is embarrassing."

She smiled at me. "Why?"

"I mean, here you are now. And I am too." I showed her my hands. "And no coffee."

She shook her head. "Yeah, no coffee. Just you and me."

"Yup. You and me."

We stared at each for another moment, and then Greta tapped her tape measure against her clipboard. "I'm—I'm going to get back to work," she said.

"Yeah, okay," I said. "I should let you do that."

She hesitated again. "I'm—I'm at the shack during the week," she said.

"During the week." I nodded.

"I get done at three," she said. "Most days."

I maintained eye contact. "Three o'clock," I said.

"I usually come here after."

"Sure."

"So . . . now you know."

"I do."

"In case you wanted to, you know, plan accordingly."

"I should. I might."

"Good," she said. Her expression remained puzzled as she walked off. I wasn't sure mine was much better.

As I passed the desk, I heard Stevie complain to Lorraine. "I wish I knew how to talk to girls like Butch does," he said.

I didn't have the heart to tell him that I didn't know what the hell I was doing.

Toya returned my call several hours later. I had spent the evening flipping channels and drinking beer—two activities that were exponentially worse for your psyche when done in tandem—and I might have been overly thrilled to talk to another human being.

"Are you watching people take their clothes off at least?" she asked.

"That doesn't have the allure for me that you think it does," I said.

"That's a damn shame."

"Ruined for life," I said.

"What's the point of getting out of bed?"

"This isn't helping," I pointed out.

"Sorry." She was quiet for awhile, and I was content to listen to her breathe.

"What are you watching?" she asked finally.

"Golf."

"Seriously?"

"It's very calming, especially with the sound off."

"Is there a drinking game involved?"

"That's too much effort."

"Do you even know how they score golf?"

"I might have cared a few beers back, but . . ."

"Ah," she said. "One of those days."

Jackie and Mrs. Chow. Ralph and his feral girlfriend. Angel and Darnell. So many complicated relationships. "Yeah," I said. "One of those days."

"Mmmm."

I heard a hint of something melancholic and dark in her voice.

"Everything okay?" I asked.

"Peachy."

She was lying. I didn't want to pry, but at the same time, I couldn't stop myself.

"We okay?"

"Sure," she said.

"That doesn't sound very convincing."

"Do you need convincing?"

My brain was fuzzy from the beer, but it wasn't completely dense. "No," I said. "I was pretty well convinced the other night."

"Yeah, so was I."

"Okay, good."

"Mmmm."

I struggled to sit up on the couch. I fumbled for the remote and turned off the TV. "What's—" I stopped myself. That wasn't going to work. She had called me because she, too, wanted to make contact with another human being, but she didn't want to talk about why she wanted that contact.

"I found Ralph," I said.

"Who?"

"The guy who tried to kill me in prison."

"Oh, that guy. Yeah?"

"Yeah."

"Why were you looking for him again?"

"He took something that belonged to a friend of mine. An engagement ring."

"That's right. Did you get it back?"

"No," I said. "He had given it to his girlfriend."

"Huh," she said.

"Yeah."

"Did you—which part of that made you feel bad?" she asked.

"She thinks they're in love," I said. "But honestly? She'll drop him in a second if he can't keep her happy."

"So you'd be doing him a favor if you broke that up."

"I suppose."

"Still couldn't do it, could you?"

"No, I couldn't."

"What are you going to tell the kid—"

"Gavin."

"Gavin. What are you going to tell Gavin? 'Sorry, man, they're in love.'"

"I'm not going to tell him that."

"What? You couldn't hit a girl?"

"She hit me."

"Did she?"

"Yeah. Cut me with the ring, in fact."

Toya laughed. "There you go."

"What?"

"Nothing. It's—what? Irony? Poetic? I don't know. It's funny. That's all."

I touched the scab on my cheek. "I suppose it is."

"He stabbed you and she cut you. These two are leaving their mark," she said.

"I guess they are."

She exhaled, and I imagined her stretching out as she did, her breasts rising under her shirt. I imagined sliding my hand under her shirt.

"You okay with how this is working out?" she asked, dashing my thought.

"Not really," I said carefully. I wasn't sure which 'this' she was referring to, and didn't want to show my ignorance.

"Is this why you are sitting at home, drinking beer and watching golf?"

"Partly."

"Well, that's good to hear."

"Why is that?"

"I was going to be worried if that's all it was."

It was my turn to laugh. "No, there's some other stuff."

"Yeah?"

"Yeah."

Neither of us spoke for a minute. I replayed our conversation. She might have been doing the same. We were talking around the things that were eating at us.

"You can't—look," she said. "You and I both know that life is this weird dance, right? That we wear these masks, and we work really hard to not let people in because—we don't know what they want. Fuck, we don't even know what *we* want. It's all shit, anyway—a lot of the time—and anything we dreamed about when we were kids never came true, and yeah, that messed us up. Messed us up good. We're going to —"

"Toya." I tried to interrupt her, without any success.

"We think we're going to undo it, don't we? We've got years and years to undo that damage. We've got time. But you know what? We don't do it. We find excuses not to. We're just going to get old and bitter about the work we never even started on ourselves. Our golden years are going to be spend wondering why we even bothered thinking that—"

"Toya."

This time she stopped.

"I don't care about the dreams I had when I was a kid," I said. "Nothing turned out the way I thought it was going to, and I don't have to spend a second wondering where shit went sideways. I know where it happened. West Hollywood. I was in a borrowed RX-7. Some dude ran a light and clipped the fender of my car. Spun me right round, as they used to say back then. Sure, I got bent out of shape about it, but that wasn't going to do me any good. Not where I ended up. I got spun around and ever since, I've been making it up as I go. That's the best I can do. That's the best any of us can do, you know?"

"Yeah," she said quietly. "I suppose it is."

That silence fell across the line again. I looked at the beer bottles on the coffee table. Regrets or not, that was the sum total of my evening. It hadn't required any effort. I could do it all over again tomorrow—the line of beer bottles, at least. It wouldn't take much effort. No one would get hurt. Least of all me. It would be the safe choice. The smart thing to do. The sort of thing a lazy bum who leaned on the *largesse* of other people would do . . .

"Butch . . ."

"Yeah?"

"I—I'm going to go, but . . . "

I held my breath.

She sang a line from the song we had heard from the janitor's radio, and I laughed.

"I'm trying," I said.

She made the noise in her throat, and it was the first time in our conversation that she sounded like the woman who had lit Philzee's chilly gallery space on fire.

After we said good night, I stayed on the couch and let my head spin. Some of it was beer. Some of it was thinking about Toya. Some of it was thinking about everything else.

Mr. Chow finally showed up. He assessed the sad state of affairs in my refrigerator, and then clucked his tongue at me. *It will shit on you if you don't move,* he said.

He wasn't talking about seagulls, but, of course, he hadn't been talking about seagulls the other time either.

Make a choice, Butch.

I imagined it was Toya's voice I heard this time and not Mr. Chow's.

CHAPTER 25

IN THE MIDDLE OF THE NIGHT, I HAD AN IDEA. IT MORPHED INTO a dream, and when I woke up, it tried to get away from me. I rolled out of bed before it could vanish, and by the time I was done taking a shower, I had it firmly in hand.

After getting dressed, I got the metal box down from the top shelf in the closet. I opened the combination lock and flipped up the lid. Inside, nestled in neat rows, were stacks of twenties. It came to a little over ten thousand dollars, and given my current lifestyle—no rent, no car payments, no debts—I expected it to last the rest of the year. Between now and then, some kind of work would show up. It always did.

I sat on my heels and looked at the cash. I thought I was a free man, but I wasn't, was I? I needed that Chow family *largesse* to keep my current level of unemployment. Okay, so I wasn't officially on the payroll, but I was getting paid, wasn't I?

No rent. No car payments. No debts.

Sing it, Butchie Boy. Sing it loud.

Had life at Tehachapi been all that different? Hell, at Tehachapi, the California Department of Corrections and Rehabilitation took care of my meals and health care too. No wonder ex-cons found ways to go back to prison. Life was so much easier when the state was paying for it.

I took out a couple of stacks, figuring that would cover a ring for Gavin. Ralph was a mess, and his girlfriend would stay devoted until he ran out of cigarette money. It wasn't my place to make their situation worse, regardless of how much grief he had caused me.

Gavin had lost his ring because I hadn't cooperated with Ralph and Kristoff that night. That was on me. I needed to fix that. I didn't need to fuck up other people's lives along the way.

I was putting the money box back on the shelf when Baby Baby started barking, as per the morning routine. The dog was right outside the window, where, every day, he peed on the side of the house.

Why does the dog pee on the side of house? I thought.

The closet was on the opposite side of the bedroom from the window, but it was . . . I knelt and looked more closely at the piece of carpet in the closet. *Who carpets a closet?* I wondered. I moved a bag aside and reached for the corner. My fingers found the edge of the carpet, and it lifted. The whole piece was loose.

I cleared out the crap I had been accumulating in the closet (tastefully minimal decor, remember?), and lifted out the large piece of carpet that had been cut to fit the closet. Underneath was a large crawlspace access panel. I pulled it up and leaned over the hole.

It was dark. It smelled musty. I went out to the kitchen and found a flashlight.

I went down into the hole. Crouching, I turned on the flashlight and directed the beam toward the corner of the house where Baby Baby always did his business.

Shiny plastic wrap winked back at me. A lot of plastic wrap.

The cash under the bungalow gave me a lot to think about, and my fingertips tingled when I backed my car out of the driveway an hour later. Now that I knew the stash was there, I didn't want to leave it, but that was a reaction programmed in by years of television and prison. The Universe screwed us all, indiscriminately. No one ever caught a break. Other people were always thinking about taking our stuff. The Man was always lurking in the shadows, waiting for us to miss a payment. Waiting to jump out and shout "Repossession! Repossession!" You're a bad risk, a bad parent, a bad person. You didn't deserve happiness. You didn't deserve freedom.

The only way to silence all that bullshit is to not play the game. I did my time. I walked away without any debts. I was a free man. I didn't need that cash. I didn't need the headaches that came with it. I didn't want to see the light change in people's eyes when they realized I was flush.

There was no doubt in my mind that the forty bundles of stacked and wrapped hundred dollar bills had been squirreled away by the family patriarch. I had had lots of time to think about why he had stashed the money. Now I couldn't stop thinking about whose money it had been before he tucked it away.

I drove over to Perks A Lot and parked near the sporting goods store. The big store wasn't open yet, but business was brisk at the shack this morning; cars were lined up in both drive-thrus. I watched Anna and Greta and a third woman spin and twirl around each other—slinging coffee, laughing with customers, ringing up orders. It was a tight little operation. Cars drove up. They drove off. I could see how it was a growing industry. You could put another shack—maybe two—in this giant parking lot, and they would all be busy.

The blue Camaro was in the lot too. A silver Subaru with a ridiculous spoiler was parked next to it. A couple of dudes, trying to look nonchalant, were hanging around the cars. They weren't all dressed the same, but there was no doubt that they were in uniform. Being visible, letting the world know this was Vista-13 territory.

After an hour, I added up the hash marks I'd been making on a piece of paper. It wasn't scientific in the slightest, but an informal survey of clientele showed a reasonably equitable split between whites, browns, and blacks. However, the clientele in the last hour had predominantly been white, and most of them hadn't left the lot. They got coffee, parked their cars, and went to work. The earlier drivers got coffee and drove out of the lot. Those were the folks who worked elsewhere. The folks who had a commute because they couldn't afford to live where they worked.

When the morning coffee rush slowed down, I got out of my car and walked over to the shack. I stood in line behind a diesel-belching pickup and practiced holding my breath. A bearded guy in a white Honda eased up behind me. He crowded me slightly, as if he didn't quite believe I was a walk-up. I was a little lightheaded when I got to the front of the line.

"Hey, Butch," Greta said. She leaned out the window. "Lose your car?"

"You have no idea how pointed a question that is these days," I said.

She raised an eyebrow and put a hand on her hip. Her hair was up today, and she was wearing a cotton tee with a few tiny buttons. They didn't go all the way down her front, but they went far enough. "You want your regular?" she asked.

"Sure," I said. "But I'd also like to talk to Anna."

The eyebrow went up again, and when I didn't offer any more, she shrugged and pushed away from the window.

Anna bopped over, looking a little harried. A long wisp of hair blew across her forehead. Now that I was looking for it, the family resemblance wasn't hard to spot.

"Hi," I said. "You remember me?"

"Yeah, sure," she said. She rattled off the ingredients of the drink that was, presumedly, my 'regular.'

"You remember the other day? When I jumped out of the line and drove off?"

Anna frowned. She didn't know what to do with her hands. "Did you?"

"You told your boss about it," I said. "She mentioned it to me."

"Huh. Okay, yeah. I suppose I did."

"You remember who else was in line that day?"

She spread her hands. "I serve a lot of people. It's hard to—"

"You know my drink, and I've only come here a few times."

"Sure, but I don't recall which days you came, you know? We learn the faces."

The guy in the white Honda honked his horn and I gave him a *I'll give you a honking you won't forget pal* look.

He honked again.

Anna fidgeted. "Look. We're busy. Can you—"

"Talk to me about your brother," I asked.

Anna froze, her mouth hanging open. "Wh-wh-who?" she finally managed.

"His name's Free," I said. "He drives a truck. Hangs out with some mighty swell dudes." I thought about the gallery preview. Free hadn't been there. "Not much of an art lover," I added.

Anna shoved her hands in her back pockets. She tucked in her shoulders and offered me a shrug. It wasn't a denial.

I glanced over at the dudes hanging around the Camaro and the Subaru. "They know he's your brother?" I asked, nodding toward the gangbangers.

Anna's eyebrows scrunched together. Behind her, Greta was wondering what was going on.

I knocked a knuckle against the wooden ledge that stuck out from the shack. "I don't know how tight he is with his pals, but they aren't good people." I looked over at the Vista 13 members. "They're going to run afoul of some other folks pretty soon. It shouldn't happen here, you know?"

Anna looked like she was about to cry. There was a hardness in Greta's eyes that was reassuring to see. She'd take care of hers.

"I'm sorry," I said, knocking against the ledge again. "It's not my fight, but I'm in it now, I think. I don't know your brother, but you and you"—I looked at Greta—"I like you both. You make me coffee, and it's always very hot and tasty. I'll try to remember that if Free and I run into each other" One more knock against wood. "I hope we won't."

Anna fled, which wasn't far, given the size of the shack, but she managed to disappear from my line of sight. I looked at Greta, who was standing there awkwardly, a cup of coffee in her hand. She stepped up to the window and put the cup down. "Your, ah, your drink," she said.

"Thanks—"

The dude in the white Honda honked again.

Greta laughed and immediately put her hand over her mouth to cover the sound.

I shook my head. "He's ruining my exit," I said.

Greta tried to hold back another laugh.

I reached for my money clip. "What do I owe you for the coffee?" I asked.

"Oh, Butch." Greta swiped at her eyes. "Seriously?"

"What? I want to pay for my drink."

White Honda leaned on his horn this time. A healthy *I'm done being passive-aggressive about this* bleat.

I peeled a twenty off my clip. "His too," I said. "Not that he'll feel a moment of guilt for being an asshole."

Greta plucked the bill from my hand, and maintaining eye contact, tucked it inside her shirt. "He's paying for yours," she said. "Your money is no good here today."

I eyed the gap in her shirt where the bill had gone. "I might want that back," I said.

"You can come get it later," she said. She toyed with one of the buttons on her shirt.

I let my hand rest on the ledge for a moment. "I—" I started.

She shook her head. "I don't want to know," she said. "Please don't bring it here, okay?"

I nodded. "Okay."

I stepped out of line and headed toward my car.

The sporting goods store had opened, and I went in and bought a couple of large duffel bags.

CHAPTER 26

I DROVE OVER TO SANTA MONICA. TONY'S RESTAURANT, THREE Hares, was tucked into a residential neighborhood adjacent to the Promenade. The building was an adorable craftsman house, and Tony had converted the downstairs area into a cozy dining room. The kitchen area took up the back half of the house. It wasn't large, but it had been thoroughly modernized and was more than enough to service the dozen tables of the dining area.

Reservations were impossible to come by, and the staff turned the room two or three times during a long lunch hour, and that was it. The food was great, of course, but the mystique was even better.

Maria, the pastry chef, and Eduardo, one of the prep chefs, were working in the kitchen when I wandered in through the back. I waved at the pair and nodded toward the closed door of the tiny office tucked in the corner. "Morning, gang," I said. "The boss in?"

Maria, who was squeezing buttercream onto a plate of tiny cakes, noticed the cup in my hand. "You bring me coffee, Butch?"

"What? The espresso machine broken?"

Maria shrugged. "I haven't looked."

Eduardo was prepping asparagus, and his hands were moving in a quick rhythm. He had a mound of green on the counter next to him. He spared me a quick *You offering to make coffee for everyone?* look.

"I don't even know how the machine works," I said.

"Tony's on the phone with one of the suppliers," Maria said. "Who knows how long he's going to be." She narrowed her eyes as I raised my cup toward my lips. "You are not going to stand there and drink coffee while you wait."

"I could go out in the parking lot," I said.

"I could lock the door when you leave too," Maria said.

Shaking my head, I navigated through the kitchen toward the espresso station at the front. "Jesus, you make coffee once and forever after, you're the coffee bitch," I muttered.

"Milk's in the fridge," Maria offered as I squeezed past her.

"Lots of foam," Eduardo said. "Please," he added when he caught my side-eye.

Fifteen minutes later, Tony came out of the office. He lifted his head, smelling the scent of freshly brewed espresso, and he caught sight of the tiny cups on the counter near his employees. "Where's mine?" he demanded.

I pointed at the cup next to me on the pass-through window. "It's getting cold," I said.

He came over and picked up the cup. He took a tiny sip, considered the taste in his mouth for a minute, and then took a larger sip. "I'm not hiring you," he said.

"I'm not looking for a job," I said.

He took another sip. "Probably for the best," he decided.

In the kitchen, Maria and Eduardo shared a look. Their cups were empty, so I knew I could safely ignore whatever snark they were thinking.

"What's going on, Butch?" Tony asked.

I eyed the staff again. "Let's go sit on the porch," I suggested.

Tony picked up his cup and led me to the front door. I grabbed a pair of chairs on my way, and when he unlocked and opened the doors, I brought the chairs out to the covered porch. I put them down so we could watch for squirrels and birds.

"Let's talk about our dads," I said when we were settled.

Tony fussed with the seam of his slacks. "Sure, I guess," he said.

"Your father was angry when you put yourself in danger with those gang members," I said. "After which, you ran away."

Tony lifted his hand and let it fall on his leg again. "I'm not proud of that, Butch. I was young. I was—it was long time ago."

"Yeah, I get it. You're not the only one who ran away from a shitty situation," I said. "It's what boys do when they're not ready to be men."

"Yeah, that's as good an excuse as any."

"You thought your dad was weak. You weren't going to put up with that shit yourself, and man, you couldn't stand the idea of seeing your father on his knees."

"Butch, I—" Tony looked away, shaking his head.

"My father was an alcoholic," I said. "He was so drunk one night that he missed the driveway and put the car through the front window of the house."

Tony's head came back toward me.

"Killed my sister. Busted my mom up pretty good. He barely had a scratch on him. He didn't know what he had done until a day later. Mom was on pain meds for a couple of days. I watched them take my sister's body away. I was the only one who got a chance to say good-bye to her. I was the only one who knew she was gone. The rest of my family wasn't there."

"Jesus, Butch. I didn't know . . ."

"So, yeah, as soon as I could, I ran away too. I stole some money from a stash I knew my dad had—fuck him, you know?—and I came out to LA. Had no idea where I was going or what I was going to do. Just a dumb kid, trying to run away from his trauma. And look where I ended up."

Tony looked mortified for another moment, and then an awkward laugh hiccuped out of him. "I'm sorry," he said reflexively. "I didn't mean—"

"It's okay," I said. "Someone has to be that poster child. Dumb stud from small town in Colorado. No acting talent to speak of. I wasn't even a decent carpenter. Had the physique of a kid who showed up for sports but never really excelled. I could take direction, and I had the necessary stamina of a young man coming into his prime. What else was I going to do?"

He fiddled with his espresso cup. "I worked at one of those peep show places," he said. "When I first got to New York."

"Really?"

"Only for about a month. It was . . . " He laughed. "It was so fucking tedious." He laughed again. "All I did, night after night, was swap tapes out of VCRs and make change for dudes who didn't want to be seen. When I caught myself wishing someone would try to rob the place, I quit. That's when I knew I had to do something else. Something that wouldn't put me in a situation like that." He shifted in his seat. "You know, the guys who rob these stores? They just need some cash, and the store is their ATM. You're in the way. That's all. If they could call ahead and ask you to step out for a minute, they would."

"Make everything easier, wouldn't it?"

"It makes you feel . . . It robs you of your identity, you know? It's not your money. It's not your store. You don't care. You don't know them. You'll never see them again. They won't even look you in the eye. Just like those guys who came in to the shop for a peep and a jerk. You don't exist to them."

Tony fiddled with his cup. He checked the seam on his pants. He looked at his watch. I waited. I had been doing a lot of thinking.

"When my dad—" Tony stopped. "I wasn't surprised when Dad went away. I mean, I guess I always knew something like that would happen, but I thought it would be more—more violent. But no, it was all about money—money they never found, by the way—and Dad rolled over for them. I knew he would. It was just like the gangs coming into the store. He didn't want me standing up to them, and he didn't stand up to the Feds when they pushed him around. He just let them shove him into jail."

He turned toward me. "Do you know he forbade us from visiting? When the cancer came, his lawyers got him out and he came home, but we weren't supposed to see him there either."

"What? Really?"

"Yeah, really. Mom said he was a proud man; he wanted us to remember him as being strong and healthy. There were specific times when we all gathered as a family, but they were well staged. You remember how much Mom fussed over Dad during those times, don't you?"

I nodded. "Yeah, okay. But I just brushed it off as your mother being who she is."

"Well, you're not wrong about that, but mostly, it was to cover Dad's illness." Tony cocked his head. "That's why he wanted you around," he said. "He needed someone to care for him, but he didn't want any of us to see him as he got sicker and sicker."

"What the hell? Your father lawyered himself out of jail so that he could die with his family, but when he got out, he told you all to stay away?"

Tony nodded. "Yeah, basically. I mean, Mom was the one who told us, but we assumed it was what Dad wanted."

I sat back on my chair, stunned by what I was hearing.

"Well, fuck," I said. "No wonder Jackie hates me."

Tony laughed. "You didn't know?"

"No, I—I had no idea. He tracked me down. Told me that he needed someone to wipe his ass and pre-chew his food. I said I wasn't doing either. He changed his tune, asked if I could keep an old man company during his last couple months. I didn't have anything else going on, so I said 'sure.' He told me to stay in the bungalow out back, so I'd be close by. After he died, your mother said that he wanted me to have it and—"

"Have it?"

"Yeah. You know, like he willed it to me or something."

Tony shook his head. "That whole property is owned by Chow Enterprises."

"What?"

"Yeah, Mom lives in the house because she's, you know, the chairwoman of the board and all, but you . . . you don't have any claim to that house." He stared at me. "Who do you think pays the taxes on it every year?"

"There are taxes? Why? I thought it was paid for."

"Butch . . ." Tony couldn't help himself, and he started laughing.

"It's not funny," I said.

"It is," Tony said. "Jesus, Butch. You never thought about why Mom kept you and Jackie apart?"

"I assumed it was because Jackie was an asshole with Daddy issues, and I kept undoing all the work his therapist had done."

"Well, I'm sure that was part of it."

I ran my tongue around the inside of my mouth. I wanted something stronger than coffee.

Tony read my desire in my eyes. "I've got—hang on." He went inside, leaving me alone on the porch.

My thoughts were all over the place. On the one hand, Mr. Chow was as vain and egotistical as they come, and a lot of the reason I had stuck around when he had asked me to was because I wanted to provide him some dignity and cover. It was the least I could do for the man who had plucked me out of prison and made me into, well, into someone who could . . .

That's where my thoughts got muddled, because, on the other hand, I was the perfect cut-out for the family.

That conspiracy theory ran like this:

The Feds get a whiff of a money laundering program where Mr. Chow is moving cash through his convenience stores. They try to squeeze him, but he folds instead, taking the income tax evasion hit and going to jail.

With Chow in prison, the pipeline is busted. The cash in transit gets shrink-wrapped and stashed under the house. Maybe everyone will forget about it. Maybe not.

Probably not.

Chow uses prison as a means to put some distance between him and the whole matter. He's already serving time for tax evasion. He's out of reach. Everyone was going to forget him.

This was a Bunko-worthy conspiracy, and oh, it had its hooks in me.

Tony came out of the house with a bottle of scotch and a pair of glasses. He poured an inch for both of us, and I absently took a glass when he offered it.

I took a sip from the glass. "What is this?"

"The good shit," Tony said. "With the amount of thinking you're doing, I figured you'd need it."

I took another sip, letting the fiery pulse of the scotch bolster my thinking. "Okay, here's my wild theory. Your dad goes to prison. He doesn't want to see the family. He doesn't do anything about the stores. They're supposed to be abandoned. Maybe they'll close. Maybe they won't. Either way, he's not involved in any way. The Feds can't connect him to the stores."

I took another sip of scotch.

"But Jackie and Marco rescue them, don't they? They step in with Chow Enterprises and bring everything under one roof. All neat and tidy."

"And legal," Tony pointed out.

"Yes, and legal. But—" I point a finger at Tony. "This is still an open sore for the Feds. Someone can't let it go. They're very patient, and they wait for someone in the family to fuck up. They never stop looking for an angle.

"But nothing ever happens. Your dad gets old. He gets cancer. He gets out. He dies. And that's it. The Feds don't have anything. It's all over."

"Except . . . except it isn't. Because they're watching me."

I nodded. "Why would the Feds try to squeeze you if the case was going to die with your father?"

"Maybe they thought he'd get remorseful and want to confess before he died."

I laughed. Tony gave me a rueful smile. "Okay. So, yeah, probably not."

"You said something about money," I said. "Cash that went into the pipeline and never came out."

"Did I? Yeah, I suppose I did."

"What if that's the smoking gun the FBI is still looking for."

Tony shrugged. "Maybe, but my father's dead. What's the point of tying it to him."

"But the people he was laundering money for aren't dead. Your brothers—who have turned a bunch of convenience stores and nail salons into a tidy little inland empire—aren't dead." I waved a hand toward the south. "Real estate is the single best investment in this town," I said. "Chow Enterprises owns more than a handful of convenience stores and nail salons.

"But the problem is your father's past. The money pipeline. The people he worked with. Jackie and Marco—whether they meant it or not—tied the family to that legacy. If the Feds ever find a bunch of money, they'll use it as an excuse to take everything. You know how they are."

Tony nodded. "Yes. Yes, I do."

I drained my glass and held it out for Tony to refill it. "So, what's the simplest way to extricate the family from all of this bullshit?" I asked.

Tony gave me another splash. "Give the Feds the other end of the pipeline," he said.

"Perhaps," I said. "But that means rolling over and giving them up. Your dad never ratted on them, and for a good reason, I'll bet. If he had talked, they would have come after his family."

Tony paled. He gulped his scotch and poured himself a healthy measure. More than he had given me.

I didn't quibble. It was his scotch, after all. And his family.

"However, there's an easier way out of this," I said.

"How's that?"

"Have a cut-out. A patsy. Someone you can blame everything on. Someone deep in all of this, but who isn't family. Someone who your dad knows—has known for a long time. Someone with a criminal record . . ."

Tony got it. "Shit, Butch . . ."

I nodded. "Yeah. Me. That's why your dad embraced me and told the rest of you to stay away. He wanted everyone to dislike me. I was an outsider, but not so far outside that there wasn't a history of debts. Owned and paid."

"But Mom—you stayed in the bungalow after he died. Why would she let you stay unless . . . ?"

"Unless she knew," I finished for him. "That's why she kept me around. I was the family's insurance policy in case anything ever happened. In case the Feds started to poke at family members. Come on, sooner or later, you would have told your mother about the FBI visits, right?"

Tony looked at his hands. "Yeah," he admitted. "I would have."

"And she'd have taken care of everything," I said. "I'm right there. In the backyard. She can give me up any time she likes."

"But . . . there's no case without a stash of money," Tony said.

"Oh, there's a stash," I said.

Tony's eyes got big. "There is?"

"You don't want to know," I said.

He swallowed several times, working his eyes down to a normal size. "Yeah, yeah," he said. "I don't want to know."

I leaned back and stared out at the street. "Do you know the dumb thing in all this?" I asked. "None of this would have happened if Jackie hadn't had a stupid idea."

"What stupid idea?"

I looked at Tony. "The night of the robbery, Angel showed up. She said you called her. You told her that I was in trouble."

Tony flushed and wouldn't meet my gaze.

"Why did you tell her that, Tony?"

"I-I don't know what you are talking about," Tony said.

"Angel wasn't coming down for smokes or a six-pack of beer," I said. "You called her and told her to come to the store. Why?"

"I-I must have heard something on the radio, and I—"

"No, you didn't," I said.

He faltered, and his gaze fell into his glass where he wished he could drown himself. When he spoke, I almost didn't hear him over the sound of a truck passing in the street.

"Jackie called me," he said. "He told me to tell Angel you needed a lawyer."

"And how did Jackie know what had happened?" I asked.

Tony shook his head and wouldn't say anymore. It was okay. I had learned a thing or two from Angel. Lawyers don't ask questions they don't already know the answers to.

CHAPTER 27

I'm disappointed you think me capable of such malevolent foresight, Mr. Chow said when I was sitting in traffic on the 10.

You mean: you're disappointed I figured it out.

Mr. Chow shrugged. *Perhaps. Or maybe it is your own shame you are feeling. I am a mirror. Look at me, Butch. Look at yourself. Did I really fail you? Was I not a better authority figure than your own father?*

You didn't love all of us equally, I said.

No father ever does, Mr. Chow said.

And what of those sons who get left behind? I asked. *Do you just say 'oops' and find some new ones?*

That's not how it works, he said.

No? Tell me about Dickie Boy and Tattoo Bob, I asked. *What happened to them after you got out?*

The passenger seat in my car was empty. No answer was forthcoming.

"Yeah, that's what I thought," I said to myself.

My phone rang. I picked it up, thinking it was Huggy. I had called him as I was leaving Three Hares to ask for a favor. He said he could do it, but it would take a little while.

"Hello? Mr. Bliss? This is Lucas. From the dealership?"

"Oh, yeah. Hi, Lucas. What can I do for you?"

"Well, we've received the other car—" He stopped to clear his throat. "And, well, we're a bit disappointed about the condition of the vehicle."

"Lot of that going around today."

"Pardon me?"

"It's—never mind."

"Of course, we'll be happy to take care of repairs to the body and fender, and, uh, new wheels, I guess. Again."

"Sure," I said. "Can you just charge it to the account?"

"Well . . ." Lucas cleared his throat again. "We'll, uh, we'll need a signature on a repair order for that, and . . ."

"And you'd like me to come down and sign that order, wouldn't you?"

"If you wouldn't mind," he said.

"I'm sure I can do that," I said. "Later today be okay?"

"That would be fine, Mr. Bliss. Oh, and sir? We found a package in the console. In case you want to pick that up . . ."

Package? Ah, yes, the earrings from the pawn shop. The ones I had bought on a whim, thinking that I could give them to . . . Well, it didn't matter, did it?

"Yeah," I said to Lucas. "I'll get those when I drop by."

He thanked me and ended the call. I drummed my fingers on my steering wheel as traffic inched along. Thoughts kept banging around my head.

Mr. Chow wasn't forthcoming with any more commentary or advice.

I got off two exits later and swung by the BMW dealership, where I suffered a couple long exhalations from Lucas and a few pinched glares from other executives. The repair order for body work and new tires came to a couple grand. I made an illegible scrawl that looked more like an abstract drawing of a dodo than a legal signature on the document, and Lucas handed over the paper bag with the earrings.

He was in a better mood when I left, and I couldn't blame him. The dealership was making good money on the repair work. Their markup on services was astronomical.

☆

Huggy still hadn't called back, and so I went by the house next. I filled the duffel bags with bundles from under the bungalow. As I was loading them into the trunk of the car, Baby Baby barked at me from the house. He worked himself into a tiny frenzy, and eventually Mrs. Chow came to the sliding glass door and opened it for him.

The dog launched himself off the deck. He circled the car, barking ferociously at the trunk. I closed it and leaned against the car, watching the Pekinese make himself hoarse. When he approached the back tire and lifted his leg, I stomped noisily. He got a dribble of urine out before he scampered off.

Mrs. Chow remained in the house, staring at me through the sliding glass. *She knows about the money,* I thought. *She has to.*

Was I trying to convince myself?

Baby Baby bounced around the car. An idea occurred to me, and I went back to the bungalow. I unlocked the front door and went in, leaving the door open behind me. A couple of seconds later, I heard the scrabble-scrabble of tiny nails on the hardwood floor. Baby Baby bounced past me and leaped onto the couch. He wrestled with one of the pillows.

I went into the bedroom and opened the closet. I removed the carpet square and pulled up the access hatch to the crawlspace.

Baby Baby came tearing into the bedroom. As he rushed toward the closet, I scooped him and dropped him in the hole. "Knock yourself out," I said as I put the access hatch back in place. I put the carpet down and closed the closet door.

I locked up as I left. Mrs. Chow had seen her dog go into the bungalow, and she had seen me come out. The dog's barking was muffled, but I could still hear him. He sounded . . . well, he didn't sound panicked or angry. He sounded . . . happy. And why not? He had finally found the source of the elusive scent that had been tormenting him for years.

"Your dog fell in a hole," I said loudly. "I think he's okay, but maybe you should get him out sooner than later."

My phone buzzed. I dug it out of my pocket and glanced at it. A text message from *Bear*. It was a ten digit phone number. Huggy had given me the landline number of an apartment in Palms.

"What are you doing, Butchie Boy?" Mrs. Chow pushed open the sliding glass door and came out onto the deck.

"I'm solving problems," I said.

She shook her head. "You don't know what is—"

"What? What don't I know?"

She snapped her mouth shut. A vein pulsed in her neck.

I dialed information on my phone. When the operator came on, I asked for the number of a custom car shop. "It's on Exposition," I said. "Near the freeway."

The woman asked me to wait. I did. Mrs. Chow and I stared at each other. The woman came back and read me off the number for Jackie's shop. "Would you like me to connect you?" she asked.

"Absolutely," I said.

The line went dead, and then I heard the gamboling scramble of a number being dialed. It rang twice before it was picked up. "C-c-custom Auto Designs, this is R-r-ralph," a voice said. "H-h-how can I help you today?"

I was so startled by the voice that I nearly dropped the phone. "I, uh, yeah," I said, getting my shit together. "I'm looking for Jackie Chow. Is he in?"

"Sure. Let me connect you. Can I tell him who is calling?"

"Sure," I said. All my thoughts over the last twenty-four hours coalesced into a white-hot ball of fire in my head. "Tell him it's Butch Bliss."

I heard Ralph gasp. He sputtered for a minute, and then the line went dead.

"Little fucker hung up on me," I said to Mrs. Chow.

I redialed information and started to ask for the number again, but Mrs. Chow cut me. "Don't call him back."

I lowered my phone. "Do you know who answered the phone at Jackie's shop? It was the guy who tried to kill me in prison. He was one of the two shitbags who came to the store the other night." I laughed. "He works for Jackie. Jesus Christ, lady. Your son hired the dumbest kid on his crew to kill me during an attempted robbery at one of his stores."

Mrs. Chow shook her head, and I laughed again.

"The other robberies—they were Vista-13, weren't they? The Mexicans were making a move." The white-hot ball of energy in my head expanded. "I thought the Feds had floated a rumor—a little something to get under everyone's skin. But it's not that, is it? Your husband was cleaning money for Mafia Mexicana, wasn't he? That's why he kept his mouth shut when he went to jail, because if he hadn't, he wouldn't have lasted a week."

"You don't know what you are talking about—"

"No, you don't know," I growled. "You don't know how things worked inside."

She gave me a death glare, but she didn't contradict me.

"He cut a deal with Zalo. They knew that Chow wasn't going to squeal, and so they left him alone. They gave him his little coterie to play with, and he kept to himself. But he knew it wouldn't last. He knew someone was going to get bent about unfinished business—sooner or later. He had keep the family safe somehow. That's why he tried to bury it all and leave the ground fallow. But Jackie fucked that up, didn't he? Several—"

Mrs. Chow launched herself at me, her hands extended like claws. I was caught off-guard. This was a woman who never let anyone forget she had been a world-class hand model. She didn't do anything that might leave a mark on her fingers, even though it had been years since she had done any work.

I nearly lost an eye as she raked her nails across my face, and I may have lost my temper a bit when I clouted her on the side of the head. She spun away from me, and when I pressed my palm against my face, it came away bloody.

Baby Baby's bark grew more urgent, as if he knew his master was in trouble.

Mrs. Chow's icy impassiveness had been replaced with unglamorous fury. I didn't like the way her eyes glittered. Physically, she was no match for me, but that didn't mean she wasn't thinking about a hundred ways to hurt me.

The dog made a noise that neither of us had ever heard before, and her eyes shifted away from me.

I took that opportunity to take a step back, putting some distance between us. I got out of her way, if she decided the bungalow was more important than trying to shove a well-manicured finger into one of my eyes.

Her hand shot out, fingers extended, and I nearly jumped. "Key," she snarled. "Give me the key."

I got my house key off the ring and tossed it over. I wasn't going to get any closer to that hand.

She caught it with a snap of her fingers. Like a trap closing. "Walk away," she said. "Leave the car. Leave the money. Just walk away."

I shook my head. "No."

Her face darkened. There was murder in her eyes. So much murder.

"You knew," I said. "You knew about the money."

Her hand tightened around the house key.

"You wanted a solution, but you didn't want to make a choice. Well, I'm going to make it for you. I'm going to tell all the wrong people about what's under the bungalow. If you're lucky, everyone will shoot each other. If not, well, you might have to decide which of your children you love more."

"You're a bastard," she said.

I shrugged. "No, I was just saved by one."

As I drove away, I dialed information and asked to be connected to Jackie's shop again. This time, I was put through. "It's Bliss," I said when Jackie answered. He started to say something, but I cut him off. "I know where the money is," I said. "Your mom knows too. She's always known."

Jackie didn't say anything, but I could hear his tense breathing.

"I know you hired Ralph and his pal Kristoff to hit the store," I continued. "I know you told them to make it look like an accident. When it didn't work out, you had Tony call Angel, because you knew I would trust her. You knew she would want to protect me. She would never realize that her own brother had set this up."

Jackie made a noise in his throat, but he didn't argue with me.

I glanced at the cross traffic and made a left. My face felt stiff, and when I glanced in the rearview mirror, I didn't like what I saw. Mrs. Chow hadn't marked me permanently, but the scratches made me look like I had tussled with a wild animal.

"Did you know who Ralph was when you put him up to this?" I asked. "Did you know about his history with me?"

Jackie stopped breathing for a second, which was answer enough.

"Jesus, Jackie. He's part of a white power group. He's been harboring a grudge against me for a decade. He has ties to people who knew that your father had a relationship with the Mexicans." My voice was getting louder. "You invited the Double-Z to make a move on both your father's legacy and the Mafia Mexicana. No wonder Bunko—"

I stopped. My thoughts were moving faster than my mouth.

Jackie filled in the blank for me.

"That fucking reporter," he ground out. "He kept digging and digging. Picking at it. Trying to ruin my father."

"Your father ruined himself," I interrupted. "Bunko was just there to tell the rest of the world about it. Until those idiots took another shot at me."

The traffic light ahead turned red, and I slowed my car to a stop. A seagull hovered over the intersection, dancing in a thermal. *It'll shit on you if you don't . . .*

"You fucked up, Jackie," I said. "You should have done the work yourself. People died because you weren't man enough." I laughed. "Hell, your father took care of his own business. Did you know he killed a man in prison? I did an extra nickel because your father stabbed a man in the shower. I was a better son to him than you were, Jackie."

"I'm going to fucking kill you, Bliss," Jackie said.

"Well, get to it, Jackie Boy," I said, using the same tone of voice his mother did with me when she gave me that nickname. "Tick-tock. Tick-tock. You're running out of time. The money isn't going to be there forever."

"Where is it?"

The light changed.

I hung up on Jackie.

CHAPTER 28

I DROVE PAST THE RED EAGLE, COUNTED THE BIKES OUT FRONT and the cars in the lot. Spotted the *wife's* car up the block. I turned my head as I passed, just in case Detective Lorenzo looked. I went two blocks up and parked on the same side of the street, and my view of his vehicle was blocked by a delivery van. Which was fine, as I was more interested in who might be leaving the Red Eagle.

I pulled up the text from Huggy and dialed the number he had sent me. Apparently, if you had an address and you knew the right people, you could find out the associated phone number. Yet another reason to pay cash for everything and own nothing.

I laughed, thinking about the duffel bags in the trunk. The call connected, and my laugh turned to a choking cough.

"Hello?"

"Where's—is Ralph there?" My voice was rough, making the subterfuge easier.

"Ralph? Who is this?"

"I ain't got time for this shit, Sooz," I said, dragging out the last letter. "This is Kristof. We gotta move. I need him right fucking now."

"Wait, wait." Suzzana tried to calm me down. "He's—he'll be here any minute. Really. I promise."

"Promises ain't worth shit," I snarled. "It's put up time."

"Is—is he in trouble?"

I gave her a hard bark of laugher. "Trouble? It's fucking payday, toots. This is what we were promised."

Toots? Whatever. I wasn't trying for an Oscar.

"Hold on a sec. Let me . . ."

"You tell him I know where the money is. We gotta shot at it. But we need to go now. Tell him we gotta get to Chow's place. Quick."

"I—hang on! I hear him. He just drove up."

Of course he did, I thought. True to his nickame, Rabbit ran as soon as he got off the phone. Where else was he going to go when I spooked him?

I shouted my address into the phone, like I was busy running. "Tell him Kristof said to get to Chow's place." I shouted the address one more time. "Tell him to meet me there."

I hung up the phone and dropped it into the center console.

While I waited, I wondered how badly Suzzanna was going to mangle my message. Was Ralph still the dumb kid who had tried—twice—to kill me at Tehachapi? Could he manage a thought of his own with Suzzanna barking at him. *He said something about money. You gotta go now. There's money!*

Ten minutes went by, and then someone came out of the Red Eagle. Seconds later, a car came careening out of the lot. It turned right and accelerated past me. Scar—*Kristof*—wasn't looking left nor right. His hands were tight on the wheel because he had places to go.

Thirty seconds later, Detective Lorenzo drove by. I waved, though I didn't think he saw me.

Looks like I won't have to call the Feds, I thought.

I started up my car and drove in the opposite direction. Leisurely. Not like some folks who were in a hurry to tussle over a couple hundred grand in cash.

Jackie was going to be pissed when I didn't show up at the house. I suppose if he had spent a decade listening to his father spout off about the art of conflict avoidance while doing tai chi, he might be less surprised. *It's not about where they think you should or shouldn't be*, Chow would tell us. *It's about being somewhere else entirely.*

☆

Frank was the only one working at the *Venice Voice* when I wandered in. His desk was covered with a blizzard of newsprint. He hadn't slept, shaved, or changed his undershorts in a few days.

I dropped the duffel I was carrying next to the couch, and sat down gingerly on the uncomfortable cushions.

He stared at me as if I was an apparition that would disappear if he doubted me hard enough. "What happened to you?" he asked when it was clear that I wasn't an imagined phantom.

"Cougar," I said.

His eyebrows moved as he tried to decide if I was being literal.

"Deadlines?" I asked.

He glanced at the weight of paper that was planning on smothering him. "Always," he said.

I nodded. "You running Toya's piece on Philzee's opening?"

"Of course."

"She going to get shit for it?"

He gave me a *When does a woman like that not get grief for everything she says or thinks?* look.

"She around?" I asked. Trying to sound casual, as if she wasn't the real reason I had dropped by.

Frank cocked his head. "No," he said. "She's taking a couple of personal days."

"She always do that after writing a shit-stirrer for you?"

He shook his head. "No, she only does it when her father hurts himself."

"Her father, huh?"

A tired smile crept across his face. "She didn't tell you."

"We had other things on our mind," I said.

Frank leaned back in his chair and put his hands behind his head. "Well, technically, I'm not allowed to talk about the personal lives of my employees."

"Good thing I didn't ask," I said. "I'll wait for her to bring it up."

"You might be waiting awhile."

I shrugged. "I'm a patient guy."

He chewed on the inside of his cheek. I looked around the office.

"Jesus Christ," he said after a couple minutes of silence.

"See?" I said. "I'm good at waiting."

"What do you want, Bliss?"

"She's an amazing writer, isn't she? She's the reason you're still in business."

"Yeah," he said. "She is."

"You give her those shit assignments because she pisses people off. Angry people buy papers. They write letters. Conversations happen. Keeps circulation up, doesn't it?"

Frank held up his hands like he didn't understand how it all worked, but by gosh and by gum, it wasn't his place to interfere with the natural order of things.

"She said you give Philzee an op-ed slot after she slags him, and it drives a whole bunch of traffic to his gallery. Sells a lot of paintings."

He shrugged as if the idea had never crossed his mind.

"Philzee buy a lot of advertising space in the paper?" I asked.

Frank made a face. "Everyone around here does."

"The circle of life in action."

"Look, Bliss. You know show business works. This isn't any different."

"No, I don't suppose it is."

We stared at each other for another minute.

"What are you going to do when someone from the *LA Times* poaches her?" I asked.

Frank flinched as if I had slapped him.

"There's a spot open on the Metro desk. She's got a healthy— what do you call it?—a healthy *CV* for that sort of thing. They'd probably offer her what? Two? Three times what you're paying?"

HARRY BRYANT

Frank's lips were a thin line, slashing across his face. "Yeah," he sighed. "She'd probably talk them up to four times what I'm paying her."

I smiled. "You're a tight-fisted bastard, aren't you?"

A spark flashed in his eyes. "I know how far I can stretch each dollar before it comes back to bite me," he said. "That's how you survive in this business."

"How long do you think she'll last at the *Times*?"

My question surprised him. "Excuse me?"

"You can barely contain her. Do you think she's going to tone it down for the big leagues?"

He laughed. "She won't. She's going to make them crazy." He paused. "It's going to make her crazy."

"But she'll do it, won't she? Because of her dad." I thought about her reaction when she realized she had slept over at my place. She hadn't fled because she had been embarrassed. She had fled because someone had needed her. "He needs constant supervision, doesn't he? And that sort of care isn't cheap."

He hesitated for a second. "It isn't," he admitted. "But . . ." He indicated the office around him. "I can't match what the *Times* will offer."

"No," I said. "But you know how to focus her. She knows the line with you. That's worth a lot."

"It doesn't pay for in-home care."

"True," I said. I glanced at the bag at my feet, and decided it wasn't enough. I dug into my pocket for my car keys. I tossed them to Frank, who caught them awkwardly.

"What's this?"

"Keys to a silver BMW parked in the alley," I said. I picked up the duffel and slung it over my shoulder. It contained, among other things, the paper bag with the emerald and mother-of-pearl earrings. "I was going to—well, it doesn't matter." I nodded toward the keys in his hands. "You should move the car before it gets towed," I said.

266

I headed for the door.

"Bliss."

I stopped and looked back. Frank had an exasperated look on his face. "I'm not your fucking valet."

He tossed the keys. They hit me in the chest and fell to the floor. I looked down at them.

"There's close to two hundred thousand dollars in the trunk," I said. "After today, it's clean money. No one will come looking for it." I looked at Frank. "You really should move the car."

I left the keys on the floor and walked out of his office.

I got an ice cream cone and strolled along the boardwalk, a duffel bag with forty thousand or so in cash slung over my shoulder. A woman in tight shorts and tall socks went whizzing past me on roller-skates. Men, tanned a deep bronze by the persistent California sun, flexed and strutted in a parody of the peacocking that went on in prison yards. On the beach, kids and dogs chased one another. The surf was up, and a dozen or so hardy souls were trying to catch waves. I wondered if Chaz was among them.

I wasn't in any rush. I had enough money for awhile. I didn't owe anyone anything. Mr. Chow had killed a man—maybe to protect me, maybe to put me under his thumb. It didn't matter. I had done the time for him. My debts were well and truly paid.

My phone rang. I looked at the display. *Heartbreaker.*

I popped the last bite of my cone into my mouth. "Hello," I managed.

"Hey," she said.

"Hey," I said.

"I heard you stopped by the office, looking for me."

"I did. You weren't there."

"No, I—I'm taking a couple of days off."

"Okay."

Toya was quiet for a minute. "Aren't you going to ask . . . ?"

I looked up at the sky. Curling clouds flirted with the sun. "You'll tell me when you want to," I said.

"I'm—I'm not sure . . . I'm not sure if I want to," she said.

"Okay."

"Is that going to be a problem?"

"Does it sound like I have a problem with it?"

"I might."

I shrugged, even though she couldn't see me. The duffel strap dug into my shoulder.

"I don't know if I'm . . ."

"Toya," I said, interrupting her meandering defensiveness. Or obtuseness. Or whatever. "Look, it's been an interesting week, and I doubt either of us needs to make a decision about anything right now."

Out of the corner of my eye, I thought I saw Mr. Chow, but when I turned my head, it was an old black man eking out a snail's pace on a wooden skateboard. He wobbled on the board, but he didn't fall. A fat grin lit up his face. He wasn't moving fast—the roller girls were whipping past him, making his hair flutter—but he was moving. God, he was moving, and that was enough.

"I do have a couple of things I need some help with," I said. "If you're, you know, interested."

"I might be," she said cautiously.

"Okay."

After a minute of silence, she laughed. "Okay, okay. Yes, Butch. Yes. I'm interested."

"Good." I switched ears with my phone. "Listen, I have something like eight hundred minutes on this phone," I said.

"What?"

"I bought a bunch of prepaid minutes," I said. "Remember. I need to use them."

She laughed. "Do you need someone to talk to, Butch?"

"I do."

"Yeah, I might be able to help you with that."

"Great, and the second thing is I need some help picking out a ring."

She didn't reply for a long time, and when she spoke, there was a tremor in her voice. "Butch, I—God, Butch. Don't. It's too soon—"

"What? For you?" I played up the false indignation. "You think I'm talking about a ring for you?"

"I—what—I don't—"

"Shit, woman. You remember the first day we met? You didn't even want to make out in the back seat of your car. What makes you think that I—"

"What am I supposed to think?" she snapped.

"Jesus, you think you're such a fantastic lay. One time with you and—"

"Hey, it wasn't just the one time!"

"Fine. Two times. You think two times is going to make me lose my mind?"

"It sounds to me like you've lost your mind."

"I'm not buying *you* a ring," I said. "It's for Gavin."

"Who?"

"The kid who got shot at the store. Remember?"

"Which kid? Oh, right. The store where those guys . . ."

"You don't remember, do you? I told you all about it in Frank's office."

"Wait? Was that when you and I were in the office, or when you and I were there with Frank and Chaz?" Her voice had lost its edge.

"Yeah, the later time."

"Oh, I wasn't listening to a damn thing you were saying then. I was too busy thinking about . . ."

I watched a seagull float over the boardwalk. It drifted toward me, and then the wind shifted and the bird went with it.

It's just a dumb bird, I thought. *It's not a fucking metaphor.*

I briefly wondered about how many cars were parked in the driveway at Mrs. Chow's house. I wondered if Baby Baby was still trapped under the house. I wondered if the Feds had shown up. I wondered how long Jackie would hold a grudge.

Missed your chance, Jackie Boy, I thought.

"Are you listening to me?" Toya asked.

"Absolutely," I said.

"Liar."

"You're right. I was busy thinking about how that dress came off you that night."

"Were you?"

"I was."

"Mmmm."

"You don't believe me, do you?"

"I don't care, really. *I'm* thinking about how that dress came off. And now I'm thinking about what happened after that."

I smiled. "Of course you are. I was amazing."

"God, you're impossible."

"So is that a 'yes'?"

"A 'yes' to what?"

"A 'yes' to anything you want it to be for," I said.

She hesitated. "Yes," she said. "I'm saying 'yes.'"

"All right then. Can I call you tomorrow?"

"Yeah, you can call me tomorrow."

More Bliss

Building a relationship with my readers is one of the marvelous parts of being a writer, and the best way that relationship grows is through interaction. The only way I know these stories are making you laugh, cry, or shake your fist in joy is by hearing from you. The easiest way you can let me know that you'd like to see more Bliss is to leave a review.

Reviews don't have to be complicated. All you need is a place to leave a few words about the book (the retailer where you purchased this book, an online review site, or—heck!—even a hand-drawn sign works). Let me know what you think about Bliss.

Also, the Harry Bryant mailing list is very low-traffic. It's the best way to stay informed, and signing up lets me know that you're a fan and you'd like to see more.

http://www.harrybryantwriter.com/mailinglist.php

Thanks for your support!

ABOUT THE AUTHOR

Harry Bryant lives in the Pacific Northwest with a house full of pretty books.

Find him on the web at http://www.harrybryantwriter.com

www.ingramcontent.com/pod-product-compliance
Lightning Source LLC
Chambersburg PA
CBHW030612120726
47904CB00006B/1871